THE CRIMSON FOG

THE CRIMSON FOG

Paul Halter

Translated by John Pugmire

The Crimson Fog

This book is a work of fiction. The characters, incidents, and dialogue are drawn from the author's imagination and are not to be construed as real. Any resemblance to actual events or persons, living or dead, is entirely coincidental.

First published in French in 1988 by
Editions du Masque – Hachette Livre as *Le Brouillard Rouge*
THE CRIMSON FOG
Copyright © Paul Halter & Editions du Masque, 1988.
English translation copyright © by John Pugmire 2013.

Prix du Roman d'Aventures 1988

For information, contact: pugmire1@yahoo.com

FIRST AMERICAN EDITION
Library of Congress Cataloging-in-Publication Data
Halter, Paul
[*Le Brouillard Rouge* English]
The Crimson Fog / Paul Halter;
Translated from the French by John Pugmire

November 1888

There are occasions when one sees one's life passing before one's eyes with a perfect lucidity, as if projected by a magic lantern. And it's always during the most intense of moments that it happens.

The little room is miserable: poorly furnished, with no taste, unless you count the engraved print above the mantelpiece, entitled (with unintended humour) The Fisherman's Widow.

My hands are sticky and I am wet with perspiration from having worked for two hours without a break, in an attempt to make this room more lively and colourful. I did my best to decorate it with the means at my disposal, with improvised garlands hung around the print frame and the jewels laid out symmetrically on the table for all to see.

The walls and ceiling are now aglow with warm colours. There's no doubt I've succeeded in bringing a bit of life to this squalid lodging, all the while exercising the greatest discretion. And in record time! With the stump of a candle stuck in a cracked wine glass as the only illumination.

There, it's finished. Now I can light a fire in the hearth.

Before leaving, I look around with the satisfaction of an artist contemplating his masterpiece.

PART ONE

1

May 1887

'Make your mind up, sir. The train's going to leave at any moment.'

After one last hesitation, I stepped down on to the platform. The shrill blow of the whistle startled me as the train began to pull out, leaving behind a long plume of steam.

I strode purposefully through the white barrier towards the station hotel, where I could charter a cabriolet. The coachman, a short fellow with rough features, asked me my destination; I replied briefly:

'Blackfield.'

There was a crack of the whip and, after hitting a large bump and shaking violently, the carriage rattled forward.

Blackfield! After so many years.

Blackfield. Scene of my childhood. But this was not the moment for sentiment. Definitely not. I would need all my faculties to accomplish the mission I had set myself, and which would be far from easy. Knowing that chance—and therefore improvisation—would play an important part in my carefully thought-out plan, I felt I had envisaged every possibility.

For I have no equal when it comes to improvisation, even if I say so myself. I know that my brain reacts with lightning speed, whatever the danger, the disturbance, or the state of my mind, and always finds the perfect response.

This ability has led to an impressive number of professional successes.

There was only one part of the plan that caused me concern. I had, on occasion, needed to modify my appearance, but doing so for an evening among strangers was one thing; deceiving a whole village for weeks was quite another. An ill-conceived disguise could arouse suspicion.

But why did I need a disguise, in any event? My adolescent years were far behind me. In view of the years that had gone by, my neatly-trimmed beard and moustache—very fetching, I'm told—should make me unrecognisable.

Certainly I need not fear that Major Morstan, with his lorgnette, would recognise me. But there were also Rose, Eleanor Burroughs, Celia Forsythe, Dr. Griffin, Tony Ferrers the inn-keeper, and several others to worry about.

Not without emotion, I watched the pleasant, verdant English countryside slip past. It was a beautiful spring afternoon: little clouds drifted peacefully towards the east in an azure sky. All the sylvan scents of the gently rolling Surrey hills mingled, under the already blazing sun, with the incomparably sweet smell of meadows after their morning shower. The chant of a cuckoo could be heard at regular intervals.

The horses' hooves pounded rapidly on the road bordered by a variety of trees and shrubs. Lulled by the rhythm and intoxicated by the pure and fragrant air, I allowed myself to be overwhelmed by a sensation of extreme well-being, my mind fully occupied with the difficult mission in which I had just become engaged.

I savoured the singular contrast between the present enchantment and the frightening adventure I was about to embark on. In a few moments I was going to relive a tragic past; little did I imagine the evil forces that would be unleashed as a result.

Madness slumbers in all of us, hidden in obscure crevices. Sometimes a chance word or gesture, or a seemingly insignificant combination of circumstances can provoke a breach of the rampart of conscience and reason. And suddenly everything changes and the forces of evil emerge, overwhelming the protective walls to spread terror in a spattering of blood.

Blood, a spattering of blood.

A cold shiver ran down my spine. I covered my eyes with my hands in an attempt to dissipate the growing sense of unease. In a few seconds I succeeded in clearing my thoughts. I could see nothing; all my senses were paralysed.

Strange chords pierce the silence: dissonant, muted and strident at the same time; frantic bowing on crazed violins. The sounds intensify insidiously; my eardrums seem ready to explode. Scarlet drops appear on a black screen before my eyes.

'Blackfield! Here we are, sir.'

The coachman's voice struck me like a whiplash. I came out of my reverie and opened my eyes. Behind the trees I could see the red- and grey-roofed houses.

Blackfield! The cradle of my childhood. I felt a lump in my throat.

'Where shall I drop you off?' asked the coachman.

'At the *Black Swan*.'

There was no going back. The die was cast.

A few moments later, the carriage pulled up in front of the inn. I paid the bill and added a decent tip, and the cabriolet took off in the direction from whence it came.

I opened the door of the saloon bar. Nothing had changed in the oak-panelled room: the same enormous black beams supporting the ceiling; the tables arranged next to the same green- and yellow-paned windows; the same hunting trophies lining the walls. Opposite me, at the other end of the room, was the landlord's sanctuary: the counter, dominated by an imposing tiger's head brought back from India by Major Daniel Morstan.

I went over to the counter, placed my bags on the floor, and sat down. It was four o'clock and, unsurprisingly, there was nobody else in the room.

A few minutes later, Tony, the landlord, appeared. He was a jovial fellow of medium height, with greying sideburns. There was a frank and open gaze behind the gold-rimmed spectacles.

'I have a room booked for three weeks,' I said. 'The name is Miles—Sidney Miles.'

He shook my hand with a warm smile.

'Tony Ferrers at your service. You're going to have an enjoyable stay, Mr. Miles: the weather's supposed to stay warm, and it's a pretty part of the world—but perhaps you'd like to see your room?'

'Yes, but I wouldn't mind a drink first.'

'Of course. I'll send someone out while I take your bags upstairs.'

So saying, he left. He'd treated me just like a normal customer, which meant I was over the first hurdle, although there were many more to come. And far more difficult: entering the lion's den, for example. I hadn't devised a detailed plan of approach, preferring to rely on my gifts of improvisation. But I think my idea—that of a journalist planning to write a book about the mysterious death of

Richard Morstan—was a good one. Although the simpler approach of using my real identity might have been....

'Good afternoon, sir. Would you care for something?'

Cora! The innkeeper's daughter. I'd completely forgotten about her. My goodness, how she'd changed! The awkward adolescent I'd known when she was fourteen had turned into a splendid young woman. A mass of chestnut hair swept up in a chignon, from which a few golden-brown locks had escaped to frame a lovely face with slightly pouting lips, a pert nose and heavenly blue eyes; a pearly-white complexion; a perfectly shaped figure clad in a simple cotton dress which did nothing to conceal it. I looked at her in wonder, much as Adam must have looked at Eve. She could not help noticing my embarrassment, and asked mischievously:

'Do you always stare at women like that?'

'Women?' I babbled. 'I see all of them in you, and I'm not disappointed. Quite the opposite.' I moved towards her. 'After close inspection, I think we may speak of a masterpiece of the Creator. A masterpiece which has never been equalled and never will be.'

Approaching even closer, I examined her from all angles. She remained as motionless as a statue, looking straight ahead at some imaginary object. But her amused smile encouraged me to continue:

'Remarkable,' I said confidently. 'Absolutely remarkable.'

I observed a short silence which she broke with an ironic:

'Is that all?'

'My emotions have rendered me speechless. I could do with a drink.'

'In the circumstances, maybe something strong?' she suggested.

'That would probably not be prudent,' I said with a smile. 'It would probably give me the courage to propose to you.'

She burst out laughing, and I joined in. There was now a bond of friendly complicity between us.

'It's past four o'clock. Suppose I make you some tea?'

'That would be more prudent, dear madam.'

She disappeared with a rustling of skirts.

My stay was taking an unexpected turn, and a very enjoyable one, I had to admit. How she had changed. Cora, the shy little girl. Maybe she was married. She wasn't wearing a ring. Curious, though, that such a pretty girl, already...let me see, fourteen plus nine equals twenty-three years old, was still unmarried. What were they thinking about in Blackfield? Maybe there was a fiancé somewhere?

There, I was getting jealous. It wasn't the moment; I had to get back to work. Now I thought about it, Cora would make an ideal ally. She knew the Morstans very well, and she and Rose were very close once.

My plan of action was in place in a matter of seconds.

Cora returned with the tea and some slices of cake which looked delicious.

'My speciality,' she announced, pouring me a cup.

The tea and the cake were both of excellent quality and I complimented her, adding:

'I think I should warn you: you're going to have to put up with me for three weeks. I've booked a room here.'

'In the name of—?'

'Sidney Miles.'

I sipped my tea, congratulating myself for the turn of events, when the bomb burst:

'You're not Sidney Miles.'

There was a silence. The house of cards had collapsed. Cora had recognised me.

'No,' she continued, 'you're Bluebeard. The lady-killer!'

My relief probably registered on my face for a fleeting instant. She appeared not to notice, and I tried to recover by stroking my beard with a knowing air.

'I knew Bluebeard was a handsome man,' she said, tongue in cheek, 'but I never imagined him to be as handsome as this.'

She was entering into the spirit of things. I shot back:

'And what's the name of his next wife and victim?'

'Cora Ferrers. I'm the daughter of—.' She stopped, annoyed with herself for falling into the trap. 'Very well,' she added, with an air of resignation, 'all that remains is for me to let myself be murdered. By the way, what does Bluebeard do when he's not killing his wives?'

'He's a journalist for the *Daily Telegraph*.'

'Sir's from London, the capital,' she said mockingly. 'So why is he taking his holidays in a backwater like Blackfield?'

Now we were at the heart of the matter. Careful: one slip and the whole edifice would crash down. Looking down into my cup, I asked:

'Have you ever read *The Moonstone* or *The Woman in White* by

Wilkie Collins?'

She shook her head.

'Or *The Widow Lerouge* by Gaboriau?'

'I've heard of the Wilkie Collins books, but I've never read them.'

'What about Edgar Allan Poe?'

'Yes, but I find his stories horrible, particularly those about the black cat and the red death.'

'So you must have read *The Murders in the Rue Morgue*?'

'Is that the one where the woman is found stuffed in the chimney?'

'That's right. There's also the body of an old woman in the courtyard, whose throat has been cut so deeply that her head falls off when they try to lift her up. But I'm getting into too many bloody details.'

She didn't let the opportunity pass:

'It's quite natural. You are Bluebeard, after all.'

I liked her sense of humour, which was similar to my own, as I had sensed from the very start. But I was far from happy with the Bluebeard analogy, so I let her remark pass and went on:

'What's interesting is how the first crime was committed. The flat was found to be hermetically sealed, so that nobody, apparently, could have got out of there after the murder. It's a crime which appears to have been impossible to commit.'

'Very interesting. So what?'

There was a silence.

'I'm going to write a novel where a mystery of that kind occurs.'

Cora shivered, her eyes wide with fright.

'My God,' she exclaimed. 'Now I'm beginning to understand. You want to base your book on Richard Morstan's murder, the one that's never been solved. What you call an impossible crime.'

She started to tremble, a faraway look in her eyes. In a childlike gesture of defence, she hid her face in her hands. I took the opportunity to seize her by her shoulders.

'Cora, what's the matter?'

She put her hands down, revealing eyes full of sadness and fright. There was something else as well: a look which I have never seen on the face of any other woman, something primitive, even savage. Fascinated, I looked deep into her eyes, as deep and limpid as mountain lakes reflecting the azure sky. Her open lips suggested a passion, an ardour, of which she seemed unaware. She was infinitely attractive, irresistible, and my heart raced under the pretty hands pressed against my chest. I almost kissed her, but managed to control myself.

'I saw the crime committed before my eyes, more or less,' she murmured. 'There were ten of us, all young girls, including Rose, Richard Morstan's daughter. He was performing conjuring tricks. He pulled the curtain across the room so as to hide what he was doing. We waited…Nothing happened…We went to have a look…Mr. Morstan was dead. Murdered. A murder no one, absolutely no one, could have committed. And yet Mr. Morstan couldn't have committed suicide.'

Cora was one of the girls who had witnessed the murder. I'd forgotten that. It changed everything.

After a while, Cora regained her lovely smile and the mischievous look in her eye. She made a helpless gesture and apologised:

'I'm sorry. I can't help myself. Every time I think about it, the same thing happens.'

'It's not worth working yourself into such a state,' I declared, with calm detachment. 'Particularly since you will soon be joining my other wives, hanging on a wall with your throat cut.'

Removing my hands from her shoulders, she exclaimed—with a smile this time, and in a different voice:

'Horrors! You have a really macabre sense of humour. If this is a new seduction method, I doubt very much it will work.'

'You're completely mistaken. I'm not trying to seduce you.' Her eyes widened in disappointed surprise. 'I'm simply noting your exceptional beauty.' Her eyes gleamed with pleasure. 'Just a simple, perfectly objective, observation made with profound sincerity.'

Seeing her blush, not knowing quite what to say, I took the opportunity to hold her hand. There was an awkward silence which ended in a double burst of laughter. She took her hand away, reluctantly, it seemed to me.

'Well,' she said. 'Let's get back to your book. You want to draw inspiration from Richard Morstan's murder.'

'That's it. You see, by writing *The Murders in the Rue Morgue*, Poe put his finger on something important: the impossible crime. Someone is killed in a room locked on the inside, and apparently nobody could have got in or out. But one can think of other variations: a room where all the doors and windows are watched by witnesses; or a body discovered in a pavilion surrounded by virgin snow, yet it stopped snowing an hour before the crime was committed; or, a criminal is trapped in a passageway bounded by high walls which make escape impossible, yet he escapes. The theme is rich in variation. What's important, to my mind, is the notion of a murder coupled with a mystery: we're in the presence of a phantom killer.'

'You're determined for me to have sleepless nights. The notion of a phantom killer, as you call him, haunted this village ten years ago. I was only fourteen then, and I was terrified—just like all my friends, I may add. In fact, how did you come to hear about it?'

'Purely by chance. A couple of months ago, I was asked to write a piece about the development of the bicycle. As I was delving into old newspapers, I stumbled on the Morstan affair and was struck by its unusual nature. Just think, I who had wanted to write a mystery novel and who thought such stories only happened in fiction, had just found a real one. I read every article about it I could lay my hands on, and found the case had never been solved.'

'That's right. The police got nowhere. Major Morstan, the victim's brother, swore to find the killer, but had to give up.'

Her head down, Cora played with her hands. Suddenly, she looked me straight in the eye:

'So you want to find the murderer before writing your book?'

'It's not so much the killer's identity I want to find, as how he did it.'

Cora looked into the distance. I had a feeling I'd tackled the subject too clumsily.

'Needless to say,' I added, 'the backdrop to the book will be the tender love story—.'

'I can rely on you for that!' she exclaimed, laughing.

'The heroine will be young and beautiful with azure blue eyes.' Cora raised hers to the ceiling. 'She'll fall in love with a handsome young man with a superb black beard...And, at the end, they'll marry and have lots of children.'

'That's much better than all that impossible murder business.'

I sighed wearily, and declared:

'You'll see, one day there'll be so many stories on the subject that someone will do a study about it.'

'In which case the first writer he will quote will be the celebrated Sidney Miles.'

'Don't laugh. I'm serious about writing the book.'

'But first you'll have to solve the Morstan affair. It's already nine years old, don't forget. If I'm your only witness, you won't get very far. My memory isn't all that extraordinary. In fact,' she added, frowning, 'how exactly are you planning to conduct your investigation?'

I pretended to be shy and unprepared:

'I—I don't really know. Could you possibly help me?'

With her elbows on the counter and her chin in her hands, Cora looked at me thoughtfully. Her brow was furrowed. It was apparent that she was still asking herself a lot of questions about me and would be probing further. After a long silence, she asked:

'Help you? And how, exactly?'

'I don't really know. Perhaps you could introduce me to the Morstan family?'

'As far as Major Morstan's concerned, that shouldn't be difficult. He gave up trying to find the killer a long time ago, but if you restart the investigation I'm sure he'll do everything in his power to help.'

Just at that moment, the entrance door creaked open. I turned round. A striking figure came into the room: Major Daniel Morstan.

2

'Solve the mystery surrounding Richard's death in order to write a novel about it? I must say, the more I think about it the more I like it, young man.'

The major, a stocky man of medium height with a ruddy face, paused in order to fill up his pipe. Behind his lorgnette, bedecked with a black ribbon, steely little eyes looked out from under bushy eyebrows. A magnificent salt-and-pepper moustache and a small amount of wayward hair of the same colour gave a rather comic look to a personage who appeared strict, but at the same time likeable.

The three of us were seated at the second table on the left when entering the room. Each time the major dropped in for a drink he inevitably sat at the same table. In my mind's eye I could see long evenings where the major told interminable stories about his service in the Indian army to anyone who would listen: the Sepoy revolt and many others, sprinkled with strange-sounding names. When he had returned from India in 1877, this table had been the centre of attraction for the customers of the *Black Swan,* eager to hear tales of the exotic country. But, little by little, the audience shrunk and now only old Fred feigned interest, in exchange for numerous glasses of beer.

'What paper did you say you worked for?' asked the major, once his pipe was lit.

'The *Daily Telegraph.*'

'The *Daily Telegraph.* So you must know young Steve Brown. He left Blackfield when he was eighteen. His father, a jolly decent fellow, all things considered, once told me....'

Although not native to the village, the major knew everyone and followed the professional careers of its young men closely. He was proud of each of them and of their professions, whatever they had chosen, as if they were his own sons. Being a bachelor, he had no children, which may have accounted for his interest.

Cora and I listened attentively to the major's story, which evolved into another one about a dangerous tiger hunt.

While I listened, I watched Cora out of the corner of my eye. The windows were open, creating a slight breeze. The sun's rays, refracted by the small panes of glass, created coloured patterns on the waxed table, which Cora was tracing with a finger. She seemed pre-occupied, no doubt considering what approach to take with me. Would she help me or not?

'—and I felled the great cat with a single thrust of my knife,' the major concluded in his booming voice.

He removed his lorgnette, took a handkerchief out of his pocket, and wiped the perspiration from his ruddy face.

'You must have lived an extremely eventful life,' I observed.

'True, my boy. Quite true,' said the major, with great satisfaction.

'You know, Mr. Miles, the major's experience is quite without equal,' said Cora.

'I don't doubt that for a moment,' I replied, glowering at her.

Her innocent air proved to me that she was secretly deriving great amusement from watching me flatter the major.

'I must admit my experience is quite considerable,' he said modestly. 'You can't gain experience simply by reading books, you know. When you've been in the Indian army...but I digress. Cora, be a good girl and get us some more beer.'

Cora was more than happy to oblige, for she was finding it hard to contain her mirth.

'Before we talk about the murder,' continued the major, 'it's useful to understand the context in which it happened. But before that....' He thought for a few moments before going on. 'You see, the Morstans were once one of the richest families in this part of the world. Their holdings covered most of the eastern part of Hampshire. But in the last century, three heirs in a row squandered the family fortune, leaving nothing to their descendants but a house with a few acres of land. The last owner, my father, was a ruined man who led a miserable existence. Richard and I were the only two children. When he died, we learned that the house and the land had been mortgaged to the hilt. I suggested to Richard that there were ways of saving the property which would involve a further loan, but he would hear none of it. Despite my insistent pleadings, he refused categorically, in the belief that we would only sink further into debt. And maybe he was right. But I believe to this day that, if we had joined forces, we could have climbed out of the mess and saved the property. But that's all water under the bridge.

'My brother emigrated to Australia more than twenty years ago, in 1854 to be precise. He returned in 1871, having amassed a considerable fortune through gold mining. He got married down under, but his marital bliss was cut short by a tragic accident. His wife left him two children, so he returned to England with Rose and Michael in tow—aged seven and eight respectively, if memory serves—and also Eleanor Burroughs, a governess he engaged shortly before his wife's death. Richard was captivated by Blackfield and purchased Burton Lodge.'

'Where you live today.'

'Yes. After Richard's return—Ah, Cora, here you are at last. We were dying of thirst.'

Without a word, the innkeeper's daughter placed the glasses on the table and sat down where she had been before: to my right, by the window.

'Meanwhile,' continued Daniel Morstan, after having downed half the glass in a single gulp, 'your humble servant had left for India. I shan't dwell on all my various encounters, although they're not without interest, believe me.'

'If they're as fascinating as the story of the tiger hunt we'd love to hear about them,' said Cora perfidiously, giving me a gentle kick under the table to show me that when it came to obsequious behaviour, she was every bit my equal.

'The tiger hunt was pretty small beer,' replied the major, making a dismissive gesture. 'There were other encounters far more dangerous, but better to draw a veil over them. Be that as it may, I did get an enemy bullet in the knee, which precipitated my retirement and causes my left leg to drag when I walk.' He waved his walking-stick in the air. 'That happened in 1877 and I was forced to return to England. Richard greeted me in true brotherly fashion and lodged me under his roof.'

There was a brief sadness in his grey eyes.

19

'Richard was an extraordinary fellow. One might have expected his fortune would go to his head, but not a bit of it. He was simple, friendly and generous, all of which endeared him to the villagers and gained their respect. He made countless gifts to charity.' He took off his lorgnette and a strange smile lingered on his lips. 'Richard had changed quite a bit. It was a magnanimous gesture on his part to take me in. I wasn't needy, of course, but I wasn't rolling in money either. And so we got to know each other, after so many years. He was a good and generous man. Naturally, no one's perfect and he had his faults, just like everyone.'

The major paused. He seemed absorbed by some inner torment, drawing on his pipe without realising it had gone out.

'In May of 1878, two months before the murder, little Angela Wright, who was not even twenty years old, lost her mother. Her father, the worst kind of drunk, had died a few years earlier. It was one of the poorest families in the village. Angela found herself all alone, with no means of support. Richard showed his great generosity, bringing her under his roof and giving her the family name.'

'Not forgetting she was a pretty little thing as well,' observed Cora.

The major made a weary gesture.

'I don't deny it. And it's no disrespect to point out that she wasn't the brightest jewel in the box. Not that she was stupid, exactly. It's just that nobody expected Richard to marry someone so... insignificant. Not to mention the thirty year age difference. Almost everyone attributed the act to Richard's generous soul. But there was some gnashing of teeth: Eleanor, the governess, had assumed that, if ever my brother were to remarry, it would inevitably be with her. In fact, she was far from unattractive: regular features, a lively look in her eye, extremely graceful and with excellent manners. She took it calmly and said nothing, but if looks could kill...She became the strict, cold-eyed governess we know today, managing the household with energy and ruthless efficiency.

'There was also Richard's fortune to consider: the will was going to be changed. Personally, it didn't matter much to me. So what if my inheritance was a little less? I was only one year younger than Richard and I could very well die before him, especially since his health was better than mine. Michael, my nephew, was above all that.

Money had never interested him; he proved it during what followed, and still does so today. But that's another story we'll get to, in due course. As for Rose, my niece, she was only fourteen years old. She was a decisive young lady who knew exactly what she wanted. She already knew, even at that stage, who her future husband would be. They weren't officially engaged, but they were certainly more than good friends. Luke Strange—he must have been seventeen, if memory serves—already showed signs of great ambition. He was a serious young man who knew where he was going, and he and Rose were very close. Everyone expected them to marry and we were not mistaken.

'Rose became Mrs. Strange a few years later. I remember a discussion I had with my niece two or three days before the tragedy. "Papa's been hoodwinked. That little slut only wants him for his money, it's as clear as day. Uncle Daniel, do something. Try to make him see reason. He doesn't want to listen to me: he treats me like a little girl who knows nothing about life." Luke, seated nearby, appeared absorbed in a book but was, in fact, following the discussion closely. I told my niece that my brother was old enough to know what he was doing, then I turned on my heel to leave. As I was going out of the room, I looked over my shoulder: Luke and Rose were looking at each other, obviously in the grip of a very strong emotion. I can't put my finger on it, but the attitude of the two adolescents seemed very strange.'

The major paused, as if to give weight to his words, then went on:

'Michael loved his father, but didn't show it. There were frequent quarrels because of—let's leave it at that. Nevertheless, Michael, to everyone's surprise, made no comment when his father announced his marriage to Angela. His silence on the subject was tantamount to approval.

'Now we come to the murder. For her fourteenth birthday, Rose had invited a number of friends to the house. To mark the occasion, Richard had planned a surprise attraction—.'

At that moment, two men came into the room. They nodded to us politely, then seated themselves a short distance away. Cora got up to serve them.

'I think we'd better postpone our discussion,' I suggested.

The major didn't reply immediately. His hand on his mouth, his brow furrowed, he looked thoughtfully in my direction, without appearing to see me. Then he confided in a low voice:

'Nine years ago, my brother was killed, and for nine years I've been trying to lay my hands on the murderer. I often wake up in the middle of the night, eyes wide open in the darkness, asking myself: Who? Who and why? For you, Mr. Miles, it's how? It's the trick he used which interests you, for your novel. Even though our interests are not the same, we have everything to gain by working together. If we can answer just one of those three questions, the others will follow. We need to become a team. You told me you were staying three weeks in Blackfield, I believe?'

'That was my plan, but I could probably stay a few days longer, if need be,' I replied, rather too quickly.

Everything was proceeding beyond my wildest expectations. I had had some vague notion of introducing myself through the good offices of the major, and here he was proposing we form a team!

'In three weeks,' he declared, 'we should be able to get results, if we go about it the right way. Admittedly, the tragedy didn't happen yesterday, and some memories might have faded over time, but I believe the delay might be to our benefit. The murderer is no longer watchful: he believes himself to be safe. If he were to get wind of our project, he might panic and give himself away.'

'If only we could be sure the killer still lives in Blackfield.'

The major frowned:

'I don't know how to explain myself,' he said, in a slow, solemn manner, 'but I sense something bizarre is happening, a curious tension in the air, oppressive and hostile.' He grabbed my arm and looked at me with those beady grey eyes. 'Someone is on the alert. The murderer. Yes, young man, the killer is still in the village. I can feel his presence, as if he were right next to me.'

A long silence followed his words. The major leant back in his chair, motionless. Behind the ribbon of smoke which rose from his pipe, his lorgnette gleamed in the sun's rays and hid what was in his eyes.

He spoke again:

'I presume you only know the circumstances of the crime from

22

newspaper reports, which means you don't know very much.'

I nodded in agreement.

'Listen, young man, I have an idea the killer will only show himself if we provoke him. We have to drive him into the open. First, we need to gather together all the parties involved, to create a retrospective of the tragedy. That won't be easy, I'll have to think about it. For now, not a word to anyone. Not about your idea of a novel, and certainly not about your profession. Take Cora into your confidence and swear her to secrecy.'

Major Daniel Morstan had spoken in a tone which brooked no argument.

'We'll meet here tomorrow at the same time,' he announced, getting up.

We shook hands firmly, more a sign of agreement than a taking of leave. The major moved towards the door, leaning on his stick and dragging his leg.

I stood still for a long moment, and then began to think.

3

'And this is Bluebeard's room!' announced Cora, opening the door and bowing respectfully.

I waited for her to straighten up before looking her in the eye, and replied admiringly:

'Superb.'

Without giving her time to reply, I went into the room. It was spacious and comfortable, albeit with a rather low ceiling. The whitewashed walls contrasted with the well-polished rustic furniture. In front of me, on either side of a wide-open window, were a washstand and a chest of drawers. An imposing wardrobe stood opposite a bed with a floral bedcover. Immediately to my left was a small table with a lamp and a cane chair whose twin stood just in front of the window.

'You can write your memoires here,' said Cora, indicating the table. 'I'll bring you a writing-case.'

There was an ironic smile on her lips.

'But don't impregnate the walls with your horrible stories, because—.'

'Cora, I need to talk to you.'

'Ah, the marriage proposal.'

'Not yet.'

I told her about my talk with the major and our project. She was enthusiastic:

'A murderer hunt! A hunt for a ghost. How exciting!'

'We start tonight.'

'Who's "we"?'

'You and I.'

Her eyes grew wide in amazement.

'The major is unaware of this nocturnal expedition,' I explained. 'I plan to visit the scene of the crime, just to get an idea.'

Needless to say, I knew the layout of the village from my past. But the idea of seeing Burton Lodge in the moonlight in the company of Cora was irresistible.

'I need a guide. You're the only one I can ask.'

'Ah, I begin to understand,' she said, her eyes narrowing. 'It's a pretext for a romantic moonlight stroll. If you'd asked me outright, I might have been tempted. But you've misplayed your hand.'

'The idea never crossed my mind,' I protested virtuously.

'In any case, I have to help my parents with the inn. The last customers don't leave until eleven o'clock.'

'I thought we'd start at midnight.'

'Midnight?' she stuttered. 'But—.'

'It's the ideal time: it's not too late, but most honest folk are already asleep.'

'I've only known you for a few hours,' she said, professing an indignation I was sure she didn't feel, 'and you dare to suggest I meet you at midnight. It's out of the question.'

'Cora, I beg you, be reasonable. It's not a rendezvous, it's a noble enterprise: the search for the truth.'

'A noble enterprise: don't make me laugh. You want a good subject for your novel. The answer is no.'

'Cora, for heaven's sake, I beg you.' I went down on one knee—is there no limit to what a man must do to seduce a woman? 'I promise I will make no attempt to imperil your honour.'

It was all a game: she knew it as well as I. In a flash, I worked out a plan: if she accepted, I would feign extreme indifference throughout our escapade. She would quickly become disappointed and reverse the roles. The plan had only one weakness: it was very difficult to remain indifferent in the presence of Cora.

'In that case...' she hesitated. 'I'll think about it. Now I must go. Dinner will be served around seven o'clock.'

'I'm very grateful to you, Cora.'

'I haven't said "yes" yet,' she huffed with a mischievous smile, closing the door in my face.

My moonlight walk was looking promising, I told myself. I hung up my clothes, took off my shoes, and lay down on the bed. I needed to analyse the situation. First, nobody had recognised me. Not Cora, nor her parents—Tony had introduced me to his wife a short while ago—nor Major Morstan, who had looked straight at me several times. Second, I was assured of an introduction to Burton Lodge: the major would take care of that, as I'd anticipated. The mystery surrounding the death of his brother still haunted him and he'd welcomed the fact that a journalist was prepared to study the affair in order to write a novel. He had even gone so far as to propose working as a team.

Cora had not been part of the plan. Nevertheless, I'd realised immediately that she could be useful to me. Even though making contact with the major wouldn't have been difficult, these things are always better if there's an introduction from a third party. In addition, Cora was extremely attractive. And she wasn't averse to my charm. I don't think of myself as a great seducer, but I've never had any difficulty with women. My face, it seems, is pleasant and sympathetic and inspires confidence. (Bear this in mind, for it will play an important role in an "enterprise" I hadn't envisaged up to now: it will be a trump card, without which I would not be able at one point to pursue the aforementioned enterprise. This is not conceit on my part, but merely an honest appreciation of my relations with the opposite sex. You will understand at the end of my story what I am referring to. This is a point I shall make once and only once.)

Cora…images of tender scenes filled my head.

But this was not the moment to let my thoughts wander. Not everything had been perfect this afternoon. First of all, I did not appreciate the comparison with Bluebeard at all. And then there was the major's curious remark about "a curious tension in the air, oppressive and hostile," which kept nagging at me because I, too, had had the same feeling of suffocation, of danger.

From now on, I would have to be doubly cautious, analysing every word before pronouncing it, and only talking about what I was assumed to know. A moment's inattention and I would be unmasked. Particularly in the presence of Cora, who made me forget why I had come here in the first place.

On reflection, this night's escapade—if it ever took place—would be a serious test.

My eyes started to close, even though I fought to keep them open with thoughts of Cora's shapely form, her opulent hair tumbling over her graceful shoulders, her pouting lips and….

I woke with a start: someone was knocking at the door.

'Yes?' I growled.

Cora's head appeared in the doorway.

'It's almost seven-thirty. Shall I set a place at the table?'

'Yes, I'll be down soon. Wait, don't go!'

Cora shut the door and stood with her back to it.

'Thirty seconds,' she said, 'and not a second more. I'm listening.'

A smile hovered on her lips; she knew perfectly well what I was going to ask.

'Can I count on you this evening?'

'You mean this night. If you keep your promise, yes.'

'I always keep my word,' I replied, secretly keeping my fingers crossed.

A mischievous gleam appeared in her eyes; she tried to keep a straight face. The fact that I'd looked down while making the last promise had not escaped her.

'It would be best if we didn't leave together,' she said with a very convincing air of shyness. 'Someone might see us.'

'I completely understand. So, let's pick a rendezvous.'

Cora looked around nervously—even though we were the only people in the room—and pulled out a folded piece of paper from her apron pocket:

'I drew a plan. I hope you'll be able to work it out.'

I took the paper from her hand and pretended to study it hard, as if I knew nothing of the area.

'At the back of Burton Lodge, there's a little wooden bridge. I think my drawing is clear enough, all you have to do is follow the arrows.'

'I'll be there, you can be sure of it.'

'There's one more thing. You must leave by the window. The stairs creak terribly and Mama and Papa might hear.'

'Don't worry, I'm used to—what I mean to say is it'll be all right. At what time?'

'Midnight.'

Dinner had been served expeditiously, but not before I had observed the lecherous glances which lingered unpleasantly on Cora's curves, and overheard a few comments which were frankly beyond the pale. But it was all water off a duck's back and she handled everything with aplomb, distributing her smiles generously at the same time as the drinks. She missed no one out, myself included.

She was doing it on purpose. I knew exactly what she was doing, as it was part of the eternal sentimental joust in which we all participate. The lady in question, while trying to provoke me, showed masterly skill at handling the troublesome elements. I conceded she had won the first round, for, despite myself, I couldn't help but experience pangs of jealousy. I feigned utter indifference and, after a few ill-concealed yawns—which I hoped were vexing—I retired to my room.

I lay on the bed, incapable of thinking of anything but Cora. With an impatient hand I picked up the fob watch—a recent acquisition— from the bedside table: eleven-thirty. Time to go!

With one bound I reached the window sill. My room was on the first floor, but fortunately the inn sign was just below me. I waited a few seconds, scrutinising my surroundings, my ears alert to the slightest sound. Then, in a flash, I was in the street.

Burton Lodge was situated at the north of the village, at the edge of the woods, where the road turned slightly to the left: a good ten minutes walk away. A rectangular structure with simple, clean lines, it stood in the middle of a wide lawn encircled by the forest. The patches of moss on its red brick walls, its white windows and blue-grey slate roof, made it stand out against the soft green of the grass.

It was also possible to reach it from the rear, by crossing a river to the east of Blackfield, then following a path along the bank as far as the woods, then crossing a little rustic bridge to arrive opposite the rear face of the building. The advantage of this route was that it avoided prying eyes; it was the one Cora had indicated in her sketch. I therefore headed east without hesitation.

The profound silence of the village was something I was no longer accustomed to. I could hear my own footsteps on the paved surface, yet still savour the gentle calm of the night. After I crossed the river I walked along the path, savouring the fresh perfumed breath of the forest. It must have been a quarter to twelve by the time I reached the little bridge. I took a deep breath and continued my walk, when suddenly the dark roof of the forest opened on Burton Lodge.

A shiver ran up my spine. The building, which arose from the lawn bathed in moonlight, appeared frankly hostile. Suddenly, as if blown by a magic breath, a light breeze arose, causing the leaves to rustle with a menacing murmur. Death was still roaming these parts and would not go away until the truth shone on Richard Morstan's murder. Even the moon, with its rays like so many pale fingers seemed to want to penetrate the sombre mass of the house to pierce the mystery. I stood for a long moment observing Burton Lodge, which defied me in return, whilst putting me on notice.

"I've been warned," I thought, as I retraced my steps to the little bridge. I leant over it, lost in thought, listening to the furtive noises of the night creatures and the whispering of the waters beneath my feet. Ten minutes had passed before I heard soft footsteps. Cora came into view, dressed in a man's trousers and a dark shirt, and wearing a cap. Nobody would have been fooled by her masculine disguise, such was her femininity. I was about to tell her that when I remembered my vow to remain indifferent. She came to join me on the bridge. I looked at her without a word. There was not a ghost of a smile and her blue eyes were devoid of expression. The seconds went by in total silence. Then, driven by the same irrepressible impulse, we were in each other's arms, exchanging a passionate kiss, carried away by a wave of passion which left us breathless. The silence which followed was even longer than the first. There was nothing to say. Cora read my thoughts, and I hers. No words were necessary; they would only have broken the magic of the moment. My eyes were locked on hers, which, in the moonlight, took on an almost unbearable intensity: a blue of glaciers and burning lava. But she turned away to gaze at the silver ripples forming on the surface of the water.

'Cora,' I started to say. 'I'm sorry.'

'Because of your word?'

'Don't joke, I beg of you. No, it's just that…you must be engaged, I imagine. I don't want to be the source of—.'

'No, there's no one,' she interrupted tersely.

'So, a recent disappointment, perhaps?'

She smiled admiringly:

'There's no hiding anything from you, is there? But why are we here, in fact? Oh, yes, I remember: your worthy project. I suppose you've already taken a look at Burton Lodge?'

I nodded.

'Come, follow the guide. I'll show you where it happened.'

I followed her. We reached one corner of a wide dirt path separated from the nearest corner of the house by fifty feet of lawn. The rear wall of the house, with five windows on the ground floor and five on the first, formed an angle with the side wall with two windows on each floor. A door separated the two lower windows.

'What you see here is the rear face of the house,' she said, pointing. 'There are five upstairs windows on this side, but it's the one on the left closest to the corner that interests us.'

'So that's where the murderer——.'

'No, that window was locked from the inside. Notice you can also see the left side of the house, to some degree.'

'The right side, to someone looking at the front entrance.'

Cora ignored the remark:

'There are two windows on the side wall; I'm still talking about the upstairs floor. The one closest to the corner was open at the time. That must have been how the murderer got in, for it was proven that he couldn't have used any other way.'

'But it was also proven that he couldn't have got in that way, either,' I observed.

'At the time of the crime, Michael, Mr. Morstan's son, and two of his friends were playing at archery on this dirt path here. They were opposite the open window, at about fifty feet from the house.'

'Where was the target?'

'On the pathway. They were shooting in the direction away from us. So, when they were looking at the target, the open window on the side wall was to their right. They weren't watching it all the time, but they did confirm that they would have seen anyone climbing up the side wall or the rear wall, or down from the roof. They were moving to and fro along the path, according to them, so that if the murderer had got in through the window somehow, he must have done so in less than ten seconds or one of the boys would have seen him. The police tried to get them to say it could have been twenty seconds, but they wouldn't budge: not even ten seconds, maybe five at the maximum. Not only that, but the murderer didn't just have to get in, he also had to get out. He would have had to have an extraordinary agility and audacity, not to mention a great deal of luck.

'You can see there's no skylight on this corner of the roof, which is also very steep. Any acrobatics would have had to have left marks on the gutter, but there weren't any. One policeman tried and nearly broke his neck. And he left marks on the gutter.

'As to the murderer climbing up the wall, we need to stand where

31

the archers were. There's not much risk of being seen at this hour.'

We walked along the pathway to stand facing the side wall.

Cora started speaking very quietly:

'Michael and his friends were standing where we are now. Put yourself in their place. While they're playing with their bows and arrows, someone tries to climb the wall, which is practically impossible without some rope and a grappling iron. The distance separating the upstairs windows makes it impossible for him to have climbed across from the one furthest away. So, what do you think?'

I shook my head:

'Impossible. The children could never have missed seeing any kind of acrobatics.'

'And that's not all. There are patches of moss all over the walls. The murderer couldn't have helped leaving traces, but the police didn't find any. No scratches and no footprints, nothing.'

I said nothing as I stared thoughtfully at the house plunged in darkness, and more specifically at the window where death had swooped down to take Richard Morstan. Nine years had gone by since then.

'Say something, Sidney. I keep talking and you stand there as quiet as the grave.'

'I'm thinking.'

'There's even more. And I don't think there were any newspaper reports about it. Just before the fatal hour, Michael accidentally shot an arrow...into the scene of the crime. Not hearing any shouts or complaints, the boys went on with their target practice. When they heard Mr. Morstan had been killed, and under what circumstances, Michael ran away. He was only found two days later, in the woods, scared out of his wits.'

Needless to say, I was aware of all that. Nevertheless, I asked the obvious question:

'So, was he the killer?'

'Mr. Morstan was killed by a dagger in the back. The doctors confirmed that the wound wasn't caused by an arrow. Major Morstan owned two Indian daggers of similar appearance. One of them was missing: it was almost certainly the murder weapon.'

'It's all rather bizarre: someone's murdered and *a priori* nobody could have done it. Around the fatal time, an arrow is shot into the room, which could have explained everything. Yet Richard Morstan wasn't killed by the arrow. Where was it found, by the way?'

Cora hesitated before answering:

'In a rather curious place, given that the boys had clearly seen it go into the room. In the flower bed under the window. There was no blood on it.'

'The boys must have been mistaken. It probably bounced off the wall and fell down under the window.'

'That's what the police tried to get the boys to admit, but even Michael was adamant that it had gone into the room. And it was not in his interest to say so, quite the contrary.

'You have to understand: at first everyone took Michael's flight as a confession that he'd killed his father by accident. Everything seemed clear. But they didn't find the arrow in the room, they found it on the ground under the window, with no traces of blood on it. The archers counted the arrows: there weren't any missing, and none of them showed any traces of blood. The doctor stated the wound wasn't caused by an arrow, and the major confirmed one of his daggers was missing.

'When they found Michael two days after the crime, the police assured him he hadn't killed his father. He was overcome with relief, but since that day his behaviour has been strange.'

'That's hardly surprising,' I retorted. 'His father had just been murdered.'

'It wasn't grief, it was more like weariness, almost nausea. He didn't talk to anyone, and nobody saw him at the inn anymore. He stayed inside Burton Lodge until the end of his school holidays...and no one has ever seen him since.'

I remained silent.

'Notice I didn't say he'd disappeared. We knew where he was: he was continuing his studies in London. But he always took steps to avoid seeing his family, preferring to take his holidays with friends. The major received letters from time to time, and occasionally someone would turn up at the door asking for some article belonging to his nephew, but Michael himself never showed his face. Four or five years after the event, he left for America. He wrote to his uncle occasionally, without ever revealing what he was doing or where he was. We haven't seen him for nine years. At the time, Rose and I were good friends; it's from her that I learned everything.'

33

'You said "at the time". Does that mean you're no longer friends?'

'Since she married Luke, she's kept her distance—from everybody, incidentally.'

I'd noticed that, for a while, Cora had been staring at me with a gentle smile on her lips. In alarm, I asked her:

'What's the matter, Cora. Why are you looking at me like that?'

With a sudden movement, she put her hand over my chin and placed a finger across my moustache:

'Bluebeard wouldn't be bad without his beard.'

The blood rushed to my head and I instinctively pulled away. It was a crude error on my part and I attempted to make amends immediately:

'Forgive me, Cora, I don't know what's wrong with me. I'm upset. That house gives me the shivers. Come, let's go back to the bridge.'

There was something more than just concern in her eyes. I took her hand and we retraced our footsteps.

'You know,' I tried to explain, 'I don't like the comparison with Bluebeard. Since this afternoon, all we've talked about is crime and blood—.'

'Of all the nerve! You come here to stir up an old murder mystery; you fill my head with stories of perfect crimes, impossible crimes and throats being cut; you drag me to the scene of the crime at midnight, and now you say we've talked too much about blood!'

Really, I was just making one mistake after another. At a loss for arguments, I took her in my arms for a long and passionate embrace. I'd had feelings of exhilaration before, but never as intense as this. A single touch sufficed to fill me with a sense of well-being and transport me into a state of bliss.

We leant over the guardrail of the little rustic bridge, fascinated by the reflection of the moon in the water, as I started to tell her about myself. She listened intently; little dimples of amusement formed on the corners of her lips. She understood my language and could discern the truth amongst all the exaggerations. As my monologue was accompanied by sweeping gestures, it was almost inevitable that I would injure myself, which I did on a nail which must have stuck out half an inch from the rudimentary wooden rail.

'Damn! Who's the clumsy oaf who built this bridge? He could at least have hammered the nails all the way in.'

Cora took hold of my hand and examined it carefully.

'Oh, you poor thing, you're bleeding,' she said teasingly. 'We're going to have to take you home and bandage you.'

It was only a superficial wound, but enough for blood to ooze out.

Blood.

The blood is flowing, crimson, brilliant and pure.

I tried to look at Cora, in order to ward off the hideous memory which was trying to float to the surface, but she wasn't there any more. In her place was a woman with grey hair whose complexion had faded from misery and debauchery. Some of her teeth had gone and her face was streaked with red. My eyesight started to blur. The hideous vision swirled in a crimson fog.

The blood is flowing. The steel flashes against the sky, then crashes down to make the blood flow. My ears hear strange, strident, horribly dissonant chords such as a mad musician might have imagined.

'Sidney? What's got into you? Why are you looking at your thumb like that? You look as if you're terrified. It's just a little scratch, I can assure you. Come along, we're going back. It's late, anyway.'

4

Major Daniel Morstan strode into the saloon bar of the *Black Swan* at around four o'clock, somewhat earlier than planned. He looked determined and confident. He had assuredly spent most of the night planning his campaign. I, on the other hand, had spent a restless night filled with horrible nightmares. More than once I had woken up, damp with perspiration, reflecting on my blunders in the presence of Cora.

'I slept on what we discussed,' said the major sententiously, sitting down opposite me.

I was about to speak, but he raised his hand and made a sign to Tony, the innkeeper. I remembered: the major never started a speech without a glass of beer in front of him. Despite his gammy leg, he made it a point of honour to walk from Burton Lodge, no matter how long it took, which inevitably caused him to arrive out of breath. The temperature had risen since the day before, and the air was very humid. The walk must have been very painful for him; perspiration was pouring down his brick-red face.

'You shouldn't be out in this weather,' said Tony, placing two glasses on the table. 'At least, not on foot.'

'You'd be surprised by the action these legs have seen, Tony, my boy,' growled the retired soldier. 'It's obvious you've never served in India. A little scratch on the knee and a couple of miles aren't going to stop me!'

He looked around the room, even though he was well aware we were the only customers, and said, in a confidential tone:

'I've organised a small meeting for tonight, but the journalist who wants to write a novel won't be there.'

'Oh.'

'Don't misunderstand me. You'll obviously be there, but not as a journalist. Your intention of writing a novel wouldn't go down well. Quite the opposite. Some would look askance at it, and hide behind an attitude of indifference. What we need is to create a climate of insecurity and oppression. They must be made to feel they're in an inferior position. Mr. Miles, therefore, will be a detective.'

'Detective? A private detective?'

'No, an official detective: a Scotland Yard inspector.'

The announcement caught me completely off guard. I took out my handkerchief and blew my nose while I tried to decide whether this new deal of the cards was good or bad.

The major observed a brief silence, as if to give me time to digest his idea—which he no doubt thought was a stroke of genius—then persisted:

'The presence of a representative of the law, you understand, will give the investigation an official air. Witnesses won't be able to dodge questions, even delicate ones. But are you up to it? I assume that, as a journalist, there shouldn't be a difficulty. What say you?'

'Oh, I think I can do it. But how are you going to justify the investigation? You can't re-open a nine-year old dossier without new facts.'

The major held up his hand:

'Don't worry, we're not going to invent a cock-and-bull story. You're a relative of mine, on holiday: an inspector who doesn't mind lending me a hand while he's here. Even though the investigation isn't official, your very presence will make it seem so. By the way, does anyone else, apart from Cora, know you're a journalist?'

'No, but I'm still not sure I should accept—.'

'We'll get back to that later, young man,' cut in the major peremptorily. 'For the time being, let's concentrate on those implicated in the affair, and look at their psychological side, which was obviously never covered in the newspapers. Let's start with my nephew Michael, conspicuous by his absence for many long years.'

'I'm reasonably well-informed about him,' I admitted. 'Cora told me.'

I repeated what she had said, neglecting to mention our midnight excursion.

The major nodded several times, an unhappy look on his face.

'There's not much to add,' he sighed. 'We don't know any more than that. He wrote several letters from America—very vague, nothing but banalities—just to let us know he was still alive. I ask myself if we'd even recognise him if he came back after such a long time away.'

There was a moment of silence.

He bit his lip several times before he continued:

'There's the matter of inheritance. My brother left half of his fortune to his son when he came of age. But Michael failed to appear at the appointed time. Oh, he didn't refuse his inheritance, he just left it in suspense. The dispositions of the will are such—it gets pretty complicated—that, if my nephew fails to turn up in the next two years, there's a good chance that his share will go to my niece and myself. "My father's money doesn't interest me," he said, just before he left us. Even at a tender age, he showed a profound disdain for his father's fortune. But he was only fifteen at the time, so who can tell? If he really wasn't interested, there were steps he could have taken. I have a strong suspicion he plans to dangle his share in front of our noses, then claim it at the last minute. He's a strange boy, Michael.'

I cleared my throat before asking him:

'I presume your brother didn't forget you and your niece in his will?'

'I was about to explain. Aside from a few insignificant gifts to the servants, the balance of the inheritance goes to us. I already told you about Luke Strange, Rose's husband and his ambitious nature. He currently holds an important position in a London bank and he will shortly be appointed to the board of directors. He's a conscientious lad, who's climbed fast thanks to his appetite for work. He's only made one mistake in his career, but it's a beauty. Three years ago, he promised he could double our capital in one spectacular investment. I trusted him, and Rose did too, by the way. The lion's share of what we owned was invested in stock which we were happy to resell later at a tenth of their value: it was a compete disaster. I won't say our current situation is a disaster, but we no longer live in the financial tranquillity we enjoyed in the past.'

'I assume your niece and her husband still live with you in Burton Lodge?'

'Yes, along with Eleanor, the governess, who's part of the family. She it was who raised Rose and Michael. She runs the place now. She's a bitter old maid who spent the best years of her life waiting for my brother to marry her. I don't know how she took Richard's plan to marry Angela, but it must have been a cruel disillusionment.' (Here a cynical smile crossed his face: one might almost have thought the crushing of Eleanor's dreams gave him some kind of pleasure.) 'What's more, my brother left her practically nothing.

'Aside from the governess, the staff consisted of Mr. and Mrs. Hopkins and Nellie Smith. Peter Hopkins took care of the garden and the horses. Jennifer, his wife, was the cook and laundrywoman. Richard hired them on his return to Blackfield. They're an old couple above suspicion. They also happen to have a cast-iron alibi for the time of the murder. Nellie Smith, the maid, is an orphan who entered Richard's service a few months before his death. She was fourteen years old at the time, and was one of the young girls who witnessed the crime, so to speak. So she also has a cast-iron alibi. Nellie is simple, discreet, quite pretty, and does her job well. There's really nothing to add.

'My niece had invited a number of her friends to her fourteenth birthday, which Richard had promised to enliven with some conjuring tricks. That took place in a long room on the upper floor, divided in two by a curtain. On one side sat the girls, waiting for the show, together with Celia Forsythe, the school teacher, who was only too happy to be with her ex-pupils. On the other side was Richard. The show was about to begin: my brother had drawn the curtains closed. He was therefore alone in a room where every entrance and exit was either locked from the inside or observed by several witnesses...and yet he was murdered. Given the type of wound, it could not have been suicide. We'll go through all that in detail tonight.

'Celia Forsythe will be with us tonight. She's not on our list of suspects because she has a solid alibi and no motive. But I think her testimony will be valuable.

'There will also be another witness present: Angela Wright, the ex-fiancée of Richard. She had no motive: on the contrary, she had everything to lose. Fortune, which had seemed to shine on her, vanished with the death of her fiancé. Nevertheless, she was one of those without an alibi. I didn't have time to invite her but, even if I had, she wouldn't have come. She left the village shortly after the crime, with the feeling she had been robbed. In a way, I understand her.'

He stopped to refill his pipe. Aside from a few minor points, I'd learnt very little. But I had to play my part:

'Who were the two boys playing at archery with Michael?'

'Stanley, Stanley Griffin, the doctor's son. Highly intelligent. Bachelor of Medicine. Has his own surgery in Winchester. The other was Bill Hudson, a little thug, who dropped out of sight a long time ago. No idea what became of him.'

Stanley and Bill! I remembered them very well. Stanley, the studious one, who always looked fourteen years old, and Bill, the dunce, who had a way with the girls; he must have been two or three years older than Stanley. The two had nothing in common, yet they were inseparable.

'In any case, Michael, Stanley, and Bill had nothing to do with the murder. The inquest proved that. The arrow accidentally shot by Michael served only to complicate things. But let's get back to the evening in question. Those present included: Rose, Luke, Eleanor, Nellie, Celia Forsythe, Cora—What's on your mind, young man?'

He looked at me quizzically.

'Nothing,' I stammered. 'I thought she worked nights and—.'

'And you like her,' the major interrupted, with a complicit wink. 'I haven't invited her yet, but don't worry: Tony can spare her for once.'

'I don't know whether you realise this, but I could lose my spot on the newspaper if they got wind of this.'

The major replied reassuringly:

'You needn't worry, nobody will come to check up. And, in any case, I know someone at the Yard. We can always call him. Inspector John Reed, a brilliant lad who's already made a name for himself. He was responsible for solving the Bloch affair.'

I lied shamelessly:

'Oh, yes. I believe I already interviewed him.'

'He's from the village, young man. His father was very poor and his wife had left him before the child was five years old. Even though he studied medicine at first, John joined Scotland Yard...but I digress. Mr. Miles, do you think you can play the part? You would have to appear severe and supremely professional: the individuals present have to be put in their place. Do you understand what I mean?'

The major was accustomed to giving orders. He didn't ask me whether I agreed, only whether I understood. I replied:

'There won't be a problem. In any case, I'll do my best.'

There was a savage gleam in his eye as he replied:

'Perfect. We will unmask Richard's killer, young man. He shall not escape the gallows.'

5

It was half past eight. There was absolute silence in the lounge of Burton Lodge. I stood in the doorway and looked rapidly around the major's lair: oak-panelled walls and sand-coloured wallpaper on which were mounted an impressive series of hunting trophies; impressive collections of knives and pistols; Indian statues in the most amazing poses; a magnificent tiger's skin stretched out on the floor between hearth, sofa and armchairs; curtains of saffron silk masking the contents of the bookshelves, save for the central section, where the gold leaf on the titles of the leather-bound books gleamed; it all formed a harmonious ensemble in the soft light of the oil lamps.

The major, who was watching me with a look of satisfaction on his face, commented:

'You seem to appreciate good books, inspector. I'll let you take a closer look at some point during your stay. It was Mr. Reed, one of our finest craftsmen, who did the bindings.'

I thanked him with a nod as I observed the assembled audience. The haughty Rose feigned indifference. Her blue dress, trimmed with lace, complemented the copper highlights of her hair, coiled at the nape of her neck. Luke, wearing a frock coat edged with braiding and a dandy's trousers, seemed to be looking at me with disdainful condescension. I'd never liked him, with his superior airs and oily blond hair plastered down on his head. Next to him there was an empty place.

With her pink complexion and white hair, Celia Forsythe—the schoolmistress at the time of the tragedy—was as charming as ever, despite being well over sixty; a retiring yet benevolent old maid, who seemed to savour every moment of her life. Seated between Cora and Nellie, she smiled at them, happy to see them.

Nellie had an attractive profile, but a chubby face with freckles and an absent-minded, disillusioned air. She had once been a cheerful little girl with a pretty, dimpled smile.

I was beginning to wonder where Eleanor was when the major took me by the arm to introduce me and closed the door which had concealed part of the room from me. Eleanor finished lighting the last lamp, which was standing on a fabulously ornate Indian chest. She turned up the flame, and her dark silhouette emerged from the shadow, bathed in light. She turned calmly towards us and sat down on the sofa. From his golden frame, Richard Morstan watched us.

The major raised his voice:

'This is my brother Richard, murdered nine years ago.'

The only sound was that of our collective breathing. Richard Morstan was strangely present in the painting, with the surprising contrast between his powerful shoulders and his extraordinary patriarch's beard, and the gentle expression oh his face.

The major invited me to sit in one of the two armchairs placed on either side of the hearth. After taking a seat in the other one, he broke the silence:

'Allow me to present Inspector Sidney Miles of Scotland Yard, who has generously agreed to give up some of his holiday here to help me shine a light on my brother's murder. Why an investigation now, after nine long years? New elements have come into our possession which we hope will allow us to view the affair in a new light—evidence which must remain secret, for obvious reasons.'

The audience appeared to accept the explanation and sat there all ears.

'I must add also,' continued the major, looking at me with great respect, 'that Inspector Miles is their grand specialist in obscure and inexplicable crimes.'

I struck a pose appropriate to the occasion, avoiding Cora's eye, for I was finding it difficult to keep a straight face.

'These new elements which you are keeping secret for obvious reasons,' said Luke Strange, in a voice dripping with venom, 'I fail to see the proof they exist.'

I stared at him with an expressionless face, just long enough to disconcert him.

'We don't want the murderer to find out about them,' I said, pronouncing each word clearly and casting a suspicious look at all in attendance.

I was starting to like Inspector Miles. However, even though the role suited my plans perfectly, I had to be careful not to overplay my hand, lest Luke become suspicious and contact Scotland Yard.

'Richard,' began the major pompously, 'was murdered in a cowardly fashion, in this house, just above our heads.' He pointed to the ceiling. 'That was nine years ago. We're dealing with a criminal quite out of the ordinary, a diabolically cunning individual: as proof, I offer the trick he used to commit the crime. That's where we're going to start the investigation. If we succeed in shining a light on this aspect of the case, the number of suspects will be drastically reduced. I'd go so far as to say our criminal would be unlikely to die a natural death.'

There was a disconcerting gleam in his eye. Was he planning to administer justice himself, or was he counting on our mysterious murderer to do the job himself? He seemed possessed by a terrible thirst for vengeance. Legitimate though it may be, his obsession was beginning to intrigue me. He was behaving as if the crime had been committed a few days before, and he was still in the grip of grief and hatred.

I started to study the picture of Richard Morstan more closely. Here was a man with the constitution of an ox, tall—nearly six feet—but with legs a little short for the powerful body and the imposing width of his shoulders. A long beard, which he obviously took great care to keep tidy, hung down to his chest. This aggressive virility, however, was tempered by a pleasant demeanour; a peaceful expression; a warm smile; and a look of such gentle candour as to be almost childlike. In the last years of his life, Richard became increasingly generous: he never hesitated to help someone in need. Which made him highly appreciated by the inhabitants of Blackfield: a village saint, of sorts. On top of all that, he manifested a concern and an almost paternal benevolence towards children and adolescents. He organised parties and hikes through the forest, and helped Rose's friends when they had difficulties at school.

And yet there was someone who had wanted him dead.

The major picked up a large envelope from a small table inlaid with mother-of-pearl, pulled out several sheets of paper, and adjusted his lorgnette.

'I suppose you all remember the layout of the room above. Because there have been quite a few changes since the tragedy, I didn't see the point of taking you up there; the sketch I made at the time should be enough to jog your memories.'

I took the paper which the major handed me. The head of the main staircase was situated in the centre of a corridor which ran the entire length of the upstairs floor. Between the stairhead and the wall of the building where the side entrance was located were four doors, two on the left and two on the right of the corridor.

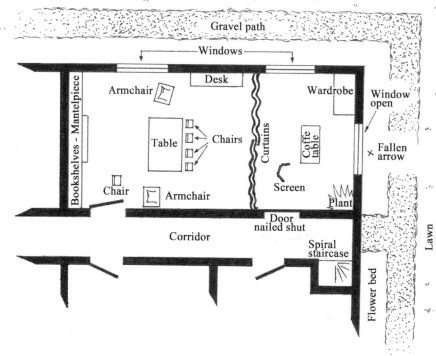

Lawn

Gravel path

Windows

Desk

Armchair

Wardrobe

Window open

Bookshelves - Mantelpiece

Table

Chairs

Curtains

Coffe table

Fallen arrow

Chair

Armchair

Screen

Plant

Lawn

Door nailed shut

Corridor

Spiral staircase

Flower bed

BURTON LODGE - FIRST FLOOR

At the end was a blank wall (above the door below), to the right of which was a spiral staircase leading to the servants' quarters in the attic. The first door on the left opened into one end of a very long room with three windows: two opposite the two doors, and a third in the side wall, overlooking the area where the boys had shot arrows. Immediately to the left—and therefore opposite the third window—were wall-to-wall bookshelves built around a mantelpiece. Two-thirds of the way down the room was a pair of curtains dividing it into two unequal parts. In the larger part were—apart from the mantelpiece-bookshelves—a table, a desk, two armchairs and several chairs. In the other part: a wardrobe, a coffee table, a folding screen with three panels and a large plant. Needless to say, these arrangements were part of the preparations for Richard's magic show.

I passed the sketch to the governess, who passed it to Luke without even a glance, and resumed her rigid posture. A strange woman, dressed all in black, with black hair in a net framing a handsome, austere face, scarcely marked by the passage of time. She was trying to appear unconcerned, but her fingers, fiddling unconsciously with the silver watch on a chain around her slender neck, betrayed her nervousness.

When everyone had had a chance to examine the plan, the major began again:

'In my notes on the matter, I've recorded everyone's movements.' He paused to glower at everyone in turn, before continuing: 'July 1878, on Rose's birthday. Before the traditional lunch, Richard had arranged some entertainment for the guests. We know there was to be a magic show and a ghostly appearance, but that's all, despite the various objects found in his small suitcase. Around half past two, Michael and his two friends started their attempts at archery. A quarter of an hour later, Rose, Cora, Nellie and seven other young girls—there's no point in naming them for the moment—entered the room Richard had prepared. My dear, I'll let you take over at this point. Cora and Nellie, don't hesitate to interrupt if you feel it's necessary.'

Rose pressed her fingertips against her forehead and closed her eyes in order to visualise the scene again:

'Yes, I remember. We went in through the door by the bookshelves. In any case, the other had been nailed up. Aside from the furniture, which had been moved around, I was most struck by the heavy velvet curtains which hid the other part of the room. I suppose we should have expected something like that.

'Needless to say, being curious creatures, we searched everywhere. The folding screen intrigued us, but far less than the door at the other end of the room, which had been sealed up by nailing three heavy planks across the width. In fact, there was only the wardrobe which could have concealed anyone—but there was nobody inside. The window between the wardrobe and the plant was open and we looked out; we saw Michael, Bill and Stanley shooting arrows, but we didn't show ourselves. The two other windows were shut. That's it. I don't think I forgot anything.'

'Good,' said the major. 'Ten minutes later, at five minutes to three, Richard himself came into the room.'

'The first thing he did,' continued Rose, 'was to lock the door behind him. Next he showed us the door which had been sealed in such a strange way, and made us check that it couldn't be opened. Then someone knocked at the other door. "That's the ghost," said my father with a smile. We went and opened it, and there was Miss Forsythe.'

'I need to make it clear,' said the charming old lady, 'that I was there at that precise moment at Richard Morstan's request. I can take over from here, Rose, if you like. Mr. Morstan asked me to take a chair near the door, to keep an eye on it. Then he locked it, all the while asking my forgiveness for not having offered me an armchair, because they were both so wide and so deep I would have sunk down and never have been able to watch the door properly. After which, he drew the curtain of the window near the bookshelves, which plunged that part of the room into semi-darkness. Some light could still be seen around the edges of the curtain, and at the top of the large velvet one.'

'You have an excellent memory, Miss Forsythe,' said the major admiringly, visibly pleased with the progress of the investigation. 'Just to be clear, the two velvet curtains functioned together just as in the theatre. Please go on, Miss Forsythe.'

'After that, he asked the girls to take a seat—no, wait, he assigned each girl a particular seat. There were four perched on the edge of the table, four others on chairs just in front of them, and two others in the armchairs.'

'I was in the armchair near the window,' announced Nellie.

'And I was in the one near the door,' added Cora. 'And if memory serves, Rose was seated on the table, isn't that right?'

Rose nodded in agreement.

With a faraway look in her eye, the schoolmistress seemed to be reliving the scene:

'I remember it very well. You were all so restless and excited. I could hear chuckling and suppressed laughter. Mr. Morstan opened the velvet curtains and fastened them to the walls. He picked up the folding screen, held it at arm's length, folded it inside out, turned it round, then placed it back on the floor. Then he went over to the wardrobe and opened it wide. It was completely empty.'

'Father wanted to prove to us there was nobody else in the room, but we already knew that from our search,' said Rose.

'His costume was really bizarre,' said Cora, smiling at the memory. 'Like something from the Middle Ages, which didn't suit him at all. He wore tight leg armour and a doublet and hat like Henry the Eighth; it all looked rather comical. He'd brought in a small suitcase which he placed on the coffee table in front of the open window.' Her expression saddened. '"And now, children," he announced, just before drawing the curtains closed, "in a few minutes you'll see a ghost appear."'

'It was three o'clock when he pronounced those words,' declared the major. They were his last. Now, I think it would be useful to find out what everyone else at Burton Lodge was doing at the time. Speaking for myself, I must admit I haven't got a particularly strong alibi. I was pruning the roses near the front of the house, but Michael and his friends told the police they saw me on two occasions as they went to collect some arrows which had overshot the target.'

Eleanor broke her icy silence:

'At that time, I was in the dining room, setting the table for a dozen people. I'd like to point out, major, that Mr. Richard had given all the servants a holiday—except Nellie, of course—despite the extra work caused by Rose's birthday. My only alibi is that the work got done. During that time, Miss Angela Wright managed to prepare some plates of toast in the kitchen.' She spat these last words out disdainfully. 'I would draw Inspector Miles' attention to the fact that the kitchen door opens directly on to the spiral staircase which leads to the attic by way of the first floor.' Again, her tone left little doubt about the implication of her words.

There was a silence. Then all eyes turned to Luke, who cleared his throat a little louder than was necessary before he spoke:

'A short while earlier, Mr. Morstan had asked me to patch up the little wooden bridge at the rear of the property. Everyone must have heard my hammer banging at the time of the crime. My alibi is therefore solid.'

'Very good,' said the major, leaning back in his armchair and folding his arms. 'Let's return to the scene of the crime.'

'So the curtains were once again in place,' said Rose, 'and we were once again in semi-darkness. We waited, eyes glued to the velvet curtains. There were noises: a sort of rustling sound, a muffled cry, a fall—or, rather, someone dropping to the floor—and other, barely perceptible, noises I can't describe. Then nothing. You must remember that, at the time, we were waiting for something extraordinary to occur. The minutes went by and nothing happened. Anxious, I suddenly called out to my father. No answer. At that moment, someone knocked on the door. I stood up quickly, not to answer the knock, but to see what was happening in the other part of the room. I pulled back the curtains, took several steps forward, and screamed. The other girls came to join me immediately. Father was lying on his stomach on the floor, between the wardrobe and the coffee table.'

'During that time,' chimed in the schoolmistress, 'I opened the door, because the knocking continued. I let Miss Burroughs into the room and bolted the door behind her. It was an instinctive gesture, I had no real reason to do it, I admit.'

'I realised immediately there was something bizarre going on,' said the governess, with her characteristic icy assurance. 'The curtains were only partly drawn, and when I got closer I could see the girls clustered around Mr. Richard. For a brief moment we all thought he was playing at being dead. But there was a wound in his back. I took his pulse: he was truly dead.

'The girls were terrified. They told me—all speaking at once—what had happened. We looked everywhere. I went to the window and spoke to the boys. They confirmed no one had climbed the wall. They came up to join us. Michael had a dreadful shock, seeing his father like that, and ran away in a panic.'

The ensuing discussion followed more or less what Cora had told me the previous night about Michael, his two friends, and their testimony.

'...and let's not forget,' growled the major, 'that Michael's accidental shot was quite feeble—Bill and Stanley testified to that—and could never have been fatal, even if it had hit my brother. As for the presence of the arrow at the foot of the wall, the explanation seems obvious: after Richard drew the curtains, it fell to the floor—soundlessly, because of the thick carpet—where Richard found it. What did he do? He picked it up and threw it out of the window. I never understood why the police spent so much time on the matter.

'So, to summarise: after Richard closed the curtains, he was absolutely alone in that part of the room.'

'And there was nobody but my friends and me in the other part of the room, except for Miss Forsyth,' declared Rose. 'And I would add that, from the moment we took our places, we never took our eyes off the curtain for a second.'

Cora, Nellie and Miss Forsythe nodded in silent agreement.

'Right,' said the major. 'We'll have to proceed by process of elimination. The murderer couldn't have got in through the door that Richard had nailed shut. Absolutely impossible, the police verified that. He can only have entered the room through the open window...or the other, which would imply Richard's complicity—a far from ridiculous hypothesis, which we shall return to later. Afterwards, he obviously needed to escape. Could he have slipped out under cover of the curtains while the girls were looking at the corpse?'

'Utterly out of the question,' replied Miss Forsythe categorically. 'I would have seen him. I didn't move from my chair. After the sinister discovery of the body, the room was inspected again in the full light of day, with the curtains drawn fully back. And don't forget the door was bolted until the arrival of the boys. There was nobody except us. The murderer had already gone.'

'That leaves the two windows. If he got out through the one we found shut, that suggests complicity. Do you see what that means? Someone present in the room must have locked the half-open window.'

'Equally impossible,' stammered Rose, who had gone pale. 'When we found the body, I automatically looked at the window, and it was closed. It might appear curious to you that I would note a detail like that under such circumstances, but I did. I recorded the fact.'

There was a painful silence, pregnant with suspicion and fear. It would not, after all, have been entirely ridiculous to imagine that the person who shut the window behind the murderer was Rose herself. That thought seemed to be written on the faces of all present. It was Nellie who came to Rose's aid:

'Mrs. Strange couldn't have been the one to do it. She pulled back the curtains to see what was happening, and had only taken a couple of steps forward before she stopped and screamed. We gathered round immediately.'

'That's right,' agreed Cora. 'She never left our sight for a second.'

The major looked relieved. Nellie's intervention had lifted a great weight from his shoulders. The fact that the witnesses had not let Rose out of their sight avoided a hypothesis he had dreaded: a lightning blow struck by the first person to reach the body.

After lighting his pipe, he continued:

'Now, let's talk about the case which Richard placed on the coffee table. It contained: two shrouds—ghost's clothes, if you prefer—a long strip of black paper, on which was drawn a skeleton, a large sheet of white linen, a small mask in black satin, a belt and six scarves. We know that Richard wanted to mystify us with the appearance of a ghost. In order to do this—and the presence of two shrouds seems to confirm it—Richard needed the help of an accomplice. It also seems probable that the accomplice was the killer. I feel that if we can work out the nature of the trick Richard had prepared, we'll have gone a long way to solving the mystery. In my opinion, the police investigation didn't probe deeply enough on this point. Allow me to draw your attention to the fact that the murder weapon—an Indian dagger of remarkable workmanship, part of my own collection—had a long blade which was both thin and sharp. The medical examiner went so far as to say: "Anyone, even a feeble woman, could have struck the fatal blow." Note, too, that only someone familiar with the site would have known where to get hold of the weapon.

'After everything that's been said, I think we can all accept the following as given:

'*One*—Richard needed an accomplice for his trick; *Two*—the murderer and the accomplice are one and the same; *Three*—the killer is one of this direct circle; *Four*—the murderer entered the room through one of the two windows; *Five*—the murderer left by the open window.

'The last two points require special attention. According to the testimony of the archers, the killer had to have got in or out of the room in six seconds or less, and the investigation revealed there were no traces on the roof or the walls. Consequently, I believe the killer did not enter through the open window, but through the other one which looks out over the rear of the property, the one which nobody was watching. And with Richard's help, of course.

'The killer is at the foot of the wall, waiting for Richard to open the window, at which point he throws up a rope. He hoists himself up by the strength of his arms while my brother holds the rope firm, a piece of cake for him. The killer is in the room without leaving a trace and without being seen.'

I looked at him in admiration:

'Your deduction is remarkable. Not only that, it's highly likely.'

'Let's not count our chickens before they're hatched,' replied the major. 'We still have to work out his escape. How could he have got out of the window in five seconds and be certain no one would see him? He couldn't have jumped: it's twenty feet to the ground and Michael and his friends couldn't have helped but hear the noise. The police tested it out. Furthermore, such a leap would have left marks on the flower bed or on the gravel path or on the lawn, and there weren't any. So how did he do it? That's the question.'

Major Daniel Morstan had placed particular emphasis on this last phrase, as if to impress upon us the difficulty of the problem and to invite a solution. Pensively, he watched the plumes of smoke from his pipe as they rose towards the ceiling.

Eleanor Burroughs broke the ensuing silence by interrupting in an impersonal voice:

'You seem to forget, major, that at one point the police thought the crime could have been executed via the sealed door, at the base of which, let us remember, was almost an inch of daylight. And let's not forget that, when I went upstairs to join the girls for the magic show—something I did not want to miss—and therefore a few seconds before the crime was discovered, I noticed a shadowy figure on the spiral staircase.'

'At the time you knocked on the door?' I asked brusquely.

'No, I was in the middle of the corridor, just after completing the last step of the staircase. I couldn't tell whether it was a man or a woman, even though the silhouette appeared quite slender...a young woman perhaps.'

6

More silence.

'The spiral staircase leads to the kitchen, inspector,' said Luke, staring at the glowing tip of his cigarette. 'The slender silhouette could well have been that of Angela Wright, who, by her own admission, was in the kitchen. At the time, I considered the possibility of her guilt, but she appeared to have no motive, alas!'

'In any case,' retorted the major, 'it was conclusively proved that the murder could not have been committed through the gap at the base of the door. Richard had been stabbed in the back, and his body was found between the wardrobe and the coffee table. I can't see how it would be possible to...It's simply unimaginable.'

'Quite,' agreed Luke. 'Your solution, dear uncle, remains the most likely one. Unfortunately, it doesn't explain how the murderer was able to leave the premises. Furthermore, even supposing that we solve that little mystery, that wouldn't necessarily reveal the identity of the killer. And I don't believe the villain is necessarily part of the family circle. Besides, the weapon has never been found. A dagger vanished from your collection, and the fatal wound was inflicted by a blade with the same characteristics, but we cannot be sure it was the weapon. Someone could quite easily have stolen your dagger in order to lead us to that conclusion and lay the blame for the crime on one of us: someone who hired an accomplice to do the work for him and give him an alibi. So, let's not jump too readily to conclusions.'

Silence descended again, and with it the veil which, a few moments earlier, had appeared to have lifted on the mystery. The atmosphere was heavy, as if a storm was approaching.

'Oh! My goodness!' murmured Celia Forsythe, in a choking voice.

All eyes turned to her.

'What is it, Miss Forsythe?' asked the major sharply. 'Aren't you feeling well?'

'It's nothing,' replied the old spinster in a scarcely audible voice. 'I thought I remembered something. No, I must have dreamt it, it's impossible. My memory is playing tricks.'

'Perhaps you could explain what it is....'

'No.' The worried expression had gone from her face. 'I'm getting old. I thought I recalled certain images, but it's obvious that...These memory lapses are terrible. One imagines things.'

Suddenly, the major sprang up from his armchair and went to the nearest of the two windows. A slight breeze was making the curtains move. He drew them back, looked out of the open window, and peered into the darkness. Then he closed the curtains and shook his head, as if doubting himself.

'Well?' asked Rose, who had gone over to join him.

'Nothing. I had the impression someone was spying on us. There was no one there. I'm starting to imagine things, too.'

Rose and her uncle sat back down. I remembered my role as Scotland Yard inspector.

'Did anyone think to examine the chimney? I know it's on the opposite side of the room, but....'

'There's a grill up inside,' said Luke, giving me a condescending look. 'And even if there'd been a staircase in there, that wouldn't have made any difference because, as you say, the crime was committed at the other end of the room.'

This fellow was really getting up my nose, with his superior air and his attempts to teach a Scotland Yard inspector his job. I continued:

'Let's move on to more serious matters. A few days before his death, didn't Mr. Morstan send everyone away from Burton Lodge on some pretext?'

Suddenly, Luke appeared disconcerted. The major, intrigued, raised an eyebrow.

'Er...yes,' mumbled the bank employee. 'Yes, I remember. It did seem odd at the time. But how do you know about that?'

I took my time lighting a cigarette, before answering sarcastically:

'Come now, Mr. Strange. Stop and think: Mr. Morstan must have had a rehearsal, and certainly wouldn't have wanted any witnesses present, even if it were just to avoid revealing the identity of his accomplice. Another thing: I assume Mr. Morstan nailed the door shut on the morning of the murder?'

This time, there was a certain admiration in the astonished look in Luke's eyes. He obviously had no way of knowing that I knew the answer already.

'Yes, it's true. I even helped him by holding the planks in place while he hammered in the nails. But how could you possibly know it was in the morning?'

'By a simple deduction: if he asked you to repair the little bridge in the afternoon, it was probably because the hammer and nails reminded him of the defective state of the bridge. Do you follow me?'

Luke looked at me open-mouthed, and the major removed his lorgnette—the better to observe me. The situation was even more comical because my explanation was far-fetched. I continued my thrust:

'Was this the first time Mr. Morstan had attempted a magic trick?'

'Absolutely,' replied the major, a curious gleam in his narrowed eyes.

'Very well. Then he couldn't have invented it. He must have got the idea from a show he saw, or a book. Have you seen any works on magic tricks or theatrical illusions?'

Rose looked at me wide-eyed.

'Wait,' she said, hesitantly. 'It's all such a long time ago, but I think so. When I went into father's study one evening—I forget the reason—he was reading, and when he saw me he slid the book under the bedcovers. That intrigued me so much I went back the next day and found it on his bedside table. I don't recall the title, but it was about magic or prestidigitation; it had a yellow cover. I can assure you it's not in the house any more. We must have thrown it away with—No, I lent it to someone.'

'To whom?' I shouted.

Everyone looked at me in surprise. Embarrassed, I repeated the question in a quieter voice:

'It's very important, you understand. To whom did you lend the book?'

Rose closed her eyes in an attempt to gather her thoughts:

'Wait. I think it was one of my friends, but I don't remember exactly which one. It was several weeks after my father died.'

'And she never returned it?' I asked calmly. 'That's strange, it's been at least eight years.'

I was in complete control of my voice at that moment.

'No, but that wouldn't be the first book which was not returned.'

'In fact, didn't you lend it to one of the girls who was present at the murder?'

Rose considered me for quite some time; there was something

anxious in her look:

'Yes, I believe so. For the moment, I can't remember who, but I'm sure it will come back to me.'

While the major and Luke peppered Rose with questions, I observed the schoolmistress discreetly. She was sitting motionless on her chair, staring straight ahead. In her eyes was a strange light, as if, after a profound meditation, she had realised some awful truth.

'We're going to have to stop here for today,' announced the major, standing up. 'The investigation is far from over, but I believe we have already made great strides towards the truth. With what Inspector Miles and I have learned, it is quite possible that an arrest will follow in a few days.'

The major dwelt on the dangers which the murderer was running; the audience was hanging on every word. The old spinster took me aside:

'You remind me of someone, inspector. That look in your eye above all.'

My blood froze in my veins. I managed, nevertheless, to appear calm and collected.

'Ah? And who would my twin be?' I enquired, with a broad smile.

'A very nice young man whom I haven't seen for a long time,' she said, lowering her eyes. 'A charming fellow, whom—alas!—I felt was not completely stable. Oh, his appearance was perfectly normal, but there was something in his eyes….I don't know how to say this…One day, a long time ago, he came to see me; he must have been about fifteen. He seemed to want to confide something important, but couldn't quite bring himself to do it. I didn't ask him any questions. All the sadness in the world was in those eyes, yet at the same time, he seemed to be possessed by an inner excitement of a frightening intensity. I became quite anxious. He was on the verge of madness. His adolescent soul was in turmoil.'

Be careful. Danger.

Had Celia Forsythe recognised me? Or did she simply assume it was a resemblance?

'I would like to talk to you, Inspector Miles, but not today. I'm tired and I need to think some more. Could you come and see me in two or three days? I live in Hill Street: the third house on the left after the inn.'

I nodded my acceptance.

The major, through Nellie, had asked Peter Hopkins to prepare a carriage to take Miss Forsythe home. He'd had the presence of mind not to suggest that we—Cora and I—take advantage of it, guessing that we would prefer to walk back to the inn together.

We watched the carriage depart into the night. When the lights of the lanterns had disappeared, Luke observed:

'That's funny. I had the impression that she'd remembered something, but preferred to keep it to herself. What did she tell you just now, inspector?'

'Only to come and see her in a few days. Nothing precise.'

The major cleared his throat loudly:

'Speaking of memory, my dear niece, I hope you'll soon recall to whom you lent that book.'

'You do understand, don't you, darling?' her husband added. 'It's extremely important. The explanation of the trick must be in there, and hence the explanation of the murder. Now that I think about it, I find it extraordinary that the police didn't pursue the point. If we ever shine the light on this sinister business, we shall be indebted to you, inspector.'

I acknowledged the remark with the appropriate humility. (What a pompous ass!)

'It wasn't Nellie, in any case, nor Cora,' replied Rose, patting her hair.

'So it was one of the other seven girls,' said Cora.

A frown of concentration appeared on Rose's brow.

'Yes, but I still can't recall which one.'

'Stop thinking about it, darling. It'll come to you when you least expect it. It's always like that.'

Luke and Rose retired to bed. It was now nearly eleven o'clock, and only Cora, the major and I remained in front of the entrance. It was a superb moonlit night, gently bewitching, and the dark mass of the forest encircled us with a scented freshness. Leaning on his cane, the major chewed thoughtfully on the stem of his pipe.

He observed suddenly:

'You were remarkable, Miles. Relatively discreet at the start of the proceedings, but very incisive at the end. An excellent tactic, my young friend. Well played! And you put your finger on a point which might well be the deciding factor.'

'Allow me to return the compliment, major. Your judicious

deductions about the movements of the parties involved set us on the right path.'

'Quite so,' replied the major, obviously satisfied. 'But all I did was proceed by a process of elimination. I think we can consider the evening a success.'

'Ah! Now I think about it, I noticed something quite curious,' I exclaimed. 'Luke seemed familiar with certain details, as though he'd been part of the household at the time of the crime, yet he was only seventeen years old.'

'Decidedly, nothing escapes you, young man,' said the major mockingly. 'I see what you're saying, but there's nothing odd there: Luke and Rose were already very close. During school holidays, he practically lived here.'

There again, I knew the answer to my own question. But Sidney Miles wasn't supposed to know.

'Well,' said the major. 'I think I'll be off to bed. Let's all give it some thought and compare notes in the morning. You can make a list of the suspects, their alibis and their motives.'

Under the pale light of the moon, the major's expression seemed to change.

'I don't know about you, but I have a strange premonition. I sense approaching danger, just as in a tiger hunt. The wild animal believes itself menaced as well; its green eyes glow in the shadows; it remains motionless; it gathers itself and pounces suddenly on its prey. Have you ever seen someone who's been savaged by a tiger, young man?'

I shook my head as I took Cora's icy, trembling hand in my own.

'Not a pretty sight, by any means. The fellow I saw was bathed in his own blood, and was missing his...well, let's just say it was butchery such as I never want to see again. Goodnight. I'll be in touch, Miles.'

7

We weren't very talkative on the way back. The major could have spared us the lurid comparison. A simple warning would have sufficed: we were all conscious of the evil presence, which was almost palpable.

Bathed in his own blood...Butchery such as I never want to see again.

I was about to wallow in hideous images when Cora's sweet voice brought me back to reality.

'You were thinking of that Poe story when you asked about the chimney, I suppose?'

'Yes and no. I wasn't expecting to find a body in the flue. But it's true, I did think about the story.'

Cora stopped suddenly and turned to face me.

'You're strange sometimes, Sidney. When the major spoke about the tiger, you went as white as a sheet and I could see you were horrified. Just like yesterday, when you pricked your thumb. Anyone would think you were afraid of blood. Rather curious for a Bluebeard, don't you think?'

'You can never understand, Cora.' I was almost shouting. 'You don't even know why...and stop calling me Bluebeard!'

Then I took refuge in an outburst of laughter—which sounded false, even to me—and continued:

'It's not really fear. And, in any case, we've already talked about it. What's more—.'

Cora was pressing herself against me, trembling. The scent of her hair intoxicated me....

We arrived at the inn in the small hours. I kissed her one last time in front of the door of her room, then climbed the stairs as quietly as a cat. I locked the door behind me and went to the open window, my head reeling with questions. The vanished book was of the utmost importance. It had to be found as quickly as possible. And had Celia Forsythe recognised me? I should never have gone to see her at the time, after what had happened. She had understood without my saying anything. Thank goodness I didn't. It's difficult to keep a secret at fifteen. Papa, my poor Papa.

With an effort, I chased that horrible memory away, in order to think clearly, and I needed all my faculties to achieve my goal. Something had severely shocked the schoolmistress: a detail appertaining to the murder; a detail that had frightened her. Everyone had noticed.

Dangerous, *very* dangerous for the schoolmistress.

I looked pensively towards the nearby houses, plunged in darkness. The night was calm, the street was deserted, the moon was pale and so fascinating…Just below my window was the inn sign.

I woke up very late, around ten o'clock. Seated at the major's table, I watched Tony serve me breakfast. He looked devastated. As soon as he put the tray down, he sat down opposite me, and sighed:

'She didn't deserve it, the poor schoolmistress. What kind of madman could have done that?'

'Someone killed her cat?'

'No,' said Tony, looking me with great sadness. 'She was murdered.'

'Murdered,' I gasped. 'It's not possible. She was with us last night. When did they find her? And who did it?'

'They don't know,' sighed Tony. 'It was Baxter, the carpenter, who discovered the body; he lives opposite Miss Forsythe. And he just missed the killer. Listen to this: he couldn't get to sleep, so he went to get some water. Knowing him, I doubt it was water, but no matter. He noticed there was a light in Miss Forsythe's kitchen window.

'That seemed strange to him. He left his house and crossed the street. The curtains had not been completely drawn shut, so he peeked in. There was an oil lamp on the table, and on the floor he could see two feet sticking out from behind a piece of furniture. There were dark stains everywhere and a spreading pool on the floor. He heard the back door creaking and went round to investigate, only to see a shadow slipping furtively away.

'I should tell you that Baxter is a burly fellow who's not afraid of anyone. I don't know many people that would have had his reaction in similar circumstances. He ran after the shadow. It wasn't a very long chase. The fugitive ran down a dead-end alley two blocks further on. He couldn't escape. Baxter swears that if there had been a door or a window open, he couldn't have failed to see it in the bright moonlight. All along the walls there were boxes and barrels. Baxter moved forward slowly, inch by inch, expecting the figure to make a run for it at any moment, and he was ready to grab him. He reached the end of the cul-de-sac. There was a large barrel standing in the darkest corner. The fugitive had to be behind it. Baxter covered the last few feet and...No one! There was nobody there. The shadow had vanished, disappeared, gone up in smoke. Baxter retraced his steps and looked into the kitchen again. The dark pool had spread! The back door wasn't locked, so he went in and saw Miss Forsythe stretched out on the kitchen tiles. Her throat had been cut from ear to ear and she'd been stabbed many times. There was blood everywhere. Baxter came here and we went together to get the police from the nearest village. Didn't you hear us when we left last night?'

'No, I was...in fact, we got in very late, around half past one, and I went straight to sleep.'

Tony removed his glasses. There were bags under his blue-grey eyes.

'Baxter wasn't drunk,' he said, stroking his sideburns nervously. 'He smelled a bit of gin, but he wasn't drunk. As for his story, what can I say? I wasn't sure I believed in the phantom killer. We reached Miss Forsythe's house, together with the police, around five in the morning. Not a pretty sight, believe me, Mr. Miles. When Baxter discovered the body, nothing was further from his mind than a ghost who vanished from a dead-end. The police grilled him for a long time, but he stuck to his story: he was right on the heels of the killer, he saw him run into an alley, then he vanished! Even though they didn't suspect Baxter—what murderer would have invented such a story?— they took a look around Baxter's house. When they came across a cupboard full of empty bottles, they assumed his story was just the ramblings of a drunkard. But Baxter wasn't drunk, I swear it. Not even tipsy. I saw him just after his macabre discovery. He's not the type to make up that kind of story.'

'And no blood on him?'

'No. Nor in his house. The police checked. That's what proved his innocence, because the killer must have been drenched in the stuff.'

'Incredible. Were there any clues in Miss Forsythe's kitchen?'

'A jug of water and two half-filled glasses on the table, if you can call them clues.'

I took a sip of coffee, thinking it was a good thing Cora hadn't told her father about Miss Forsythe's attitude the night before.

The door of the saloon bar opened and Peter Hopkins came in. After a quick look around at his customers, Tony confided:

'Everybody in the village knows.' Turning to Hopkins, he asked:

'Good morning, Peter, I suppose you've heard the news?'

Peter Hopkins had plenty of presence: tall, well-built, with the dignified air of a servant to a distinguished family. He nodded his head gravely in response to Tony, then addressed me:

'Mr. Morstan would like to see you this afternoon, inspector.'

'Let him know I'll be there. Thank you, Hopkins.'

After Peter had left, Tony exclaimed:

'It's true. I'd completely forgotten. The major told me yesterday afternoon. You're Insp—.'

With a discreet sign, I bade him be quiet:

'Yes, but I'm here on holiday. And I don't want people to know about it, do you understand? In any case, this affair is not my responsibility.'

His face betrayed his disappointment.

'Of course,' he said in a weary voice. 'I understand. But I'd still like to know who could have attacked poor Miss Forsythe like that. It could only have been the act of a madman, a monster. The police established that robbery was not the motive for the crime.'

'Was the shadow Baxter saw that of a man or a woman?'

After a weary sigh, he replied:

'A shadow, that's all he saw.'

At around two o'clock in the afternoon, I put down my pen. The small task the major had assigned me was finished:

Remark concerning those persons with a solid alibi: do not lose sight of the fact that the murder could have been committed by an accomplice.

Michael. *Motive: financial interest. The second marriage of his father would have reduced his share of the inheritance. Alibi: unassailable (unless the other archers were accomplices, which is highly implausible.)*

Rose. *Motive: the same as Michael Alibi: unassailable—unless the other nine girls and the schoolmistress were accomplices (highly unlikely.)*

Major Daniel Morstan. *Motive: the same as Michael. Alibi: not unshakeable, but given his leg wound and corpulence, difficult to envisage as the agile murderer.*

Luke Strange. *Motive: the same as Michael, because, at the time, he already expected to marry Rose. Alibi: not very strong. Based on hammer blows being heard, which could have been trickery.*

Eleanor Burroughs. *Motive: jealousy. Alibi: none.*

Angela Wright. *Motive: none. Alibi: none.*

Stanley Griffin and Bill Hudson. *Motive: none. Alibi: the same as Michael.*

Nellie, Cora and the other girls. *Motive: none. Alibi: the same as Rose.*

Celia Forsythe. *Recent events speak for themselves.*

I didn't know how the major would react to his name being included in the list of suspects, but at least he couldn't reproach me for not having carried out my assignment thoroughly.

There was a knock on the door. Cora was there. We hadn't had the chance for another *tête-à-tête* since our last kiss. The murder of the schoolmistress had left her devastated; she was as pale as death. She came to take refuge in my arms.

'It's horrible, Sidney. Papa told me.'

I comforted her, then sat down on my bed:

'I know what you're thinking, Cora. If a stupid journalist with a half-baked project for a novel hadn't turned up in the village, Celia Forsythe would still be alive. But, believe me, she didn't die in vain. She remembered something yesterday, something compromising for the murderer, who rushed to silence her.'

Cora looked at me gloomily. I raised my voice:

'Don't you understand that this proves the murderer was someone present at last night's meeting? What's more, just as in Richard Morstan's murder, the criminal seemed to vanish. Both crimes were committed by one and the same person. There's no doubt about it. A phantom killer who isn't a phantom, believe me. Because he was seen this morning. The carpenter only saw a shadow, I grant you, but at least we now know he's not invisible. And I'm going to discover his trick, believe me...Cora! Why are you looking at me like that?'

65

Her pale blue eyes looked fearfully at me. Then she burst into tears.

'Cora. For heaven's sake, what's wrong?'

I got up and took her in my arms.

'Cora, explain what's—.'

'I thought of something horrible,' she said between sobs. 'A hideous association of ideas.'

'What?'

'You won't be angry?' she asked, raising her head.

'Of course not. But what's it about?'

I had instinctively tightened my grip.

'I thought about your theories of impossible crimes…and Bluebeard, the lady killer.'

I sat down on the bed again and gave a long sigh.

'I know my black beard has glints of blue, but apart from that, do I look like a murderer?'

She smiled broadly.

'No, I admit. Quite the opposite. You could be blessed without taking confession. Oh! I must go. My parents don't take kindly to our *tête-à-tête.*'

So saying, she planted a quick kiss on my lips and disappeared.

I looked thoughtfully at the door as it closed behind her.

8

Half an hour later, I started up the drive to Burton Lodge. Halfway there, I saw Rose tending a stone vase overflowing with spring flowers.

'Oh! Inspector,' she said, affecting surprise.

She had loosened her hair; the sun accentuated the glints of copper in the long, curly locks tied together by a silk ribbon. She stood up and walked towards me, rubbing her hands on her apron.

'Please excuse my dress,' she said, looking down at her gardening clothes.

'Please don't concern yourself, madam,' I replied, bowing with amused respect; if Rose had known who I really was, she wouldn't have troubled herself with the formalities.

She tried to appear calm and dignified, but I could read the confusion and anxiety on her Madonna-like features. She lowered her gaze, and said in a pathetic voice:

'It's horrible. Poor Miss Forsythe, so good and so kind.'

Even though the crime had occurred only a few hours ago, Rose was aware of the circumstances, and I deduced it must be the same for the rest of the household. After expressing horror about the murder, she got to the point:

'Her curious attitude could not have escaped anyone's notice. It's obvious she was killed to stop her talking. Which means….'

I completed her sentence:

'…that the killer was someone in the room last night. And, by the same logic, we can conclude that person also killed your father.'

She looked down and, rather dramatically, clutched her hands to her throat:

'Yes, that's what everyone thinks at Burton Lodge. But nobody's saying anything; we look at each other in silence, waiting for the slightest gesture which might appear suspect. It's awful.'

We fell silent. I looked towards Burton Lodge. The elegant building appeared so calm and serene, standing in the centre of a verdant lawn bathed in sunlight, with the green velvet of the forest as a backdrop.

'It's hard to imagine it as the theatre for a crime,' observed Rose.

'That's just what I was thinking.'

'It wasn't the killer's first attempt...I'm talking about my father's murder.'

'Do you mean he has three murders to his account?'

Rose looked down and scuffed the gravel with her ankle-boots. She didn't reply immediately. Then:

'Oh, I haven't any proof, but I have serious suspicions.' She looked up. 'This has to stay between us.'

'You have my word. In any case, I'm only here on official business.'

'Let me start with a question. Didn't one of the testimonies last night strike you as strange? A little too good to be true?'

After a moment's reflection, I replied:

'I assume you're talking about the governess and her story about the shadow on the spiral staircase.'

Rose looked at me open-mouthed in admiration. I didn't give her time to speak:

'Just as you say: "A little too good to be true." A fairy tale. Yes, it struck me, too. But I don't give her testimony any weight. She wanted to throw suspicion on your father's ex-fiancée, that's all.'

Rose looked at me thoughtfully, then pressed her point:

'Particularly since her testimony didn't happen straight away. She only made the declaration two or three days after my father died, as if she'd hesitated a long time. But no one was fooled: it was obvious she wanted to harm Angela.

'Inspector,' she added, in an embarrassed tone, 'I must tell you that I didn't welcome the arrival of a policeman coming to rake over the coals of a past tragedy. I know that you're here at the request of my uncle, but...Do you understand?'

I answered with a knowing nod.

'I saw immediately that you weren't like your colleagues,' she went on. 'Without posing too many painful questions, you achieved certain results and...well, I feel we can trust you. You have tact and you have style.'

'Thank you, madam. But don't forget I can be persistent if need be.'

Poor Rose. If she only knew!

'If I understand you correctly, the murderer is none other than Miss Burroughs?'

She nodded once more:

'I repeat, it's only a suspicion. I was raised from the age of six by Eleanor Burroughs; she was not a warm person, but I have nothing to say against her. My father hired her a few weeks before my mother's death. She was young and beautiful, and I thought she looked at him strangely. You know, children can sense these things. My mother used to go for a horseback ride every evening after dinner. One evening, we heard her return, but she didn't come to join us right away, as she usually did. Then the horses started whinnying, which they had never done before. Father, Michael and I rushed to the stables. To our horror, they were in flames. For several seconds, just before it all became a blazing inferno, we tried to open the door, but in vain, for it was locked from the inside. Michael burned his hands trying. Father as well.

'There was almost nothing left of the stables: everything had been burnt to the ground. Although we never found out exactly what happened, it's not hard to imagine. Mother stabled her horse as usual, being careful to lock the door behind her. Somehow the oil lamp fell into the straw. In their panic, the horses must have kicked her and she only regained consciousness after it was too late. It was horrible: the red flames in the night and my mother screaming... I was only six years old.'

Nodding my head, I sympathised in silence. Rose continued, with tears in her eyes:

'The following year, we left Australia for England. But I've never been able to forget—I still have those images in front of my eyes. Nor can I forget another scene, so strange, whose significance I only realised much later. It was one evening, a few days after the tragedy. Father, Michael, Eleanor and I were sitting at the table, after supper. Father gave us a long lecture about God, eternal life and I don't remember what else. Michael and I were crying as if our hearts would break. Mama would never return, we knew. Eleanor nodded approvingly at Papa's words, adding a comment from time to time. Then Papa and Michael left the room. Eleanor took my hand and said: "It's horrible what happened. Horrible." She repeated the word several times, like a litany, with a strange, distant look in her eyes, which seemed twice as large as usual. They were burning like hot coals, as if reflecting the inferno again. I had gooseflesh without quite knowing why.

'When Papa announced his engagement to Angela Wright, Eleanor maintained a dogged silence, but her eyes flashed daggers; she was mad with rage and jealousy.'

'Your uncle already explained the situation,' I observed. 'She had the idea firmly planted in her head that your father would marry her some day, isn't that right?'

'Yes, and to have oneself supplanted by a young girl of twenty...You should have seen her. She bore a grudge against Angela, but she hated my father with a passion. We were seated at table one evening just after his death, and my uncle was eulogising him. Eleanor had the same look in her eyes as after my mother's death, and she kept chanting "It's horrible what happened. Horrible," in the same way.' Rose came closer, panting breathlessly. 'That's when it dawned on me, the significance of that look. Despite her words, the look on her face was joy. Pure joy.'

I grimaced doubtfully:

'Granted, Miss Burroughs is jealous, possessive and intolerant of any woman close to the man of her dreams. Your mother's death left the field open; your father's gave her the satisfaction of not seeing him in the arms of a rival, that's all very possible. But that doesn't necessarily mean she threw a match into the stables and murdered both your father and the schoolmistress.'

'I know,' sighed Rose, studying the tips of her boots. 'They're only assumptions, and that's why I asked you not to talk about them, inspector. But I thought it was my duty to draw your attention to the tragic *accident*.'

'You were right to do so, Mrs. Strange. By the way, where was she at the moment the flames were noticed?'

'She was walking in the woods.'

'So, no alibi?'

'No alibi, she was alone at the time.'

'Curious, though. Because she doesn't have one for the time of your father's death, either. No alibi and a powerful motive. And she's the only one who satisfies both conditions. Curious.'

'And now, Miss Forsythe.'

'And, naturally, Miss Burroughs has no alibi once again. For I assume one can leave Burton Lodge at night without being seen?'

Rose hesitated for a moment:

'I prefer to tell you straight away. Luke is very restless and has trouble getting to sleep. We are not in separate rooms, but he sometimes sleeps on the sofa in his office. Last night's meeting made him very upset...he slept in his office.'

'So, in fact,' I said, in a voice tinged with irony, 'nobody has an alibi?'

She changed the subject.

'Are you married, inspector?'

'No.'

'I've known my husband since I was thirteen years old. In fact, I even knew him before that. You must understand....'

She turned towards the vase, looking lovingly at the floral arrangement as if it were her husband. It would never have occurred to me to think of Luke as a flower. A vegetable, perhaps: say, a pickled gherkin. How did Rose become infatuated with a fellow like that?

'...that if there is someone who is inherently incapable of committing a murder, it's my husband. A wife is never mistaken about that kind of thing.'

I could have cited numerous examples proving the opposite, but I stoically restrained myself.

'As for my uncle,' she continued, 'who limps and is far from possessing the suppleness of a cat, it's difficult to see him slipping out of Baxter's fingers. But I suppose you came here to meet him?'

I nodded.

'He's out walking in the woods, but he won't be long. Luke didn't go to work today, so he'll certainly be in the lounge.'

We exchanged polite smiles and I proceeded towards the house.

'Whisky?'

'It's an offer I seldom refuse. A dash of water, please.'

Luke appeared slightly less stuffy than the previous day. Was it due to the rebellious tuft of straw-coloured hair which stuck straight up, or the cigar which he chewed nervously? Be that as it may, his approach to the matter in hand was more or less the same as Rose's. The murder of the schoolmistress had appalled him. He, like she, had not *particularly* appreciated a policeman coming to untangle the past affair, but, as the evening went on, he had understood that the logic behind my deductions, my way of analysing the facts, the correctness of my judgements, *et cetera, et cetera,* did offer some hope of

71

elucidating the murder of Richard Morstan at last. As to the identity of the murderer, he had his own ideas:

'There's no doubt that the murderer had eliminated the schoolmistress because she remembered—or he had believed she remembered—a compromising detail. You're going to tell me that the killer must therefore have been someone in the room yesterday evening. Nothing is less certain. The windows were open and anyone could have overheard our discussion. And remember that the major had the impression that someone was spying on us. The major is a man whose ability to reason is debatable, but I have complete confidence in his impressions. His instincts are almost never wrong.

'I've had my idea as to the identity of Richard Morstan's killer for a long time, and the savagery which he unleashed on poor Miss Forsythe serves only to reinforce it. The spilling of all that blood was not a careless act, it was a message destined for the Morstan family: a warning. You'll see what I mean in a minute. I already shared my suspicions with my spouse, but she flew into a rage and treated me like a...anyway, that's the reason I didn't talk about it last evening.'

Ensconced deep in his armchair, Luke gave me a smile he clearly thought was cunning:

'A question to start with, inspector: who profited from Richard Morstan's death?'

I shrugged my shoulders:

'His heirs.'

'Obviously. Let me rephrase my question.' He seemed to be exaggeratedly courteous. 'Who profited *most* from Richard Morstan's death?'

'The son,' I replied, in the same voice.

Luke nodded his head, apparently satisfied with my response.

'Michael Morstan,' he continued in a voice at once honeyed and sour. 'Half of his father's fortune came to him and the marriage was no longer a factor. Are you aware of the details of the will, in fact?'

'Yes, the major explained them.'

'Good. So you know that Michael has still not renounced his inheritance, despite his professed disdain for his father's fortune. He remains, therefore, the number one suspect—at least to my mind.

'The fact that he was only fifteen years old and had a cast-iron alibi meant that he was rapidly eliminated from the list of suspects. He could quite easily have turned the execution of the crime over to an accomplice.

'What to think about the wayward arrow he claims to have shot accidentally at the time of the crime? A curious coincidence was it not? Then his two-day escapade—note that he didn't go far at all: just stayed in the neighbourhood. And after that, the sinister comedy where he insisted he'd unwittingly caused the death of his father through that careless shot—even though Bill and Stanley said the shot was too weak, and it was conclusively established that Richard Morstan was killed by a blow from a dagger.

'Do you know what I think about all that? A subtle plan. At first sight, everything seems to point to him, but then we twist ourselves in knots to convince him of his innocence; we even feel sorry for him. Everybody went along with it, led by the police—myself included, I admit.

'All modesty aside, I must tell you that I'm far from being a poor judge of character. But, as far as Michael is concerned, I'm reduced to conjectures. A strange young man indeed: behind the look of a deer at bay flickered disturbing glances; he seemed to bear a grudge against his whole family, particularly after the murder of his father. As for me: he simply ignored me. I didn't exist in his eyes. And how to explain his attitude? Why doesn't he show himself? Do you want to know what I really think, inspector?'

I didn't answer, but sipped placidly at my whisky.

'He hates us!' said Luke, almost shouting. 'He wants to push us to the limit. I'm quite sure he's going to appear at the last minute to claim the fortune he's been dangling in front of us. You'll see.'

He took hold of himself and continued in a more measured tone:

'His first step is to secure his fortune by eliminating his own father with the help of an accomplice. The crime is a masterpiece, let's admit: nobody suspects him. After which, he disappears and, once he comes of age, doesn't even bother to claim his share. What admirable disinterest, don't you think? In everyone's eyes, he's the last person to want to kill his father. I started to realise what was going on when the solicitor told us that, for the time being, we couldn't touch it. From that moment on, I've seen Richard Morstan's murder in an entirely different light. I spoke to Rose about it, and she told me I was talking nonsense.'

Luke paused. He was gripping his glass so hard I could see the whites of his knuckles. In vain, he struggled to remain impassive; his face was twisted by a strange mixture of hate and fear.

'The fellow has two crimes on his conscience already and I'm in no doubt he'd commit another to increase his fortune. He's not supposed to know about our delicate financial situation, which is temporary in any case. But he wouldn't hesitate, he detests us so much.

'He started last night. I told you, the savageness of Miss Forsythe's murder was no accident, it was a clear message to us. Yes, Michael's back; I can feel his presence. He's not far away.'

Luke finished his drink in a single gulp. He leant forward to confide in me:

'I fear the worst, inspector. We have to put that wild beast where he can't harm us, before he—.'

Luke fell suddenly silent and turned round. Major Daniel Morstan was standing in the doorway.

9

Even though the major seemed slightly tired from his walk, he insisted our discussion take place away from Burton Lodge. We walked along the path which wound its way though the forest. The trees, their leaves dotted with luminous points, tempered the heat of the sun, enveloping us in a welcome freshness. Only after a ten minute march did the major lift the veil of silence:

'In a way, we've succeeded beyond our wildest expectations: the tiger is panic-stricken and has come out of his lair.'

'I prefer to think he's shown his claws. And, speaking of panic-stricken beasts, I know another one who's in a delicate position: if the police learn why the old maid was assassinated, they're going to interview the suspects, who will undoubtedly talk of a certain Sidney Miles, inspector at the Yard. This business may cost me dearly.'

'Don't worry. I saw the police this morning. They're convinced it's all the work of a madman and the case will be filed rapidly. What's more, nobody at Burton Lodge is anxious to shout from the rooftops that the murderer was one of theirs. I gave instructions to Hopkins and Nellie; I feel confident they're not going to say anything. As for you, young man, if our combined efforts result in the discovery of the murderer, you'll be able to offer the *Daily Telegraph* a sensational report. And you won't need to stretch your imagination to write your novel. The affair is already rich enough in mysteries, if I'm not mistaken.'

I was like a tightrope walker on a high wire. From now on, I was going to have to be extra careful, because my situation was becoming very complicated: for Cora and the major, I was a journalist passing himself off as a Scotland Yard inspector; for the Stranges, I was Sidney Miles of Scotland Yard; for the inhabitants of Blackfield, a peaceful tourist (assuming Tony held his tongue), whereas in reality....

But, for the time being, everything was in hand. My project continued to progress as planned, although the death of the schoolmistress had not been on the programme.

'Rich in mysteries, indeed. What did you think of Baxter's testimony?'

The major stopped. After wiping his damp forehead with the back of his hand, he grimaced:

'This morning, I had a look at the dead end where the fugitive magically disappeared. There were cases and barrels all along the walls. Baxter was quite firm: he'd gone down it step by step, inspecting every nook and cranny, and no one had gone past him. If indeed he'd proceeded as he said, then it would have been impossible for anyone or anything, including a cat, to have got past him without being seen. I don't really know what to think about it all. I know Baxter very well, and he's not the sort of fellow to make up stories. What is certain, however, is that we're dealing with a particularly cunning killer.'

'I'd even go so far as to say a phantom killer, as in the case of your brother.'

'Yes, he signed the murder, even though he didn't leave a card.'

'Written in red ink.'

The major raised an incredulous eyebrow.

'Excuse me?'

'Oh, it's nothing,' I replied. 'I was thinking of my novel. A phantom murderer who leaves behind calling cards written in red ink; that would be a nice touch.'

'It seems to me that we have other fish to fry, for the time being,' replied the major tersely.

'Quite so. Are there any clues so far?'

'Nothing, alas. The two glasses of water on the kitchen table confirm our suspicion: Miss Forsythe knew her killer. One doesn't offer a drink to a stranger in the middle of the night. Those dolts of policemen didn't think that was important. Just as well, in fact, because it means we won't have them stepping on our toes. But they're not the only imbeciles,' he fumed. 'While we were all hounding Rose about her memory lapse, we failed to pay proper attention to the schoolmistress who'd remembered something important. So important that someone slit her throat two hours later.'

'Especially since she wanted to talk to me. If I'd only known.'

'Quite! We've all behaved like imbeciles. All except the murderer. But that doesn't—Good grief!' he exclaimed, in consternation. 'The book!'

'Do you remember whom your niece lent it to?'

He readjusted his lorgnette and looked at me wild-eyed.

'No, unfortunately. But just think: if that book represents a danger for the killer, all he has to do is eliminate——.'

'Your niece? I hardly think so. It would even be ridiculous, for we could always lay our hands on the book by interviewing all of her friends. It might take a while, but we would inevitably find it.'

The major's expression changed again: he now wore a sphinx-like smile. He clicked his fingers and declared:

'We've got him. I've just had an idea. Exploit the wild beast's panic to set him a trap. If the contents of the book are a danger to him, he won't hesitate to go after it, head down.'

'I understand. Even if we haven't found it, we can always make him believe——.'

'Exactly! But let's not rush into it. I'm going to mull it over with a clear head. The slightest error could have grave consequences. There's nothing more dangerous than a wounded tiger. Now, have you done the homework I gave you?'

I handed him the list of suspects.

'Brief, but concise,' he said after he'd read it. 'And you left no one out, even the good old major! But you did the right thing, for, after all, I am one of the suspects.'

There was silence, then he asked, artfully:

'Who, in your opinion?'

Confident that I'd gauged his reaction, I replied:

'If financial gain is the motive for the murder, I vote for your niece's husband.'

There was evident satisfaction on his face as he responded:

'Luke Strange. I have to admit, that's my opinion as well. I always thought he'd married my brother's daughter, rather than Rose herself. And his alibi is not very strong, as you yourself point out.'

'I spoke to your niece not long ago. She admitted her husband spent the night in his office. So, once again, no alibi.'

'As to that, Miss Forsythe's murder doesn't get us any further forward, because anybody could have slipped out of Burton Lodge under cover of darkness. I did a little investigation of my own, but in vain. I examined the bathroom and all the water outlets in that poor woman's house very carefully, and there's not a single drop of blood to be found. I believe the killer was wearing old clothes which he stripped off and threw away after he'd finished. It's quite likely he took a bath in the river to get rid of all traces, for he must have been drenched in blood. That's one thing at least the police are certain of. As I think it over more carefully, I find it difficult to imagine Luke committing such a murder. The gratuitous cruelty, with the attendant risk, really isn't his cup of tea.'

Our footsteps and the whistling of the major's breath were the only sounds to disturb the ensuing silence.

'Major, there's one witness I'd like to question.'

'If you're thinking of Michael, forget it.'

'Not Michael. Your brother's ex-fiancée: Angela Wright.'

The major stopped, as if turned to stone:

'Angela? Angela Wright.'

'It's vitally important. Do you know where she's living?'

'Yes. Eastbourne, but—.'

Evidently discountenanced, he frowned and tugged at his moustache.

'Is there any objection?' I persisted firmly.

'No. No, of course not. If you really think it's necessary. But be careful, there's no love lost there. She's quite capable of inventing stories for the sole purpose of discrediting us. That's why I don't feel it's indispensable to go all that way to see her.' He shot me a brief glance, then capitulated. 'Very well, I'll give you her address. But it's quite possible she's no longer there.'

10

The next morning we sat watching the pleasant countryside of Sussex roll past as our train carried us towards Eastbourne. Cora was seated at the window, opposite me. We were the only occupants of the compartment; we could already detect the tang of the sea air.

Just as in that day in June, Cora was radiant. I caressed her with my eyes as the sun flecked her hair with gold.

'A penny for your thoughts, Sidney.'

'I'm thinking about you, me...us.'

She smiled enigmatically.

'I know very little about you, Sidney, other than you're a journalist for the *Daily Telegraph*. You never talk about yourself or your family, your mother, your father.'

Cora had touched a sensitive nerve, though she couldn't have known it. I lowered my head. There was a crimson screen in front of my eyes with shadows moving on it....

A rasping voice which chuckles and sneers...an odious screeching... violins starting to groan, about to emit perfect dissonances....the tension increases... an oil-lamp diffuses a purple light. On a table, a long, shimmering blade...eager fingers grasp it...steel slices the air...blood...

'Sidney?'

Cora's musical voice brought me out of my torpor.

'My parents? Yes, well, you see, I didn't know my mother for very long. She—I'll explain another time. In fact, I lived a very dull life until the day when....'

'When?'

'A fairy appeared.'

'Hmm, I see,' she said, rolling her eyes to the sky.

'A fairy about whom I know nothing, other than she suffered a disappointment.'

Cora gave a deep sigh before she started to talk:

'That's another banal story. A boy I met in London: a thug but I didn't know it. I stayed with him for almost a year, in his miserable little flat in Brick Lane.'

'What? Brick Lane in London?'

'Yes,' she admitted, after a brief hesitation.

Brick Lane, a street which crosses Spitalfields, Whitechapel; one of the most infamous parts of the capital, and one which I knew well. A labyrinth of sordid alleys and passages where thieves, vagabonds, beggars and prostitutes crowded together.

I shook my head in consternation.

'I know what you're thinking,' said Cora, whose eyes had clouded over, 'but I was madly and blindly in love. I would have followed him anywhere. It was the first time...I was completely inexperienced, a young provincial girl, easy prey for someone like him.'

I was overcome by a wave of anger and jealousy. The question was out of my mouth before I knew it:

'What was his name?'

'Larry. Larry Jordan.'

I made a mental note of it. But it would be best for me—and, above all, for him—if I didn't lay hands on the scum who had dragged a girl like Cora into that depraved and degenerate place.

'One evening, I surprised him with another girl, a little slut. Their behaviour left me in no doubt of their relations. It was a brutal shock, but I learnt my lesson. I realised how stupid I'd been, and I left him straight away. I went back to Blackfield with indescribable joy. What a contrast with those squalid streets and that miserable flat.'

'I can understand.'

'I needed time to recover; the sordid experience had left me disgusted with men. Until the day....'

There was an agreeable silence, followed by another, no less agreeable.

'Have you ever been to Eastbourne?' Cora asked, patting her hair back in place.

'No. All I know about it is it's supposed to boast the most days of sunshine in the country, there are beautiful walks, several theatres, golf courses, a beach and—above all—a certain Angela Wright.'

'I'm willing to bet she's not there any more.'

'It's more than likely. But we shall see.'

'Sidney, if we have time, I'd like to show you The Seven Sisters. It's a magnificent spot.'

'Agreed. But we'd better not miss the last train, or your father will get suspicious. He's already been kind enough to allow you out today, and I don't want him to think....'

Cora shrugged her shoulders with a mischievous grin.

'Given the way you look at me all the time, he must already be more than suspicious. Oh, here we are.'

At about eleven o'clock, we rang the doorbell of 4, Carow Road, only to find that Angela Wright had departed for Lewes several years earlier. As Lewes was on our way back, and there were several hours before the next train, we hired a cab to The Seven Sisters.

Shortly thereafter, Cora and I lay on the edge of the high cliffs, caressed by the breeze beneath a radiant sun. I had never felt such bliss in my life. Without exchanging a word, we expressed our love.

A few hours later, we knocked on the door of Angela's new address, thankful the old lady in Eastbourne had written it down.

'Don't declare victory too soon,' warned Cora. 'The nameplate says Mr. and Mrs. Hudson.'

'Angela married someone called Hudson, that's all.'

'Hudson,' mused Cora. 'That name rings a bell.'

'We'll soon know. I hear footsteps.'

The door opened and Angela appeared. She was still just as beautiful, with her jet black locks tumbling over her shoulders, her blood-red lips and olive complexion inherited from her mother.

She frowned, then her eyes opened wide in recognition.

'Cora! Cora Ferrers. My, how you've changed! Do come in. Your husband, I suppose?'

Cora started to open her mouth, but I got there first.

'Sidney Miles, her fiancée. Delighted to meet you, madam.'

Angela led us to the lounge. I let Cora and our hostess exchange a few banalities, after which I got to the purpose of our visit, without mentioning the death of the schoolmistress. After I finished, Angela gave a deep sigh:

'So the major decided to dig up the past. I find that strange, particularly since it's almost certainly a family member who killed him. By the way, was it the major who asked you to come to see me?'

'No, it was my idea. I think your testimony could be useful.'

'I thought as much.'

She spoke those words in an amused, almost ironic, tone. I looked at her, intrigued, and asked her to elaborate.

Angela remained thoughtful for a moment, then obviously decided to speak frankly:

'After all, I've nothing to hide. I'm no longer a secret. But I fear you may be wasting your time, inspector.

'In early 1878, Mama became seriously ill. I was nineteen years old and not working. Papa had left us three years earlier and our situation was desperate. But you know all that, don't you, Cora?'

Cora nodded her head silently.

'At which point,' said Angela with an embarrassed smile, 'the village saint came to our aid. He did more than that, he consoled me...in a manner of speaking. I didn't find Richard attractive, but what choice did I have? Needless to say, there was no talk of marriage at that point. Three months later, I realised there was a good chance I was pregnant...a catastrophe. But when I thought it over, it didn't seem such a catastrophe after all. I gave Richard an ultimatum: either he married me or there would be a huge scandal. I don't know whether it was my charm or the fear of scandal that did it, but he agreed to marry me. We announced the news shortly before Mama's death.'

'And to think that many saw it as a sign of his bountiful spirit,' said Cora bitterly.

Angela gave a fleeting smile:

'But the bad luck continued. Richard was murdered before the marriage could take place. I think you can guess my opinion about that, inspector?'

'Yes, indeed,' I sighed, 'but we have no proof for the moment. Please continue.'

'The major offered me a large sum of money to leave the village. A very large sum, in fact, which would have kept me in food and shelter for a long time. But I'd become greedy and I could see he was ready to do anything to avoid scandal. The family honour was at stake. His brother was a saint and he had no intention of his name being sullied in such a manner.

'So I asked for three times what he'd offered me. He became purple with rage, but he agreed after making me swear I would never return to the village and never reveal the existence of the baby-to-be. I had always thought the major to be a kind man, but I had to think of my future and the baby's. I'd always lived in misery and I was so close to a comfortable life.'

'Aside from the major, did anyone else know about the baby?'

'Dr. Griffin, of course, the governess...and Rose and Michael, I think.'

'And what about the baby?' asked Cora.

'He was stillborn. But I have two others. They're sleeping like angels right now. And I think you know their father, Cora.'

'Hudson. Bill Hudson!' exclaimed Cora, clapping a hand to her forehead. 'I saw the name on the door, but I failed to make the connection.'

Angela's dark eyes gleamed with pleasure:

'He was a handsome fellow at the time and he courted me assiduously, but I was only seventeen at the time. I met him again, purely by chance, a year after the murder. We've never left each other's side since.'

Purely by chance. Knowing Bill, I suspect he might have forced the chance somewhat. The house, though not luxurious, exuded a certain level of comfort. Leave it to Bill: a beautiful girl, a handsome "dowry"...he wouldn't have let that go to waste.

11

At eight o'clock that night, I rang the doorbell of Burton Lodge. It was Eleanor Burroughs who answered.

'Good evening, inspector. You're here to see the major, I presume? He's in the village. Apparently the police have made a discovery in Miss Forsythe's house.'

'Do you know what it is?'

'I don't. The major will doubtless inform you upon his return. If you care to wait....'

She let me into the lounge, where I installed myself in an armchair. Eleanor appeared on the point of retiring, but changed her mind and sat down on one of the chairs. I pretended to be preoccupied, but watched her discreetly. Sitting straight as an arrow on the chair, with a distant look in her eyes, she waited impassively. But for her almost inhuman coldness, the severity of her coiffure which held her opulent hair in check, and the sombre dress which deprived her of all femininity, she could have been beautiful. Only her trembling hands displayed any life: white and beautiful against all that black, they opened and shut incessantly, betraying their owner. Impatience, disarray, excitement, embarrassment? Perhaps a mixture of all of these.

After a silence which she obviously had no intention of being the first to break, I told her:

'Please don't think that I'm involved in this investigation for my own pleasure, miss. When the major asked for my help, I couldn't possibly have foreseen the turn of events.'

'The major,' she repeated, with the semblance of a smile, 'the major and his brother...his *dear* brother...the dear brother for whom he nursed an affection, or rather an adoration, which I would characterise as quite excessive.'

I appeared unconcerned as I stoked the fire:

'As a policeman, I've frequently encountered individuals bent on vengeance for a loved one, but the major pursues the unknown murderer with a hatred that time seems not to have abated.'

Again there was silence, then the governess replied in a quiet voice: 'The brothers were not always on such good terms, did you know that?'

I shook my head and she went on:

'When their father died, the major—who was not yet a major—wanted to keep the ancestral property at any cost. Richard was against it, convinced it was a lost cause.'

'I knew about that; the major told me.'

There was an ironic look in Eleanor's eyes:

'His brother tried in vain to get him to change his mind, but Richard had made his decision. He remained inflexible and called the major an imbecile, a sentimental dreamer, and other terms best not repeated. There was a terrible struggle and they came to blows. The major packed his bags and, as he left, accused Richard of not being worthy to be called a Morstan and promised not to show him any mercy if their paths were to cross again. According to Richard, his brother was beside himself with rage, and prepared to kill him. The brothers didn't see each other for nearly twenty years. Then the major came back from India. Richard, wishing to put an end to a quarrel he felt had gone on too long, welcomed the major with open arms. It was a moving reconciliation.'

Another point the major had neglected to mention. But then, he was under no obligation to reveal all the family secrets to a journalist.

'A decent man, Mr. Richard Morstan,' I said, waiting for her reaction.

'A decent man,' she said grudgingly, 'who had his qualities and his faults.' She looked down and sighed. 'He disappointed me, bitterly disappointed me. I'd devoted all...but let's not dwell on that, he's dead. What I wanted to point out, when I spoke of an ancient quarrel, was the strange behaviour of the major, who, having once threatened his brother's life, then proceeds to venerate him beyond all—.'

The lounge door opened suddenly and the major walked in, his expression sombre, and muttering incomprehensible words. After shooting me a look to remind me our conversation was secret and worth reflecting on, the governess left.

'Incredible, incredible,' muttered the major, filling two tumblers with whisky. 'This case is getting beyond me. Guess what the police found in Celia's house. You'll never believe it.'

I emptied half the glass and waited to hear, incapable of uttering a sound.

After lighting his pipe, the major looked enquiringly at me:

'What's wrong, young man?'

'Nothing,' I stammered. 'It's nothing.'

'This is no time to lose your grip,' he growled. 'Don't forget, you're a Scotland Yard detective.'

'Get to the point. What did you find at Miss Celia's?'

Surprised by the tone of my voice, the major looked hard at me, then continued:

'The police determined that theft was not the motive for the crime, given that nothing of value was taken. But a neighbour came forward to say that Miss Forsythe owned a number of family heirlooms which, following a series of local thefts two or three years ago, she kept in a place known only to her. Although not completely convinced, the police redoubled their efforts, and one of them had a flash of inspiration when re-examining the old lady's bedroom, on the walls of which hung an etching with a biblical motif, a portrait of a young woman, and a watercolour of a garden scene. This last, rather clumsily done, depicted precisely what he and his colleagues had seen in Miss Celia's own garden: a weeping willow in the middle of a small lawn, a stone bench and a few flowering shrubs. Taking down the picture, he discovered that the watercolour had been folded back on itself inside the frame, and that on the hidden part was a cross indicating a spot at the base of the willow and just in front of the bench. After that discovery, they wasted no time: Baxter supplied them with picks and shovels and the jewels, along with several pieces of gold, were recovered from a chest buried two feet down.'

The major stopped. Something told me that wasn't the end of the story. I was not mistaken. He continued, but at a more deliberate pace:

'Another of the policemen thought there might be a second treasure buried below the first; after all, that had happened before. He dug more deeply in the same spot, and there he found, not more treasure, but a body. That is to say: not precisely a body, but human remains.'

I drained my glass in one go.

'It was Baxter who alerted me,' continued the major. 'He was in quite a state. When I arrived, Dr. Griffin was already there. He had been summoned to give his opinion, ahead of the medical examiner. In his view, the remains were those of a middle-aged woman who had died more than ten years ago.' He shook his head in despair. 'It's incomprehensible. Who is the woman? Who buried her there? To my knowledge, there were no persons reported missing from Blackfield at the time. What troubles me most is that the death of this stranger coincides almost exactly with the death of my brother. Say something, Miles, don't just sit there wide-eyed.'

'I wouldn't say no to another glass.'

'You're still young, my friend,' he said as he served me. 'Obviously, you can't have had my experience. Here, drink. And now tell me all about your visit to Eastbourne.'

I related our interview with Angela in great detail. His expression changed several times and he puffed furiously on his cigar, which resulted in a veritable fog of smoke around his head. When I had finished, he waved his hand to disperse it.

'You must understand, Miles, that I couldn't have done otherwise. In a place like Blackfield, the birth of that child would have been a bombshell. The villagers would have done the calculation and realised that—I couldn't allow my brother's memory to be sullied. I owed him that much! If the marriage had taken place, things would have been different: a few tongues would have wagged, but that's all.'

'I understand.'

'I bought Angela's silence and ordered her to leave Blackfield. I admit it.'

The major sat deep in thought for several minutes. He smiled:

'So Bill married Angela. Not a bad choice, I must say.' There was a note of irony in his voice. 'It's curious though, that she gave herself an alibi for the death of Celia Forsythe without appearing to do so.'

'I haven't checked with the neighbours.'

'Never mind, we can always do so, if need be. As for Richard's murder, she didn't tell you anything new.'

'No, she didn't hear anything, didn't see anything, and never left the kitchen. We drew a blank there.'

The major looked at the ceiling thoughtfully:

'Suppose for a moment they were both complicit in my brother's murder. Bill had a perfect alibi: he was playing at bows and arrows with Stanley Griffin and Michael. The executioner of these works in high places must therefore have been Angela.'

'And Bill must have craftily distracted his friends at the moment his accomplice escaped by the window?'

'It's a possibility. It doesn't explain how Angela managed to leave the premises so quickly—remember, all three of the boys said the killer would only have had a few seconds at his disposal—but at least it means she could have acted at the right time, when Bill was distracting the others.'

I looked doubtful:

'And the motive?'

The major shrugged his shoulders:

'That's where my theory breaks down. If Bill and Angela had been after the money, they would have waited until after the marriage, obviously.'

'Quite.'

'In any case, I've never seriously considered Angela as a suspect. She was a decent girl who'd only ever known misery, and I feel what I did after Richard's death went a long way to compensate her. You have to admit, young man, that the trip to Eastbourne was a waste of time.'

Although I didn't take issue with the major, I remained convinced of the opposite. I had put my finger on something important, and the culmination of my efforts was approaching...the goal I had set myself many years ago.

'Despite all this,' the major said, looking fiercely at the tiger skin at his feet, I'm convinced the beast is living his last hours of liberty. He knows it, and he's afraid. And I can sense that fear. I can't explain it, but I know it to be true.'

'By the way, has Rose remembered her friend's name yet?'

'No, but it's on the tip of her tongue. We're not going to wait for that to happen, however. Forget about the book: after all, there's no guarantee it will shed light on the murderer's identity. We're going to set a trap for him tomorrow night. Towards the end of the evening, say around half past nine, Rose will pretend she's suddenly remembered, and announce the name of the person to whom she lent the book. Needless to say, I shall arrange for the whole household to be present. Because it's late, we shall delay our visit to the person in question.'

'And, at nightfall, a shadow will slip out of Burton Lodge to try and retrieve the precious document. And we'll be there to intercept him!'

The major shook his head with an indulgent smile:

'Not exactly, young man. The murderer, whose diabolical talents are a matter of record, could quite easily avoid our net without being seen, and silence Rose's friend. Don't forget, we already bear the responsibility for the death of the schoolmistress.'

'So, what do you suggest?'

'We'll mount guard around the house of the "goat," so to speak. It's clear that, if we catch him while he's trying to get in to someone's house, in the middle of the night, armed with a knife—his favourite weapon—on him, he'll be in a difficult position. He might talk, due to the effect of the shock.'

I thought for a moment, then enquired:

'What will the "goat" do?'

The major pulled a face.

'I'm not quite sure yet, I'll look at that tomorrow. Of the seven other girls that were present at the time of the murder, there are only three or four left in Blackfield. Nellie, who knows them every bit as well as Rose, will be able to advise us.'

'Nellie, the maid?'

'Yes, I've told her about it. She's prepared to help us. We can trust her, she's very discreet.'

'And your niece?'

The major drew on his pipe and slowly let out the smoke:

'I'll assign her her role at the last minute, without being too specific.'

At around nine thirty, I was in my room, lying on the bed, my hands crossed above my feverish brain. In my mind's eye, I could see Richard Morstan. The good, the powerful, the charitable Richard Morstan, who reigned over Blackfield until the day that *someone* dispatched him to the hereafter. Who, why and how? Those were the questions that had troubled the major's nights over the years. But he wouldn't die without knowing, I gave him my word. I would offer him the truth on a plate, I and no other.

That mysterious *someone* had caused blood to run a second time—to ensure his own safety, to be sure—but under what circumstances! The schoolmistress' body had been reduced to a bloody pulp. He had enjoyed every minute of it.

The killer liked to see blood, fresh blood.

And something told me he wouldn't stop, now he had started, particularly if he was provoked. You didn't provoke a wild beast.

Furthermore, the major seemed to be underestimating it, this wild beast, which I felt to be a grave error. After all, it knew how to become invisible if need be.

My other worry was Cora. I was soon going to have to tell her the truth about who I was. For a brief moment, I considered turning the clock back and getting away from all this—with Cora, of course.

There was a knock on the door. I opened it and took the new arrival into my arms.

A few minutes later she said:

'Well, I walked into an ambush, it seems.'

'You haven't seen anything yet.'

After an even more passionate repeat, I told her about my meeting with the major.

'...as for the skeleton found in the garden,' I concluded, 'I really don't know what to think. If I had to guess, I'd say it had nothing to do with the present case. Consider: we know poor Miss Forsythe was killed to stop her talking. In and of itself, her life was of little interest to us. It matters little if she killed a rival, or a relative, or whatever else. It's merely a coincidence.'

'He's handsome, Bluebeard, when he climbs on his high horse,' whispered Cora.

'Enough of the Bluebeard.'

'Do you prefer I call you "inspector"?'

At that moment, more than at any time before, I wanted to reveal my identity.

'Let me remind you that it was the major's fertile imagination which created the idea of a Scotland Yard inspector. And, at the rate things are going, Blackfield will be honoured with a visit from a real inspector.'

'That would be amusing, you could meet your old colleagues,' replied Cora, teasingly.

'I shan't be there to meet them, you can be sure of that.'

Cora placed her hands on her hips:

'So you would abandon your fiancée, just like that?'

In an emotionless voice, I replied:

'What's this talk of abandonment? You'll pack your bags and we'll leave together.'

Cora's tender smile vanished as a thought occurred to her:

'If the Yard were really to come here, one or other of the Morstan family would be sure to mention Inspector Sidney Miles, who, of course, doesn't exist. But Sidney Miles, the journalist? One of them will surely have heard of you.'

Yet another thing I hadn't thought of. Cora's reasoning was impeccable, given that she thought Sidney Miles was my real name.

'Thank goodness we're not at that point yet. But you're right, it might happen. I'm digging myself into a deeper hole every day.'

'What would you do if it happened?'

'What could I do? I'd have to tell them the truth and find myself out of work…in the most optimistic case.'

'You wouldn't leave, then?' Cora persisted.

'No. No, of course not.'

This time, the comedy had gone on long enough. My triple role was starting to become too taxing.

I owed Cora the truth:

'Cora, I—.'

'You're in dire straits, I know. But whose fault is that? Let's not dwell on it. As for your tiger trap, I can't help wondering how it will end.' She looked at me with eyes full of reproach. 'Suppose there's another murder?'

At that moment, there were three discreet knocks on the door.

'Yes?' I growled.

The door opened and Cora's father peered in.

'Am I troubling you?'

'Troubling us?' I protested respectfully. 'Why, not at all, Mr. Ferrers. Do come in.'

After a quick look at Cora—who looked modestly at the floor— Tony said pleasantly:

'There's a young girl to see you, inspector. She's downstairs. Shall I send her up?'

'A young girl?' repeated Cora, shooting me a murderous look.

'It's the Morstans' maid,' Tony explained, with a mocking smile at his daughter.

'Tell her to come up, please.'

After Tony had gone, Cora and I exchanged puzzled glances.

There was another knock on the door.

'Come in,' I said.

It needed only one look at Nellie to tell there was something seriously amiss. She was haggard, her hair was dishevelled, she was out of breath, and there was a wild look in her eye. Everything about her indicated haste and disarray.

'I ran all the way from Burton Lodge,' she gasped, looking around for somewhere to sit.

I offered her the little cane chair, and she plumped herself down with a sigh of relief.

Cora's hands went to her throat:

'Don't tell me there's been another murder, Nellie?'

Nellie shook her head:

'No. But Rose has talked.'

My blood froze in my veins:

'The book?'

'Yes. It's Patricia Morrison who should have it, if she hasn't lent it to someone else in the meantime. We were all in the lounge when Rose remembered, a quarter of an hour after you left, inspector. The major fears the worst.'

The danger was obvious. We needed to act right away.

'She talked in front of everyone?' I cried, fists clenched. 'But that's insane! It's idiotic! Our whole plan is ruined.'

'I assume the major has given you new instructions,' said Cora, in a strangely calm voice.

'Yes, he's going to try and keep everyone there until eleven o'clock,' said Nellie. 'After which he'll lie in wait in case anyone tries to leave Burton Lodge. Meanwhile, sir and I will keep watch at Patricia's home. That way, there'll be a double surveillance. If he doesn't see anything suspicious, he'll join us at one o'clock in the morning.'

'Hmm, for an improvised plan, it's not too bad,' I muttered. 'And Patricia Morrison, what do we do about her?'

Nellie looked at me nervously, her eyes wide:

'I went round to see her, sir. There's nobody at home and I think her parents are away. As for her, I think she's with her friend, and should be back soon. The major thinks we should not frighten her by explaining what's happening. He just asked me to try and find the book.'

'Fine. It's quarter past ten,' I said, consulting my watch. 'That leaves us forty-five minutes, assuming that the major can keep them there until eleven o'clock.'

'It would be best to leave right away, sir,' said Nellie. 'We might be able to intercept Patricia. It would be awkward knocking at her door at eleven o'clock to get a book.'

'You're right.'

'There's something else,' she continued hesitantly. 'I wonder if it wouldn't be better to explain the situation to Patricia. Maybe we could protect her better that way.'

I replied with a calculated deliberation:

'"Explain the situation"…and how would she react? I can only see two possibilities: either she thinks we're mad and asks us to leave, or she believes us and panics. Let's stick to the major's plan: we'll both watch the house from the outside, and no one will——.'

'Both of you? And what am I supposed to do while all this is going on?'

Cora wanted to be involved! I closed my eyes and tried to stay calm.

'Would you mind waiting downstairs?' I asked Nellie. 'I'll join you in a few minutes.'

She nodded and left. After a few tense moments I said to Cora in a solemn, persuasive voice:

'All this is very dangerous. And your presence there would be a distraction. And——.'

'And?'

'I love you,' I shouted. 'And you know it.'

'You have a funny way of showing it,' she said, lowering her eyes.

'Cora, this is not the time…'

She smiled wanly.

'And what do you think my feelings are for you?' A tear appeared at the corner of one eye. 'Oh, I know I'm not very brave, but to think of you out there, in the dark, waiting to confront a madman…when I'm here, scared to death, awaiting your return.…'

'Don't worry, Cora. Nothing's going to happen to me. I'm used to this kind of thing.'

She looked up, startled:

'What do you mean, "used to this kind of thing"?'

'I…Look, I have to go. Stay in your room and wait for me, there's a good girl. Trust me.'

12

The Morrison house, a square block of weather-stained grey stones, sat in the middle of a lawn surrounded by chestnut trees.

'What are we going to do?' whispered Nellie, in a trembling voice.

I didn't answer right away, as I was attempting to analyse the situation. The property was in total darkness, save for the occasional break in the clouds allowing a glimpse of the baleful moonlight.

'There are no lights. Patricia's not back yet, it would seem. Let's wait a little while for her.'

'And after that?'

'Let's do the rounds of the house first, and then decide.'

After that was done, I explained:

'You're going to stand behind one of the trees along the street, so you can observe the front of the house and the side wall on the left. I'll find somewhere on the diagonally opposite corner, so I can watch the other two sides. From either of our positions, it's about fifteen yards to the house. You can't see much, I know, but if we concentrate hard, I don't think anyone could get into the house without being seen. And our eyes have become accustomed to the dark.'

Nellie shivered:

'I hope he doesn't hear my teeth chattering. Do you think he'll arrive by the street?'

'Surely not. That's why I put you there. I'm sure he's going to come through the fields and through the vegetable garden to the rear of the house, and that's when Inspector Miles will intervene.'

'Which reminds me. Rose and I talked about it yesterday. You probably know John Reed: he's also an inspector at the Yard.'

'Ah, yes, the major told me about him. He comes from Blackfield, apparently. I may have spoken to him once or twice.'

'So you know him? He must have changed quite a bit since then. What's he like?'

The situation was becoming grotesque. I should never have agreed to the role the major had suggested. But I couldn't stand there and say nothing:

'Well, he's a conscientious sort of fellow. I've nothing against him. And, as I told you, we've only met once or twice. But when I see him next, I'll be sure to talk about Blackfield and its pretty girls.'

Nellie's eyes shone with pleasure; she said, conspiratorially:

'You know, Rose liked him a lot then. I'm sure if he'd shown any interest, she wouldn't be Mrs. Strange today. But please don't say anything. If Luke heard about it, he'd dismiss me on the spot.'

'Of course, Nellie. Your secret's safe with me.'

Just then, we heard the sound of voices. We ducked behind a fence and kept an eye on the street .

'It's Patricia and her fiancé,' murmured Nellie. 'They seem to be arguing. That's not going to make it any easier. What excuse can I invent?'

'Blame it all on the major. Tell your friend he's adamant about having the book, but he didn't tell you why. He'll have plenty of time to make up a reason.'

'Look! Her fiancé has turned on his heels. Patricia's coming up the street. You'd better go.'

I ran quickly to my position and waited. A few seconds later, I detected the sounds of a conversation between Nellie and Patricia. A sudden gust of wind disturbed the leaves of the chestnut trees and hid their words from me. Then a door slammed. I waited a few minutes and rejoined Nellie.

'What happened?'

'She was furious, sir, and refused to listen.'

'Did she say whether she still had the book?'

'She wasn't sure, but she thought so. I'm supposed to come round tomorrow.'

I looked thoughtfully at Nellie in the shadows. She seemed worried, as if preoccupied by some inner torment. She kept touching her cheek with her hand. Strange Nellie. Strange last-minute ally. Strange young girl, who seemed oblivious to the danger we were in.

'It must be eleven o'clock by now,' I said. 'The killer may arrive at any moment. It's only a ten minute walk from Burton Lodge.'

Nellie didn't react, but kept looking at her hands.

'Tell me, did you hear Patricia bolt the door behind her?'

Nellie didn't answer immediately:

'She slammed the door and...no, I don't think she did.'

Beckoning her to follow me, I led her to her observation post.

'Get behind that tree, so nobody will see you. That's it. Now take a look and tell me what you see.'

'The front and left side of the house,' she replied angrily. 'I'm not stupid, inspector. Please stop treating me like a child.'

'Nellie, you must never take your eyes off that part of the house. It's very important.'

'Inspector, I repeat: I know what I have to do.'

'I'm sure you do. But it's very hard to see anything and, what's more, we don't know how long we're going to have to wait. The slightest lapse of attention could have frightful consequences. That's why I insist: your eyes must remain glued on this part of the house.'

After thinking for a moment, she replied:

'All the windows of the house are closed, except one at the back on the first floor. Did you notice?'

'Of course, Nellie, I'm an inspector! Don't worry, it won't be out of my sight for a single moment. But there's also the front door, which might not be locked.'

'And if I see someone,' said Nellie, suddenly anxious, 'what do I do?'

'You shout, and I'll come running. I have to get back to my post now. No need to go over it all again.'

The rear face of the house had four windows: two on the ground floor, separated by a door with a canopy overhead, and two on the first floor. The one on the right was open, but the curtains were drawn closed, allowing only a sliver of light to pass—Patricia's room, no doubt.

The light was suddenly extinguished, plunging the rear of the house into total darkness. I had brought along my watch, but it was impossible to read the time: half past eleven, perhaps. When my eyes became accustomed to the darkness again, I realised how easy it would be to reach the young woman's window by climbing on to the canopy.

'Inspector, why are you running like that?'

'Didn't you see anything, Nellie?' I asked in a breathless voice.

She looked at me in astonishment.

'No. Or I would have called out.'

'For heaven's sake,' I groaned, punching the palm of my hand with my fist, 'I'm sure I didn't dream it. I just saw a shadow turn the corner of the house.'

'Which corner?'

I pointed to the corner formed by the left wall and the rear left face.

'That's ridiculous. It's obvious that I couldn't have helped seeing anyone approaching that way. Where did the shadow come from, anyway?'

I clutched my head with my hands.

'I lost my concentration for a moment. There was a noise from the garden. I looked over my shoulder. Not for very long: four or five seconds, that's all. When I turned back, I saw a shadow disappear around the corner of the house. I rushed here straight away.'

'You came round the corner of the house and ran towards me. There was no one ahead of you, believe me.'

'There's an area of shadow at the foot of the wall,' I observed. 'By creeping along there someone could eventually—.'

'Inspector,' Nellie sighed in annoyance, 'I would have seen it. And, when you ran towards me, you could see the length of the wall.'

'And there wasn't anyone,' I agreed. 'It must be my imagination playing me tricks.'

'It's strange,' continued Nellie, 'the major should be here by now. It's almost two hours.'

A fortuitous ray of moonlight allowed me to consult my watch:

'It's barely one o'clock. This wait has caused us to lose track of time.'

Suddenly, Nellie was seized with terror:

'The killer,' she stammered, 'the phantom killer.'

After an icy silence, I said:

'Come on. So much the worse if we wake her.'

We ran to the front door which groaned as I opened it.

'It's as I feared,' I observed. 'She forgot to lock it.'

We went in and stopped at the foot of the staircase.

'Miss Morrison?' I called.

Silence.

'Miss Morrison,' I called again, louder this time.

Still no reply.

Nellie grabbed hold of me, shaking like a leaf.

I tried to reassure her:

'She might have taken a sleeping draught after the quarrel with her fiancé.'

I struck a match. The flickering flame showed a corridor with pale yellow wallpaper, almost waxen, like Nellie's features.

Suddenly a powerful, commanding voice made us jump:

'What's happening here?'

I turned round: the major was standing in the doorway, a walking stick in one hand and a dark lantern raised in the other.

I explained the situation. He stood there thoughtfully, his eyes fixed to the staircase, then said to Nellie:

'Don't move from this spot.'

He and I raced up the stairs.

'I think it's the room over there,' I said, pointing to a door.

Without a moment's hesitation, the major struck it several times with his stick.

The response was a deathly silence.

We exchanged glances and went in.

His dark lantern swept the room and stopped, the ray shining on the bed. Patricia appeared to be in a deep sleep. We approached. The major stepped back:

'In God's name!'

The murderer had struck again: Patricia's throat had been cut from ear to ear.

13

The following day, Friday, in the middle of the afternoon, the major came to find me in my room. Cora, seated by the window, watched him enter, her expression inscrutable. I had spent the morning trying, in vain, to entice a smile out of her. Although she gave no external sign of grief, I could tell she was deeply affected: the light seemed to have been extinguished from her beautiful blue eyes.

The major waited a while to recover his breath, then dropped into the small cane chair which Cora pushed towards him, and which almost didn't support his weight. He placed his hat on the table and sponged his forehead with a handkerchief.

'Two atrocious crimes in forty-eight hours,' he began. 'The village is on full alert, and the police also. I fear, young man, that this business might fall into other hands.'

'What did you tell them finally?'

'Just what we agreed; I dropped by on Patricia at 9.00 in the morning to collect a book, and, since she didn't answer and the front door was open... To cut a long story short, they accepted my story.'

'Let's hope so,' said Cora.

'Yes, indeed,' muttered the major. 'And we still haven't found that damned book, despite all our efforts.'

'The killer took it,' I said. 'After all, that's what he came for, isn't it?'

With a brusque gesture the major removed his lorgnette and looked angrily at me:

'You told me that from half past eleven to the discovery of the crime, you didn't see a single beam of light at the Morrisons. On top of that, we spent over an hour examining every room in the house, and apparently nothing was out of place. I find it hard to imagine the killer feeling his way around in the darkness without leaving a single trace.'

'We may conclude,' I replied, clearing my voice, 'that he didn't have to look very far. Here's what I think: Patricia took the book to bed with her, to try and understand why Nellie had tried to obtain it at such an ungodly hour. Don't forget the window to her room had a light behind it for a good half hour. After killing her, the murderer simply collected it from her bedside table, in all probability.'

The major nodded in agreement.

'You're probably right,' he said. 'But that doesn't explain how he got in and out of the house. Unfortunately, I wasn't able to keep everyone in the lounge until eleven, as I'd planned, only until half past ten. Luke retired to his office, where he spent the night. A few minutes later, Rose and Eleanor went to bed as well. From that moment, I started my surveillance of the exterior of Burton Lodge. A complete waste of time, because it would have been child's play for the killer to slip out without me noticing.'

I started to pace the room, deep in thought.

'Nellie and I arrived at the Morrisons at quarter to eleven. It would have been hard for the killer to have got there ahead of us. On the other hand, he could well have been on the premises by eleven o'clock, because when Patricia slammed the door, I went over to Nellie to question her and give her instructions. The rear of the house was left unattended for two or three minutes: quite long enough for the killer to get into Patricia's room, using the canopy over the back door. That's what must have happened, because afterwards it wouldn't have been possible for him to get in.'

'Let's assume you're right,' replied the major. 'There's still the problem of the disappearance: around one o'clock, after a few seconds of inattention, you think you see a shadow fleeing round the corner of the house. It was obviously the killer who had just climbed down from the window. Just as in the case of Richard's murder, he was able to execute the operation in a few seconds, but this time we saw him, which is already not bad. However Nellie didn't see anyone go round the corner of the house! Just as in the case of the schoolmistress, he vanishes into thin air. Baxter may have taken a drop too much, but Nellie?'

'I told you, it was very dark,' I muttered. 'Oh, yes, he's very clever, I don't deny it. But he was helped by the darkness in both cases. I'm sure he couldn't have got away in broad daylight.'

'And at what time of day was my brother killed?' retorted the major, with an exasperated smile.

The sun glinted on the major's lorgnette and simultaneously a light shone in my brain: *I knew who had killed Richard Morstan*, and, by the same token, Patricia Morrison's murder had been disconcertingly simple.

'Although it was the same killer, that murder didn't resemble the others.'

'I don't follow,' said the major, frowning.

'Your brother's murder wasn't premeditated. Which wasn't so for the other two. Take the murder of Celia Forsythe: why was she killed?'

'Because she remembered something!' replied the major, beginning to lose his temper.

'And what do you deduce from that?'

'I just told you, for heaven's sake! She constituted a danger to the killer and he had to get rid of her.'

'Miss Forsythe remembered something,' I continued calmly. 'Miss Forsythe: she, and she alone, that's very important. And just as important is the interest the killer had in the book on magical illusions. He proved that tonight by taking a considerable risk to get hold of it. He could just have knocked Patricia out, but he didn't hesitate to kill her, because she could have remembered something essential.'

The major turned scarlet:

'We've known that for a long time, dammit! The trick Richard wanted to perform could give the killer away.'

'But why? Why would the discovery of the trick identify one particular person? Have you thought about that?'

The major hesitated. 'Frankly, no.'

'So, to summarise, the testimony of Miss Forsythe and the explanation of the magic trick your brother was practising were crucial, in the murderer's eyes. How's Nellie, by the way?'

The major appeared surprised:

'Nellie? I'd say she's doing remarkably well, in the circumstances.'

'Can I ask you two detectives a question?' demanded Cora suddenly. She had been leaning on the window-sill, looking up at the sky. 'How many more women are going to have their throats cut before the killer is arrested? This blood-crazed madman, this….'

She turned to face me. She hadn't pronounced the word "Bluebeard," but I could read it in her eyes.

The major gesticulated haplessly:

103

'My dear Cora, please understand. We're only doing our duty: my brother's killer must be brought to justice. I quite understand your attitude towards us. Yes, we're largely responsible for what's happened, I'm only too well aware of that. But, believe me, these murders will not go unpunished.' A vengeful light came into his eyes. 'Remember, no tiger ever emerged alive from the hunt! Do you hear me? Never. The wild beast is desperate. It's cornered. There's no way out. The end is near, and it knows it.'

'I'm also of that opinion,' I said. 'The ideal would be to gather the suspects together tonight and interrogate them thoroughly. It's possible the killer might crack.'

'It's as good as done. Tonight, at eight-thirty.'

So saying, he picked up his hat and left. No sooner had he left the room than Cora was in my arms.

'Sidney,' she said after while, 'I'm under the impression you suspect someone.'

I whispered a word in her ear.

'Oh, my God!' she exclaimed. 'It's not possible!'

'Yes. It's the only person who could physically have killed Patricia Morrison, the only person who could have disappeared from the corner of the house.'

'Of course, but what was the motive? The motive for the murder of Richard Morstan?'

'I'm not sure yet, but I have an idea. I need to talk to Dr. Griffin again.'

'Dr. Griffin?'

'Yes. He cannot be unaware. You see, Cora, the village "saint" was a very unusual parishioner.'

I explained my suspicions, which were not disproved by what she then told me; far from it.

She fell silent for a long moment, before starting to talk in an expressionless voice:

'I had gone into the woods to see if the blackberries in the clearing were ripe enough to pick. I'd just left the path when I saw him sitting on a tree trunk. Full of smiles, he invited me to sit down next to him. I didn't dare refuse. He put his arm round my shoulders protectively and talked to me about nature and the beauty of it all, and he even recited poetry. I felt uncomfortable and tried to leave, but he only hugged me more tightly. Then he tried to kiss me.'

'And did you let him?' I asked angrily, feeling a pang of jealousy.

'No, of course not,' she replied. 'He scared me, his eyes were terrifying, and his hands...I managed to free myself with a great effort. I ran away. I was more agile than he was.'

'The blackguard. And did he try again?'

'Once or twice. But I was on the alert and didn't let him get close.'

She stopped, lost in sombre thought, her eyes empty of all emotion. I didn't dare break the silence, but gathered her more closely against me.

'Sidney,' she said in a very small voice, 'I hope that....how can I say this? If ever we catch the murderer, can you arrange for him to be given a respite of twenty-four hours before the arrest? ...Give him a chance to escape?'

'Rest assured. I would have done that anyway. There were extenuating circumstances, to say the very least.'

Even though I was already a quarter of an hour late, I took the path which ran alongside the river to get to Burton Lodge. I had found the route pleasing and I wanted to cross the little bridge where we had exchanged our first kiss.

The setting sun cast a long shadow on the lawn of Burton Lodge. I could only see one window illuminated: that of the lounge on the ground floor. No doubt the major would be furious about the delay, puffing furiously on his pipe while his face turned purple. Come to think of it, why not do a bit of eavesdropping?

I crossed the lawn and made my way along the side of the house as silently as a cat, until I reached the lounge window, where I stopped to listen.

'You have to agree, major,' said Luke's voice, 'that I did the right thing by going to Scotland Yard this afternoon to report this whole business. As for you, Superintendent Melvin, I'm grateful to you for having taken the time personally to attend.'

Superintendent Melvin! I felt my knees go weak.

'It was the least I could do,' replied the policeman. 'Two atrocious crimes of a particularly mysterious character in the space of forty-eight hours, and this curious Sidney Miles fellow passing himself off as one of us: that was more than enough.'

'I think it's perhaps time for you to explain yourself, uncle,' said Rose.

After a long silence, the major spilled the beans:

'Well, since I haven't got a choice…It was my idea to have him play the role of an inspector of the Yard. He's actually a journalist for the *Daily Telegraph.* My brother's murder had intrigued him by its mysterious nature, and he wanted to solve it in order to write a novel. It seemed like a good opportunity to revisit the whole murky business. But I didn't want to introduce him as a journalist because I thought an inspector of the Yard would have more impact.'

'When did you meet him for the first time?' asked the superintendent.

'At the beginning of the week. Monday afternoon, to be precise, in the village inn where he had rented a room.'

The veins in my temple were throbbing as I pressed myself further back against the wall and waited for what would follow:

'I know all the journalists on the *Daily Telegraph* personally,' replied the policeman tersely, 'and I can assure you there's no one of that name working there.'

There were expressions of consternation and the sounds of movement. Even though I hadn't yet risked a look, I knew that the whole household must be present. Poor Major Morstan: I didn't fancy being in his place.

'Incredible,' he said in an unrecognisable voice. 'Incredible. Well, we'll soon get the whole story: he'll be here at any moment.'

A silence filled with hidden thoughts ensued. Luke could stand it no longer and attacked, in a voice hoarse with excitement:

'He's neither a police inspector nor a journalist, yet he's interested in a ten-year old crime. Instead of coming directly here, he makes your acquaintance at the inn, uncle, as if by accident. Needless to say, it's not an accident. He knew very well he'd find a sympathetic ear in you, and someone ready to help him with an investigation which was nothing more than a pretext to get inside Burton Lodge. Who is he and what does he want?

'During our discussion last Tuesday, he made several deductions which appeared to be almost miraculous in nature, to wit: Mr. Morstan had sent the staff at Burton Lodge away for a day, one week prior to the murder; and he'd nailed the door of the murder room shut the morning of the crime. Now, I don't believe in miracles and it's obvious he must have known those details before he set foot in Blackfield. We may therefore conclude that we're not dealing with a stranger, but with someone who's a friend or a relative whom we didn't recognise because we haven't seen him for a long time. May I also draw your attention to the impressive black beard which covers half of his face.'

I have to admit that, in the field of deduction, Luke didn't disgrace himself at all. I smiled as he continued his brilliant demonstration.

'What are his intentions? To answer that question, I propose we look at the facts: what has he done since his return to Blackfield?'

Another silence.

'I repeat my question: what important events have taken place since his return at the beginning of the week?'

Eleanor Burroughs replied in an icy voice:

'Two women have had their throats cut.'

'My dear Luke,' thundered the major, in a voice which rattled the window panes, 'I'd like to know what's behind your question.'

'To sum up: someone who knows us all well, whom we haven't seen for some time and who holds no love for us: Michael Morstan!'

After the ensuing commotion, Luke, at the request of Superintendent Melvin, narrated the circumstances surrounding the murder of his father-in-law and the evening preceding the death of the schoolmistress.

After he had finished, some thirty minutes later, Nellie chimed in about the murder of Patricia Morrison, and ended by saying:

'Now I know why he insisted so much on me not leaving my observation post; he was able to kill Patricia without being disturbed. Oh, my goodness, if I'd known...And to think I believed his story about the shadow which he'd seen—*him*, mind—and which I should have seen but hadn't. Everything's so clear now.'

'So clear,' exclaimed Rose, with tears in her voice. 'But you're completely mad. Michael could never have done such a thing. In any case, it wasn't Michael: I would have recognised him.'

'Calm yourself, darling,' replied Luke, 'and try to think. We haven't seen Michael for ten years. Just like the fellow who calls himself Sidney Miles, he has blue eyes, regular features and black hair. And you can't see much of his face besides his eyes, moustache and beard.'

'So be it,' said the major in a confident voice, 'let's suppose it is Michael. Let's suppose also that he killed Miss Celia Forsythe and Patricia Morrison. In that case, he also killed his father—even though

I can't see how. I only have one question, my dear Luke. Why, in that case, did he come back to investigate his own crime?'

'But don't you understand, uncle, he wishes us all dead, he wants to frighten us and——.'

'Why?'

'Don't you remember his attitude after the death of his father? He wouldn't speak to anyone. And that part of the inheritance that he's dangling in front of us. It all indicates a ferocious hatred of us.'

'I'll ask you once more: why?'

'To tell you the truth, I don't know the precise origin——.'

'That's what I thought, you don't know anything. So, from now on, please refrain from unfounded accusations. This Sidney Miles is a decent fellow, and I know men. It's not because he gave me a false name that he's not a journalist. He's honest, intelligent and in the habit of conducting investigations. Let's not forget that together we've made giant strides.'

'It's true,' observed the superintendent, 'but at what price? If you'd have come to us with your conclusions the day after the death of the schoolmistress, we would certainly have been able to avoid that of Miss Morrison. The job of a detective isn't based on improvisation, major: it's not a game of chess where pawns are moved about. Moreover, I'm about to assign this case to one of the Yard's best sleuths. He's from...Hell's bells! I think I understand.'

14

Above the treetops, the baleful light of the moon turned everything pale. I closed my eyes, took a deep breath, and went round to the front of the house to knock on the main door. Hopkins opened it. Without uttering a word, he showed me into the lounge.

The assembled household looked at me as if I were a ghost, but not Superintendent Melvin, who regarded me with amusement.

Not feeling very proud of myself, I sat down on a chair with my head down and waited. The moment of the great discovery had arrived.

It was the superintendent who spoke:

'Please raise your head, inspector, so that people can see you better.'

'Inspector?' exclaimed Luke in a strangled voice. 'But I thought—.'

'I think you ought to know him. He was born in Blackfield. Weren't you, Inspector John Reed?'

There were exclamations from all sides:

'John! Oh, John!' exclaimed Rose.

'John Reed. Well I'll be damned,' said the major, letting his pipe fall to the ground.

'It was stupid of me not to have grasped the situation right away,' continued the superintendent. 'John had often spoken to me about Blackfield and the strange Morstan business, which he hoped to clear up one day. When I found out he'd been on holiday since the beginning of the week, I immediately made the connection with the mysterious Sidney Miles. John is one of our best detectives; you've probably read about his exploits in the newspapers. Not only does he rarely make an error in his deductions, but he's very effective in the field. Quite often, in certain notorious areas of London, when a dangerous criminal needs to be taken from his lair, we have to disguise ourselves. There again, there's no one better than John. And, on top of it all, he's as agile as a monkey, and has no equal—.'

'Thank you, chief. You're too kind,' I said, looking round the assembled household.

Rose seemed thrilled to bits, which didn't sit well with her husband, who smiled grimly—apparently just as jealous as in the past. The major was torn between anger and pride. As for Eleanor and Nellie, it was impossible to guess their feelings.

'What's all this about, John,' grumbled the major. 'Why all the play-acting? To think I asked you to play the role of an inspector.... You must have been laughing inside.'

'At the time of your brother's murder, I was already thinking of going into the police. I wasn't really interested in medicine. I've always loved mysteries, and a particularly perplexing one had happened right there in my village. I tried to carry out my own modest investigation at the time. Do you remember how many times I asked you questions, Rose?'

Rose nodded and smiled, under the wrathful eye of her husband.

'My efforts were in vain, of course. My father died a few months later, and I never returned to Blackfield until now.'

'I liked your father very much,' said the major. 'He would be proud of you, John, if he were still alive.'

I was moved by his words, and gave him a grateful look before I continued:

'I left Blackfield with the solid promise to myself to return one day and solve the mystery, which was to become an obsession with me: how could the murderer have carried out his crime? The obsession grew over the years. When I made the decision to come back to pursue my investigation, I was fully aware of the difficulties involved: I was a police inspector, certainly, but I was also John Reed; knowing me would make it easier to avoid my questions. What should I do?'

The major gave a deep sigh:

'I must confess, I fell hook, line and sinker for your story about a journalist, here to write a novel.'

'I only misled you on two points: my profession and my identity.'

'In John's defence,' interjected the superintendent, 'he's been thinking about writing a novel for years. But we're still waiting.'

The major smiled indulgently, then frowned suddenly:

'Let's put all that behind us and get back to the crime. I got a distinct impression this afternoon, John, that you'd worked out part of the puzzle. What exactly do you know?'

'Just about everything.'

My response created a deathly silence.

The major took off his lorgnette and looked at me suspiciously:

'Do you know who killed my brother?'

'Yes. The murders of Miss Forsythe and Miss Morrison led me to discover how it was done. I'm still not completely sure of the motive, but I should know that by tomorrow.'

The major settled further into his armchair and puffed on his pipe:

'Is the person in this room?' he asked in a dangerously soft voice.

'Absolutely.'

'And do you know the trick he used to disappear in such a miraculous fashion after the two last murders?'

'Let me just say that, in the case of Miss Morrison, it was ridiculously simple. So simple it's hardly worth calling it a trick. The murderer knows very well what I mean by that.'

'Something tells me that, even if your superior officer orders it, you're not prepared to reveal the name tonight.'

'That's correct.'

'Can I know the reason? You seem to forget, John, the atrocious ferocity of Miss Forsythe's murder. We're dealing with a wild beast. Your silence could—.'

'For a start, this is not a wild beast. This person is more like a victim...of another kind of monster.' I looked the major straight in the eye. 'If what I learn tomorrow confirms my suspicions, major, you'll be able to appreciate the consequences of your *own* silence about certain matters. Without trying to diminish my own responsibility, I nonetheless believe that, if I'd been in possession of all the facts, I could have solved the case more quickly and avoided at least one murder.'

The major sat as still as a statue.

'I hope you know what you're doing, John,' said Superintendent Melvin, looking at me thoughtfully. 'Up until now, I've given you full rein. But if your assumptions are not well-founded, and another murder occurs....'

'The killer will not strike again, of that I'm certain,' I said, looking in turn at everyone in the room.

The fact that Superintendent Melvin was the major's guest was somewhat of a relief to me. His presence in Burton Lodge was a clear danger to the killer, and he would certainly not risk another bloody incident. All things considered, there was only one way out for him, if he sought to escape the gallows.

I was at that point in my thinking as I arrived at the inn. The last customer was just leaving and Tony was about to close the door.

'Good evening, Mr. Ferrers. Is Cora still up?'

Tony smiled with ill-concealed irritation:

'She's very tired, Mr. Miles, and—.'

'I'm not Mr. Miles anymore. My name is Reed, John Reed.'

Although the lamp in my room illuminated Cora's lovely features, I couldn't tell if she was suppressing a seething rage or a fit of helpless laughter.

Her eyes welled with tears, which didn't clarify matters. At last she spoke:

'Sidney…I mean John…I must confess…Why didn't you tell me earlier?'

'Put yourself in my place, Cora. I came here to fulfil a dream I've had for nearly ten years. I wanted to keep my cards close to my chest and not reveal my identity before I discovered the truth. On Monday, when I met you, I was bowled over—and I believe I conveyed that message to you.'

'You certainly did. No one ever spoke to me like that.'

'At that point, I was looking to enliven the investigation—if you see what I mean.'

'Only too clearly,' she replied, affecting a vexed air. 'But do go on, pray.'

'Little by little, over the course of the five days, I realised that what I felt for you was something I had never felt before. To make things short, I realised I was in love with you.'

'Why make things short? You can develop the subject….'

'Cora, please. Don't be so scathing. It's hard enough already to explain. It's past midnight already and I still have a lot to tell you. So, I was in love with you and—.'

'You're not in love with me any more?'

I kept my self-control with an effort and ignored the remark. I continued in a shaky voice:

'As I was saying, my love for you was growing at the same time as my anxiety at having to tell you at some point that I'd….'

'Deceived me. I think that's the word you're looking for. Do you

112

remember last night's discussion, where I was worried about what might happen if the Yard got involved?'

'Cora,' I implored, 'I was on the point of telling you, I swear it. But you interrupted me and your father knocked at the door.'

She looked at me incredulously, then admitted:

'It's true. And I remember you didn't seem very sure of yourself at the time.' She smiled, lost in thought for a moment. 'I'll tell you something in confidence, Sid—I mean John, even though you don't deserve it: at the time, I thought you were a handsome boy, even though you were nearly twenty years old.'

'And you were fourteen, looking at boys already?' I retorted, feigning jealousy.

'I didn't say I looked at boys. Only one: you.'

Having run out of arguments, I picked her up from the chair and put her on the bed, where I kissed her. From her response, I concluded I was forgiven.

'I've something else to tell you,' she said, some time later. 'I don't want to hurt you, but....'

'Go on.'

'Frankly, there are moments when you frighten me. Your eyes cloud over, you turn deathly white, and you give the impression you're mad. I'd like to know what's in there,' she said, tapping me on the forehead.

I stood up, picked up a cigar, and took my time lighting it.

'It's a memory. An old and terrible memory. Let me begin at the beginning. As you know, I have no brothers or sisters. I have very few memories of my mother. She left us when I was only five years old.'

'Yes, I know, Papa told me.'

'She was very beautiful, it seems: too beautiful and too frivolous. The quiet life she led with a man who went out of his way to please her in every way bored her. She found it confining and annoying. One day, she left with the nephew (and heir) of the richest customer of our bookbinding shop. My father started to hate his pretty boutique and well-equipped workshop. He left London to come to Blackfield to be near his father, who was becoming infirm.'

'That must have been awful at five years old.'

'Not really. As far as I could see, Papa didn't show much anger. As for me, it didn't really change much. My mother had been far too pre-occupied with herself to pay attention to a little kid whose outbursts

113

of affection might ruffle her impeccable hairdo. It was Papa who looked out for me, nurtured me, told me stories. Truth be told, my mother's departure only served to increase the attention lavished on me by my father. As for the village, I had more freedom here than in London: my grandfather taught me hundreds of things city dwellers never learn.'

'Tell me, John, did your father tell you all that?'

'No, Papa never talked about my mother. But one day, when he was away in London, I overheard a conversation between Grandfather and Dr. Griffin which shocked me to the core. I was twelve at the time. Grandfather quickly realised I had heard things not intended for my ears and took it upon himself to tell me everything, without passing judgment.

'Even though I scarcely remember my mother, there's an image of her engraved in my mind. It was one Christmas Day and I had just found a superb rocking horse under the tree. Papa had splashed out to get Mama a fur muff and a bottle of French perfume. She was delighted. I left my horse and climbed on her knee to press myself against her, my nose on her soft and deliciously scented cheek. A moment of perfect happiness. Later, when the perfume bottle was empty, she gave it to me and it became one of my little treasures. It was all I had left of my mother. From time to time, I opened the bottle to remind myself of her.

'But that day I threw my precious bottle in the river. My father came home and I kissed him warmly. He looked at me in surprise and gave Grandfather an enquiring look. What he saw in the old man's eyes caused him to sigh deeply and put his arm around my shoulders. We didn't need to say anything.

'My father was never short of work. Some of his customers even came to Blackfield, for he was the best at what he did. He would have liked me to follow in his shoes, but accepted it without rancour when I chose another career. When I left for college, it was very hard for him—and me as well. I was his sole reason for living. Grandfather had died the year before, as serenely as he had lived.

'One evening in the summer of 1873, when I was fourteen, we were preparing to spend a peaceful evening together. It had been a strenuous day. The night before, a bolt of lightning during a violent storm had split the ancient weeping willow in the garden of a neighbouring cottage. Rain had swollen the stream which flowed at the bottom of our gardens and the tree had been uprooted by the torrent and flung across the stream. Papa, Baxter and Tony had worked flat out the whole day to clear the stream and chop up the willow. We were sitting down to a well-earned meal when the door was flung open by a woman. A hideous, repugnant woman with dirty grey hair, pale skin under a heavy layer of make-up and a look in her eyes that I cannot find the words to describe. I was terrified and nauseated. The woman was my mother, Cora.

'His face chalk-white and his hands trembling, Papa bounded out of his chair and pointed imperiously to the door. The woman—my mother—rushed towards me as I stepped back, horrified, and screeched in a tremulous voice: "John, my little John, my one and only child."'

I stopped, devastated by the memory of that degrading scene. I swallowed several times before I was able to continue.

'Of course, it was money she wanted. Her young aristocratic lover had left her and she had fallen low...very low. Papa, whose anger and indignation was growing by the minute, continued to point to the door, saying nothing so as to avoid a scene. But she taunted him, chanting: "No one has the right to separate a child from its mother."

'Papa, trembling in every limb, picked up the bread knife. She sneered disdainfully: "You miserable wretch, you daren't touch me." They stood there in confrontation, their faces, illuminated by the light from the oil lamp, frozen in mutual hatred. She opened her mouth again to hurl more insults. The knife cut the air once, twice, I lost count of how many times. Mother's face was striped in red...the blood trickled and spattered on the tiled floor. My vision clouded in a crimson fog.'

Cora took my hand:

'Calm yourself, John. I understand.'

'I did manage to tackle my father before he killed her. She left and we never saw her again.'

'Was she seriously wounded?'

'No, I don't think so. Superficial wounds, but which had bled a lot. You can't begin to imagine the effect of that scene on me. I very nearly went mad. Papa, distraught, withdrew into a dogged silence. And I, who needed so much to talk, to confide in someone...I went to see Miss Forsythe to unburden myself of everything that was in my heart. But I couldn't do it.

'Cora, do you remember Tuesday evening, when Miss Forsythe took me to one side, a few hours before her death?'

'Yes, you told us she'd asked to see you.'

'She also said something else. She alluded to the day when little John Reed went to see her. She'd seen the madness of that terrible scene in my eyes and concluded that I wasn't entirely normal. Did she recognise me or did she just think it was a chance resemblance? We shall never know. But at the time, I was afraid I might be unmasked.

'When I was seventeen, I was admitted into a faculty of medicine, specialising in surgery. Every time I attempted an operation or a dissection, my vision clouded and a crimson screen appeared, with the image of my mother's blood-streaked face on it. I fought against it with all my force, not wanting to disappoint my father who, despite declining health, continued working in order I might continue my studies. I gave it up two years after my father died, in 1881, the year I should have graduated as bachelor of medicine and master of surgery.'

'And you went into the police.'

'Yes, that might seem odd for someone frightened by the sight of blood. It's hard to explain, but I've always been a lover of mystery. Have you ever read—.'

'John!' she exclaimed, taking me by the shoulders. 'We've already talked about all that.'

'That's true. I'd forgotten, darling. It was even one of the first things we talked about.'

'And the book you wanted to write?'

'It's true I've written nothing yet, but it will happen one day, you'll see.'

'And it will be based on the Morstan affair?'

'I think so,' I replied, smiling. 'It seems to me it's rich enough in mysteries, with a phantom murderer who strikes three times. It's curious, though.'

'What's curious?'

'Since I've been in the police, the terrible image of my mother hasn't come to haunt me. And, heaven knows, there's been opportunity enough, particularly in certain areas of London where murder is considered as an everyday event. So, I thought I was definitely cured, until the day I—.'

'Came back to Blackfield,' finished Cora.

'Yes. I hadn't even got as far as the village. Then, when I cut my thumb on the rustic bridge: do you remember?'

'I'll say. You should have seen yourself. You looked like a—.'

'Bluebeard, I know. You already told me. Talking of beards, I'm going to shave mine off at the earliest opportunity.'

Cora didn't react, but looked thoughtfully at the lamp.

'Are you thinking of the murderer, Cora?'

'Yes. It's terrible. I still don't believe it.'

'Ah, little girl,' I sighed, 'if only you'd talked to me earlier about the liberties the Master of Burton Lodge felt free to take with his female parishioners. And when I say liberties....'

'How droll,' she snapped. 'How was I to know that had anything to do with the murder? Everyone, including you and the major, thought it was all about the inheritance. And it's not the sort of thing that gets talked about. Because I, too—.'

'Enough!' I shouted. 'Please let's not go over that again. By the way, I owe a debt of thanks to Angela Wright, for it was she who set me on the right track.'

'And, in any case, I wasn't the only one to know; starting with the Morstan family.'

'I'll have a clearer picture tomorrow, after I've talked to Dr. Griffin. He's going to have to spill the beans, because as of tonight I'm here in an official capacity.'

'Officially?' repeated Cora with a strange smile. 'I asked you for twenty-four hours grace for the killer and you agreed. And now you're acting officially?'

'I hope that the individual we think is the one has already chosen the only route possible. I've no desire to put him in handcuffs.

'If I hadn't intervened with my investigation, Miss Celia Forsythe and Miss Patricia Morrison would still be alive. I'm fully aware of that. It's awful, Cora, I bear a heavy burden of responsibility. My excess of zeal turned out to be disastrous.'

Cora closed her eyes and put her head in the hollow of my shoulder. The scent of new-mown hay intoxicated me. I said to her, gently:

'It's one o'clock in the morning. You need to sleep, my darling. You're dead tired.'

15

The following day, in the early afternoon, I left Dr. Griffin's house fuming with rage.

The odious individual. And to think no one dared lift a finger against him. If only I had known at the time, I would have beaten him to a pulp. His end was too good for him.

My discussion with Dr. Griffin had been very informative: there was no longer any shadow of a doubt. Each piece of the puzzle was now in place. As for the Morstan clan, only one merited consideration: Michael.

I returned to the inn and locked myself in my room. I tried in vain to cool my fevered brain. If the innkeeper hadn't been there, I might just have packed my bags on impulse. But I knew I had to stay to keep my word: I was going to have to explain the whole sordid business from beginning to end, down to the last detail.

If the murder of Richard Morstan hadn't been of such a mysterious nature, with its invisible killer, I would never have given it even so much as a passing look. But it was an "impossible crime."

Impossible: the word that always resonated in my mind as a challenge. Meet the challenge, solve the mystery, whatever it might be, had become an obsession with me. The dogged search for the truth had always gained me high marks from my superiors, but I strongly doubted I would be congratulated in the present case.

On the stroke of five, Cora and I arrived at Burton Lodge. An oppressive atmosphere—which was not entirely due to the hot June day—greeted us in the lounge, and it was in a hostile silence that Hopkins served us refreshments. After lighting the cigar the major had just offered him, Superintendent Melvin opened the proceedings:

'As you can see, John, everyone is present: Mr. and Mrs. Strange, Miss Burroughs, Major Morstan. Except—.'

'Except Nellie!' thundered the major. 'Nobody has seen her since last night, and she's not in the habit of disappearing without warning. We fear the worst.'

'I warned you last night, Inspector Reed,' said the superintendent, whose calm voice held a note of menace. 'If another murder occurred....'

'It's not a case of murder.'

'To be that sure of yourself,' smiled Luke perfidiously, 'you must know where she is.'

After a moment's reflection, I asked my chief:

'Have you searched the house?'

'She's not here,' he replied. 'This morning Hopkins noticed that the door next to the kitchen was not locked. What should we conclude from that, inspector?'

'Nellie left last night and I don't think she's far away. She's either in the forest or the river.'

The major's eyebrows shot up in surprise:

'In the river? Do you mean she's dead?'

Even the imperturbable Eleanor Burroughs appeared startled.

'More than likely,' I agreed, staring at the bottom of my glass. 'She chose the only avenue open to her.'

'So, a suicide?' asked the superintendent, still calm.

'Yes. The murderer and Nellie are one and the same.'

Silent consternation greeted the announcement, followed by expressions of incredulity and indignation.

'Nellie?' protested Rose. 'But she couldn't have killed my father. That's impossible. And what reason would she have had?' Her voice trailed off.

'I don't know whether you realise it, John,' replied the major in a caustic voice, 'but you've discredited the testimony of a dozen witnesses.'

'No!' I retorted, snapping my fingers. 'The witnesses reported what they saw. 'But I think we should start with the real criminal.' I rose from my chair to point to the portrait of the deceased master of Burton Lodge. 'Richard Morstan.'

The major gripped the sides of his armchair.

'The good, the venerable, the generous Mr. Morstan,' I persisted, stressing each syllable, 'was the worst kind of sexual fanatic. I've just seen Dr. Griffin. At the time, he was treating three adolescents who had been raped. The good Mr. Morstan who organised walks in the woods and helped young girls with their homework—I leave the scenes to your imagination.

120

'The good Mr. Morstan who showed such great generosity towards the poorest families, among whom—by the most amazing coincidence—there was always a young girl of twelve or thirteen years old. It's easy to buy the silence of the poor, especially when you're Richard Morstan.

'Children of twelve. Some kept quiet, out of shame. Some were treated as crazy by their parents. Those who threatened to go to the police found themselves generously compensated. But I'm not telling you anything new. You were all in the know, except possibly you, Luke.'

Luke, distraught, stood up and looked around, then lowered his head. The looks on the faces of his wife and uncle said it all. Eleanor remained an impassive statue.

Superintendent Melvin signalled to me to continue.

'A few months before his death, Mr. Morstan took a young and pretty orphan into his service: Nellie Smith.'

I turned to Cora, who cleared her throat and explained:

'Nellie confided in me several times. At first, she said that Mr. Morstan was a little forward, but later she complained he was perverted and a lecher. She was on the point of handing in her notice.'

After a pause, I looked questioningly at Rose. She burst into tears.

'Nellie spoke to me, too,' she sobbed. 'Papa was a sick man, yes, sick.'

'As for the motive for the murder,' I declared, 'I don't think there's much more to be said. Resigned to being a victim, she endured the assaults of the monster—or sick man, if you prefer—until the day when the opportunity to escape from his claws presented itself. The murder, which I would characterise as legitimate defence, was not premeditated. A combination of circumstances gave her the possibility of ridding herself of her despicable master and passing the crime off as an accident. I would add that she demonstrated an extraordinary *sang froid* as well, but we'll return to that later.

'Now let's take the case of Michael. I'm doing this especially for you, Luke, as I believe the rest of the household understands his feelings and what motivates his strange behaviour.

'He's not proud of his father's activities. Their frequent quarrels were about the latter's "sickness." And I imagine the passivity of the rest of the family only served to stoke his anger and disgust.

'He was probably relieved to learn of his father's impending

121

marriage, which meant he would no longer be assaulting the girls of the village, for Angela possessed all the attributes necessary to calm the ardour of her future husband. Furthermore, he must have realised his future stepmother was pregnant. So, as far as he was concerned, his father was ready to get back on the straight and narrow.

'And then comes the murder. Michael, believing he was responsible for the death of his father, hides in the forest. Which proves his feelings towards his father were not entirely hostile. They find him two days later and explain that he wasn't responsible, after all. Whereupon his uncle, regardless of the rights of the unborn child, takes it upon himself to exile Angela Wright. It's all too much: his father who's a sex maniac, his uncle who'll do anything to safeguard the family name and his sister who'll remain utterly passive whatever happens. He makes his mind up: he's never going to see them again, and to hell with his father's fortune.

'But he was only fifteen at the time. When he reached adulthood and it came time for him to inherit, he must have told himself to put aside the disgust and disdain he had for the other family members, for the day might come when he needed the money. And so he took the necessary steps.

'The fact that he regularly sends news of himself, although without specifics, leads me to believe that at the proper moment he'll turn up to claim his share. But that's just my opinion; you're better placed than I to appreciate the situation.'

There was a terrible silence. Rose and the major were distraught and Luke seemed to be thinking of everything except the inheritance. Silent and motionless, the governess sat with her head down. It was not difficult to guess what she was thinking: "If Richard had only married me, none of this would have happened."

The major, furiously rubbing his lorgnette, muttered:

'You're clever, John, very clever.' His forehead was covered in perspiration. 'It never occurred to me for one moment that the motive for the crime could be of that nature, otherwise, obviously, I would have told you about my brother's sickness. Every man has his strengths and his weaknesses, you know.' He recalled his old quarrels with his brother and the warm welcome he had received on his return from India. 'Very few men would have reacted the way Richard did; I haven't forgotten that and I never shall,' he concluded looking emotionally at the portrait of the deceased.

After a moment's silence, he added:

'Despite his conduct, I tried my best not to allow his memory to be tarnished. I owed him at least that.'

The superintendent let some time go by before speaking:

'This afternoon, the major explained the circumstances of the crime to me in great detail. If you can show convincingly how Nellie carried out her crime, I'll take my hat off to you, John.'

A glimmer of interest lit up the eyes of those present.

'Let me first say, major, that the trip to Eastbourne and then Lewes, was not futile, far from it. I learnt from Angela how your brother consoled young girls. To which were added—much later—Cora's confidences on the same subject.'

Cora blushed.

'Nellie wasn't Mr. Morstan's only victim,' she said, looking around in confusion. 'He also—.'

'Enough,' thundered the major, bringing his fist crashing down on the armrest. In a gentler voice he added: 'Let's not talk about it any more, I beg of you. We know the motive now, so let's not dwell on the subject.'

'This,' I continued, 'forced me to look at the case from an altogether different angle. Let's now look at the murder of the schoolmistress. The killer rushed to silence her because she remembered a detail. But what was it? She had practically not left her chair. What could she have seen?

'There's only one possible answer: she'd noticed something bizarre in the room. Nothing immediately striking, but something apparently insignificant which in retrospect pointed the finger at the killer. In fact, it's not that she saw something she shouldn't have; it's that she *didn't see* something she should have.

'Miss Morrison's murder told us that the killer wanted the book on magic tricks at any price. We can deduce that identifying the trick which was being rehearsed would be the same as identifying the killer.

'There again, why? Think about it: we know that Mr. Morstan had made changes to the room—.'

'I understand,' said Superintendent Melvin, who had put the tips of his fingers together in meditation. 'The trick depended entirely on the disposition of the furniture.'

'Exactly. And Mr. Morstan had already done some of it before he

123

was killed.' I addressed myself to the major. 'Can you give me back the sketch of the murder room?'

While he was looking for it, I continued:

'Only one person could have killed Patricia Morrison: Nellie. And straight away, all the mystery surrounding the murder vanishes. While I was watching the rear and the right side of the house. Nellie simply walked through the front door, which Patricia had forgotten to lock. After killing her friend and recovering the book, she performed some acrobatics which not only gave strength to the idea of a shadow vanishing by magic, but, above all, removed her from all suspicion: profiting from a lapse on my part, she clambered over Patricia's window sill and dropped gently down to the ground; she then ran back round the house to her original observation post. If I'd reacted a second earlier, I'd probably have seen her disappearing behind the tree.

'As you can see, the explanation is ridiculously simple. I ask myself why I didn't spot it right away. But, at that moment, Nellie wasn't a suspect, and I still had Baxter's description of the shadow vanishing in mind. Speaking of which, I believe Baxter reported what he had seen accurately enough, but his faculties had been impaired by alcohol. Nellie had, in all probability, hidden behind a barrel at the opening of the alley and had disappeared once Baxter had walked far enough down.'

The major nodded in agreement, then placed his sketch on the table.

'As for the savagery of Miss Forsythe's murder,' I continued, 'it's not impossible to imagine Nellie, terrified at the thought of being accused, transferring all her hatred of Mr. Morstan on to poor Miss Forsythe, which would explain the fury of the attack.'

'All very well, so far,' said the major. 'It's all perfectly clear. Now we come to Richard's murder.'

I thought for a moment, and then asked:

'What did Mr. Morstan do before he closed the curtains separating the two parts of the room?'

'He said we'd soon see a phantom appear,' replied Rose quickly.

'Yes, but before that?'

'He'd drawn the curtains back, and shown the screen and opened the wardrobe.'

'In other words, he wanted to show there was nobody else in that part of the room.'

'And there wasn't,' said Rose categorically. 'I'm prepared to swear to it.'

'Don't do it,' I said with a smile. 'Because Nellie was there.'

'That's not possible. I repeat, there was nobody in that part of the room.'

'Here's a question which should make it clear to you: what did your father do to move the screen?'

'He walked behind it, lifted it up and—.'

'Even though nobody described it precisely on Tuesday evening, that's what I assumed: he passed behind the screen. That's where Nellie was hidden. So, he passes behind. Nellie grabs hold of his shoulders and hoists herself off the ground on to his back, which allows your father to lift the screen up without anyone suspecting she's there. Don't forget his choice of costume which, with the tight-fitting leg armour, seemed to show there was no one behind him. The illusion is perfect, no one suspects the presence of an accomplice hanging on Mr. Morstan's wide back. When he puts the screen back down on the floor, she can drop down again.'

The major stubbed out his cigar, muttering to himself.

'Naturally,' I continued, 'the execution of the trick requires great precision of movement to obtain a perfect illusion. Mr. Morstan didn't hesitate to send everyone out of the house the week before, in order to do a full rehearsal with Nellie. I can't tell you exactly what trick they planned to perform, but I don't think it's important.'

'Now we can follow the events in the chronological order in which they occurred. Mr. Morstan decides to perform a magical illusion with Nellie's help. He nails the second door shut during the course of the morning and it's certainly he who asks the boys to practice archery not very far from the window. All of that, naturally, to create a "sealed" room. Around quarter to three, the ten young girls—including Nellie, of course—enter the room. Intrigued, they search everywhere and establish there's nobody there apart from them. Ten minutes later, Richard comes in. He leads them into the other part of the room, places the small suitcase on the coffee table and shows them the door nailed shut with planks. At which point, the schoolmistress knocks on the door. That was also part of the plan: remember Miss Forsythe told us she went upstairs at Richard Morstan's request. "That's the ghost!" he exclaims, inviting the girls to go back with him, through the separating curtain, to the door where someone has just knocked.

'Everyone follows him, except Nellie. And that's the moment, I think, when the arrow falls on to the carpet. It's also the moment when a terrible thought occurs to Nellie: kill the man who has dishonoured her and make it look like an accident. She knows perfectly well what's supposed to happen next, and she knows there's a dagger in the suitcase which Mr. Morstan had borrowed from his brother for the trick—a dagger with a thin, sharp blade, a perfect weapon. And now the arrow shot accidentally by one of the boys.

'While this is happening, on the other side of the curtain, Mr. Morstan plunges the "public" part of the room into darkness by drawing closed the curtain of the window between the desk and the bookshelves. In the darkness and the growing excitement he places the young spectators in the spots previously chosen by him.

'Now look at the major's sketch, and more specifically the armchair near the window where Nellie is supposed to be sitting. Remember, the schoolmistress and the girls had their eyes glued to the separating curtain and would never have had the idea to turn round to see if Nellie was really in the armchair.

'Mr. Morstan draws open the separating curtain, passes behind the screen, executes his magical illusion with Nellie, whatever it is, and opens the wardrobe doors wide. Everything goes according to plan, the spectators fall for it; they're dazzled by the illusion and nobody notices the absence of Nellie.

'For Nellie, everything goes as planned as well. The other part of the room is plunged into darkness again when the separating curtain closes. Everyone has had their eyes glued to the scene and nobody has thought to check whether Nellie's armchair is occupied or not. Her plan is to stab Mr. Morstan, thrust the arrow into the wound, throw away the knife—whether she wiped it and hid it on her person or threw it out of the window in the direction of the forest, we don't know—place herself behind the curtain to the right of the screen, wait for her friends to arrive, and take advantage of their shock at the sight of the body to mingle discreetly with them.

'The plan isn't as risky as it looks at first sight. In fact, it's more than likely that the girls will rush in through the gap in the middle of the curtain, with their attention fixed on Richard Morstan who's lying near the wardrobe with an arrow in his back. Nellie only has to slip behind them, and it's done. You only have to look at the major's sketch to convince yourselves.'

126

'Incredible,' muttered the major. 'Incredible. A young fourteen year old girl pulling off a trick like that in under two minutes. Of course, the examiner would have spotted the trick of the arrow in the dagger wound.'

'Not necessarily,' commented Superintendent Melvin, still amazed by what he'd heard. 'Given the circumstances, why would he conclude it was anything other than an accident? Nobody could have got close to the victim, a boy shoots an arrow into the room, the body is discovered with an arrow in the back...No, frankly, I don't think he would have looked any further than accidental death.'

'That was Nellie's plan, at least,' I declared. 'Before Mr. Morstan comes back from the other part of the room, she places the arrow on the outside sill of the open window, in an attempt to hide it. A useless precaution which invalidates the assumption of an accident. As soon as she finds herself alone with him, she waits for him to bend over the little suitcase before stabbing him. Then she reaches for the arrow; a clumsy move of the hand and—Horrors!—the arrow falls down to the ground below. But she doesn't panic, she gets rid of the dagger and continues to follow her plan. Richard Morstan's death will now have "impossible" overtones, but no matter. What's important is she not be caught. There, I think that just about covers everything.'

The major looked me up and down and said:

'What a remarkable tiger hunter you would have made, John!'

Coming from the major, I assumed it must be a great compliment.

'As I told you major, he's one of our best detectives, if not the best.'

'Thank you, chief,' I replied, with a suitably modest gesture. I turned to the governess with a smile:

'I assume, Miss Burroughs, that the shadow you saw vanishing up the spiral staircase was merely the fruit of your imagination?'

Something very unusual happened: Eleanor Burroughs actually smiled.

'Now I think about it, the answer is probably yes,' she said, without bitterness. After a short pause, she added:

'And according to you, what is it that Miss Forsythe remembered?'

'She didn't leave her chair until you arrived, Miss Burroughs, so she couldn't have seen Nellie slip behind the other girls after the body was discovered because her view was blocked by the curtain, which was only partially open. I don't think she noticed Nellie's absence from the armchair, or she would have mentioned it during the investigation.

'On Tuesday evening, during our reconstruction, she must have learnt something she had not known previously. If I remember rightly, she had talked about Mr. Morstan assigning the girls their seats. That's when Nellie announced that she'd been in the armchair by the window. Naturally, Mr. Morstan had arranged things so that nobody could have noticed Nellie's absence at that moment. But afterwards? When the girls went to join Rose, who had just found her father's body?

'Miss Forsythe had just learnt that Nellie had been in the armchair. She tried to recall the scene from her phenomenal memory: she tried to visualise Nellie getting up from the armchair…and she couldn't! Nellie hadn't been in it. She tried to find a logical explanation and failed. At least for the time being.

'Memory is a funny thing. Miss Forsythe knew the armchair was supposedly occupied by one of the girls and had registered the fact that nobody got up out of it, but had failed to make the connection. Until she learnt that Nellie was supposedly the occupant, and the penny dropped.

'That's my own personal theory, anyway. There could very well be others.'

'Don't be modest, John,' said the major with a broad smile. 'It's more than likely your hypothesis is the correct one.'

He fumbled for his stick, rose from his chair with an effort, and topped up our drinks. When he'd finished, he turned to the portrait of his brother and raised his glass:

'Let's make a toast in memory of—.'

He choked on the last word, looked at his glass with a strange smile, then looked up at the painting again. Suddenly, to our astonishment, he flung the contents of the glass at his brother's face.

'Now we're even, you old goat,' he exclaimed jubilantly.

Then something even stranger happened. Eleanor got up from her seat, walked in a dignified manner to the portrait, stood elegantly on the tips of her toes, and spat in Richard Morstan's face.

'Very good, Eleanor,' the major marvelled. 'Call Peter and ask him to build a fire in the chimney to burn this horror.'

16

Nellie's body was found the next day in the river, at the edge of the woods. She had tied a heavy stone to her legs with the aid of a thick rope. It was a favourite spot for the village fishermen; thus it was that Fred Turner first saw her red hair floating on the surface in the early morning light.

Personally, I would have chosen a more private place to kill myself. But it's difficult to put oneself in the place of someone who has abandoned all reason.

Before returning to the capital, Superintendent Melvin came in the late morning to visit me.

'You unravelled this extraordinarily complicated business in record time, John. It's quite remarkable.'

'I'm not sure remarkable is the right word, sir. The mystery of Burton Lodge was certainly unravelled, but at what price? Miss Forsythe, Patricia Morrison and Nellie, whom I consider to be a victim. What had she had to suffer from her master before she did what she did? I don't like to think about it.'

'At the time, three adolescents went to see Dr. Griffin to get treatment, which suggests to me there may well have been other victims. The reactions of young girls who have been raped aren't always the same. There are those who put up a struggle, those who are paralysed by terror and shame—.'

'And those who become mad,' I said, finishing his sentence.

'In a nutshell, I think you were right to give Nellie the time to…leave. She might have got extenuating circumstances for Morstan's death, but probably not for the two others.'

There was a silence.

A worried frown appeared on his brow as he went on:

'Even though everything appears to have been explained in detail, there's one thing I find strange, that I can't quite put my finger on.'

'The skeleton in Miss Forsythe's garden?'

'No, that has nothing to do with the case. It's certainly not the only body lying in someone's back garden.'

'What, then?'

'I don't know. A simple impression, that's all. Well, I'm going to leave, the horses are getting restless. Enjoy the rest of your holiday and come back fully refreshed and raring to go.' He winked. 'I'm going to set aside a special case for you, the kind you love, full of mysterious happenings.'

If I'd known what the case was that he was saving for me, I would certainly not have had a smile on my face as he spoke.

Very late in the evening, I was seated at the table in my room, copying out the crime scene sketch which the major had lent me. Cora was sitting near me, by the door, in silence. She hadn't spoken for quite some time. She was pale from fatigue and depression. I suggested she return to her room, but she would have none of it: "I want to be with you, John. I want to help you." But she didn't seem to be at all interested in what I was doing, as she sat there with a doleful expression, staring at a fixed spot on the ceiling.

Irritated by her strange behaviour, I teased her:

'Do you remember what I said this afternoon about the schoolmistress? She didn't see Nellie get up from the armchair.

'Look at the sketch now. My explanation would have been a lot more convincing if Nellie had been sitting in the other armchair, near the door, where *you* were actually sitting.'

Cora stared at the plan. Not a muscle in her face moved.

'Do you see?' I continued, 'that armchair is less than three feet in front of the chair where Miss Forsythe was sitting.'

Cora got up slowly.

'I'll be back in a moment.'

She left, closing the door quietly behind her.

I shrugged my shoulders and went over to the window. It was a dark night, but occasionally the moon came out from behind the clouds, illuminating roofs and trees alike.

I've always been fascinated by the silver disc of the moon, the symbol of the night and of mystery. By who knows what association of ideas I could see the sordid, feebly lit alleys and passages of Whitechapel, where shadowy figures flitted in the darkness. To think that, in two weeks, I would once again be hunting down criminals in that sinister quarter. Then my thoughts drifted to Major Daniel Morstan. That devil of a man was rarely mistaken in his instincts.

Except for Tuesday last, when he thought someone might be spying on us through the lounge window. But, after all, maybe he hadn't been mistaken: Peter or Jennifer Hopkins—motivated by a justifiable curiosity—may well have been outside, by the window, trying to follow our reconstitution of the crime. It's not always behind doors that one overhears conversations!

I heard the door open and close.

'Is that you, darling?'

She didn't reply.

I turned round and saw her sitting in the same place as before, sombre and silent.

I suppressed a deep sigh and returned to my cogitations. The major…Where he was not wrong was when we were on the doorstep of Burton Lodge, that same Tuesday night. Cora and I were on the point of leaving. I could hear his words: "I sense approaching danger, just as in a tiger hunt. The wild animal believes itself menaced as well; its green eyes glow in the shadows; it remains motionless; it gathers itself and pounces suddenly on its prey." And a few hours later, the tiger had torn the schoolmistress apart. The major had not been mistaken.

He also shared his hunches with me the day I arrived in Blackfield, on Monday afternoon, at the inn: "…the killer is still in the village. I can feel his presence, as if he were right next to me." There, we have to look at the evidence. He was wrong: Nellie wasn't at the inn at that moment; only he and I were there, and Cora, who was serving two customers who had just come in.

Strange, all the same, because I'd had the same feeling.

Suddenly, my ears started to ring and my vision became cloudy; the image of my mother came once more to the surface.

But this time I wasn't going to lose myself in that terrible reminiscence, I knew how to exorcise it; all I needed to do was to look at Cora.

Which is what I did. She was still seated on the little cane chair, stock still. The lamp which illuminated the table caused her to appear as a dark silhouette with a halo.

'Cora?'

Silence.

'You're very tired, darling. You should go to bed,' I suggested.

Irritated by her silence, I turned back to the window. This time, it

131

was the superintendent's words which came back to me: "Even though everything appears to have been explained in detail, there's one thing I find strange, that I can't quite put my finger on."

"It's very humid tonight," I thought to myself, as I wiped the perspiration from my brow with the back of my hand. "What's happening to you, John? You seem lost...." I realized that my brain was on fire, carrying an important message, an urgent message which I obstinately refused to hear.

I became conscious of an extraordinary tension in the room, a tension which was increasing, coming closer, like the presence I sensed behind me. I turned round suddenly.

HORRORS! The tigress was there!

Paralysed, I watched Cora, who was coming stealthily towards me, brandishing a kitchen knife. Her eyes, shining with madness, seemed to have turned green.

Even though thunderstruck by the hideous truth, I managed to stay calm. Knife raised, she threw herself at me with the agility and ferocity of a wild beast, while I side-stepped with equal rapidity. Unable to stop her forceful lunge, she hit the sill and toppled forward through the window.

The echo of her fall resonated in my head. My heart beat fast enough to break as I looked out of the window: she was lying inert on the cobble-stones. I climbed over the sill, caught hold of the inn sign, and was by her side in moments.

Her eyes were open wide, staring at the sky.

'Cora, can you hear me?'

Her eyelids flickered feebly.

'Cora, darling, don't move, don't do anything. I'm going to fetch the doctor. Cora, I...Cora, everything's my fault...No one shall know, no one...We'll get married as soon as possible...Cora, I love you...Don't leave me, I beg of you....'

She was transported the next day to London, without any great hope of being saved.

I spent the rest of my holiday shut up in my London flat, prostrate with grief and in a permanent state of intoxication.

I had analysed the Morstan affair brilliantly, but had found the wrong murderer: it was Cora, not Nellie.

She had told me about Richard Morstan's indecent advances, but had not told me the whole truth. With an effort, I pushed the thoughts out of my head.

The monster. I would have given my life to have had him in front of me, even for a few seconds, the abject, despicable individual.

Cora, whose madness I had unconsciously detected the moment I had confided my intention to investigate her own crime.

Cora, an unfortunate adolescent whom a sexual maniac had pushed to murder. Then nine years later, a sinister imbecile arrives who speaks to her of slit throats and phantom murderers—I honestly think that's why Cora added mysterious and horrible elements to her later murders—and who leads an investigation whose rapid progress forces her to commit two more crimes. Three, counting Nellie.

As soon as Cora realised that I was getting near the truth, except that I suspected Nellie, she saw a way to end the affair. First she suggested I delay the arrest of Nellie, then she arranged for her "suicide" in a relatively well-frequented location, so that the body would be rapidly discovered. How did she manage to get into Burton Lodge at night, and how did she lure Nellie outside? I don't think it was very difficult, given the virtuosity she had shown in the previous two murders.

When Nellie and I went to watch the Morrison house, Cora was on our heels. When Patricia arrived, I went to join Nellie at the front of the house. That's almost certainly when Cora climbed the rear wall to get in through the window. But what about afterwards? How did she vanish into the night when I was on her heels and Nellie didn't see her appear at the corner of the house? Also, I have reason to think that Baxter's testimony was not that of a drunk: how did she manage to vanish in that dead-end alley?

It was not until a few months later that, purely by chance in the dark passages and alleyways of Whitechapel, I stumbled upon the diabolical—but oh! so simple—trick Cora used with such success. I shall return to that at the end of my story.

If I hadn't been so blinded by passion, her guilt would have been apparent to me much earlier. She was one of the few people who could escape easily into the night—her room was situated on the ground floor of the inn. What's more, she was able to follow the course of the investigation very closely, thanks to your humble servant. Thinking about it in hindsight, it was always just after leaving me that she went on her bloody nocturnal expeditions, which also explained her obvious lack of sleep. Finally, her eyes betrayed her several times, notably when she realised that I had come to Blackfield to investigate the death of Richard Morstan—her own crime. A savage, icy light lurked behind the apparent softness of her regard; she recalled the scene of the murder and sensed the danger I represented to her. But there was something else, something even worse, which I only came to understand much later.

I haven't got the heart to point out all the ruses and theatrics to which I fell victim. Despite that, I still believe she has—or, at least, had at certain moments—deep feelings for me. As for me, I love her as I have never loved any other woman. And I will always love her.

I was the instrument of her fall, the one who tipped her reason— already unbalanced in her adolescence by a monster—into a murderous madness. I owe her help and protection, whatever happens.

For several days now, I've done something I've never done before: I pray. I pray God she will live, even if she must remain disabled.

Tomorrow, I shall return to work: to my colleagues, to Superintendent Melvin and to the London underworld. I'm getting better: whisky nauseates me. Even though Cora occupies most of my thoughts, the mists are fading and I am starting to think rationally again. A new obsession is starting to haunt me: what is the trick which Cora uses to disappear into the night?

17

June 1887

A fortnight after her fall, I was allowed to see Cora in hospital.

'A cerebral concussion which will take a long time to cure,' said the doctor. 'She should try not to exert herself, she needs peace and quiet.'

As soon as I saw her, I was struck by her strange fixed stare and the lack of any expression on her pale face. Nevertheless, I wasn't discouraged and, having stressed my total responsibility for the recent events, I asked her for her hand. She replied that she didn't know where she stood and needed time to think. She was first going to return to Blackfield. She further asked me not to try to see her for some time, which we agreed would be six months. I accepted on condition I be allowed to see her the day she left hospital, before her return to Blackfield. Although her response was in the affirmative, I detected no enthusiasm on her part. At that point, the doctor interrupted and asked me not to prolong my stay. I enquired regularly after her and was overjoyed when, two weeks later, I learned that she was to leave the forthcoming Monday. On the appointed day, in the late morning, I presented myself at the hospital.

'She took a cab to Waterloo station at about ten o'clock,' the doctor told me with a worried look. After an embarrassed silence, he added:

'I reminded her you were coming to see her, but she took no notice of my remark—she seemed in a great hurry.'

I turned on my heels and walked away with a heavy heart. I had planned to take her to Regent's Park, a stone's throw away, one of my favourite spots, where we could have strolled agreeably in each other's company for a few hours.

Alas!

If there had been nobody around, I think I might have cried, such was my disappointment. I wallowed in mental agony, and was only brought out of it when I found myself face to face with a Bengal tiger.

An icy stare gleamed in those green eyes. An inevitable and terrible recollection surfaced as I plunged forward. But nothing in the zoo, not the mischievousness of the monkeys, nor the chattering of the parakeets, nor the elephant rides for children, not even the great favourite of Regent's Park, the hippopotamus, could chase Cora from my mind.

Indifferent to the crowd, the botanical garden, the Boating Lake and the marvellous flower beds, I wandered a while longer before finding a cab to take me home.

I had furnished lodgings at 12, Shoe Lane, near the Temple. The flat, consisting of two comfortable rooms, was on the second floor. A back staircase leading up from the interior courtyard allowed me to enter discreetly when an investigation kept me up into the small hours and even to the crack of dawn.

I paid the driver, climbed slowly up the stairs, and entered my bachelor quarters, where I served myself two stiff whiskies back to back, after which I lit a cigar and threw myself on to the sofa to try to pull my thoughts together.

It was standard procedure for me during particularly tricky cases: the sofa, a cigar, a whisky and a cracking fire, and the solution appeared as if by magic. But in the present case, I had little hope of resolving a sentimental matter when one of the protagonists had clearly conveyed her deepest thoughts to the other. I had to keep in mind, however, that Cora suffered from a cerebral concussion for which time was the best remedy.

The shrill ring of the doorbell interrupted my thoughts. It was a police officer who had brought me a message from Superintendent Melvin demanding my presence immediately at the hospital where Cora had been treated.

Half an hour later, I found myself in the basement of the hospital in front of the corpse of a nurse lying in a corner, her throat slashed and her body hideously mutilated. According to the medical examiner, death occurred in the last twenty-four hours, which placed the crime between ten o'clock at night—when Sally Humphrey was last seen alive—and six o'clock in the morning at the latest. I didn't attend the inquest: it was sufficient to know that Sally had been one of the nurses looking after Cora.

What was the likelihood of Cora's innocence? One chance in a hundred, at most. A woman subject to fits of insanity, with four murders to her credit—of which two similar to this last one—who leaves the hospital in a great hurry a few hours after the murder of a young nurse without an enemy in the world; I couldn't ignore the evidence: Cora was in the grip of a madness which only my presence seemed to assuage.

In one sense, this new murder was a relief. Her sudden departure was not because she hadn't wanted to see me. At this point, more than any other I realised just how much I loved her.

I found myself in a unique situation: obliged to cover up a murder Superintendent Melvin had asked me to solve. If I did my best, and my efforts were successful, nobody would make the connection between Cora and the bloody murderer.

I owed her care and protection, whatever happened.

PART TWO

18

December 1887

As agreed, I allowed her the several months of reflection she had requested, and set my return to Blackfield for just before Christmas. If my nights and my dreams were devoted to Cora, the same was not true for my days, involved as I was with murder, prostitution, burglary, blackmail and drug trafficking. There was also the civil unrest which had begun the year before.

In an attempt to restore order, General Sir Charles Warren had been recalled from Egypt to become Commissioner of Police of the Metropolis. It was not an easy time: the man had shown a profound disdain for the Criminal Investigation Department, and had reorganised Scotland Yard along the lines of military bases. For the last few months, he had dispatched the police against the unemployed who marched every Sunday brandishing placards carrying Evangelical texts. The most bloody confrontation took place on the thirteenth of November, 1887, in Trafalgar Square, when police and grenadiers were mobilised to restrain the twenty thousand unemployed streaming through all the streets of the capital. Two hundred protesters were seriously injured and two died. The understandable hate the London working class felt towards Sir Charles after "Bloody Sunday" had repercussions for the working policemen who, in the vast majority, did not approve of their chief's conduct. The authoritarian and rigid regime which Warren tried to install had only succeeded in demoralising and exhausting them.

But my own morale was not so low, for I would soon be seeing the one I loved—who must be almost cured, because no murders had reported around Blackfield the past few months.

Two days before Christmas, my heart full of hope, I was back again in the village of my birth. Imagine my disillusionment when Tony informed me his daughter had left the day before to go back to London.

His coat collar turned up and his hat pulled down to his eyes, Detective Sergeant Walter MacNiel could not suppress a shiver of revulsion.

'Horrible! And at Christmas, too.'

'Looks as though the killer wanted to end 1887 with a bang!' observed the constable, who was holding up a dark lantern to illuminate the body.

We were in one of those dark passages off Commercial Road. At our feet lay the body of a woman, horribly mutilated, whom the press would later name "Fairy Fay," although her true identity was never discovered.

'I wonder what kind of a madman could do a thing like that,' said MacNiel, shaking his head sadly.

I didn't reply, forcing myself to remain impassive.

'You're looking very thoughtful, chief. Do you have any idea of the killer's identity?'

I shook my head in silence, secretly convinced that Cora had struck again. I still had a clear picture of the nurse's corpse in mind, and it would be hard to tell the two bodies apart. And the fact it had occurred within a day of Cora's arrival in London was too much of a coincidence.

Once again, I was going to have to muddy the waters of an investigation of which I had been put in charge.

Huddled in the back of the cab taking me home that wintry night of Christmas 1887, I repeated ceaselessly to myself: "I owe her help and protection, whatever happens."

'Nobody knows who she is or where she comes from. She spent the night drinking in a pub in Mitre Square, which closed at midnight. She decided to take a short cut home. That's all we've been able to learn.'

I was seated opposite Superintendent Melvin in his office, explaining my conclusions about the murder of "Fairy Fay." I was beginning to get the hang of things: I had managed to slow the investigation down to the point where we were unable even to identify the victim. My enthusiasm may have been somewhat exaggerated, for I had found no clue incriminating Cora, but I didn't want to run the slightest risk.

The superintendent listened with his customary politeness. Rare were those who could resist the charm of this distinguished grey-haired gentleman in his fifties. No matter whom he was talking to, he was always courteous, thoughtful and calm. His eyes were of a very pale blue, almost transparent. A bachelor, he consecrated himself to his job, which he carried out with an irreproachable conscience, which had earned him the respect of his men, his superiors and even criminals, to whom he showed a lenience which I sometimes felt was exaggerated. But it would be a mistake to think that he had attained his high position by hard work and integrity alone: he was a remarkable detective with no equal for nosing out "the small detail that doesn't quite fit." One has only to remember his remark just before leaving Blackfield, when the general feeling was that Nellie had committed suicide in remorse for her actions. He seemed to possess a sixth sense, rather like Major Daniel Morstan at the approach of danger. Which was cause for some alarm, in view of the ruses I had used to cover up Cora's recent crimes. Nevertheless, he had a weakness: I was his favourite, the idol of his eye. He allowed me free rein to conduct my investigations. All this is by way of saying how ashamed I felt to betray his confidence; but saving Cora took precedent over all other considerations. He could not have understood what it was to love a woman, he who had lived a monastic existence since I had known him. That had always appeared strange to me: he was handsome and stylish despite his fifty years and never flaunted his culture. Yet he was not known to have had any relations with the fair sex, and in that regard he remained an enigma to me.

After having looked hard at me for a long moment, he shrugged his shoulders:

'So, a complete blank. So be it. It's not the first unsolved murder of a lady of the night, nor will it be the last.' He opened a dossier, read a few lines and pulled a face. 'For women battered to death, kicked and punched, knocked out, chopped up with an axe, stabbed, or deliberately burnt alive, 1887 wasn't a good year. There were thirty-five homicides just for the Home Counties alone, and more than double that if we include infanticides. And only eight convictions, that's very few.'

I nodded solemnly.

141

'Out of those eight, five were the fruit of your work, John.'

I could see perfectly well where he was going.

'Your yield, if I may put it that way, is exceptional. I haven't forgotten, either, the sad business of the Morstan murder which you solved so brilliantly last year.' He paused, putting the tips of his fingers together with an air of concern. 'Since then, you seem....not to have relaxed, exactly, but to be treading water. Please understand, John, it's not a reproach. You're still our best detective and you know it very well.' He smiled, and his voice changed. 'In short, I'm not accustomed to have you hand in a negative report.'

I took a cigar from the box he proffered me. Between puffs, I worked on an urgent strategy. I had to find Cora as quickly as possible. If the series of murders continued, the chief would find out I was trying to protect someone. But how to do it? Finding Cora in a city like London without help from anyone was like—.

The superintendent didn't give me time to finish my thought:

'By the way, John, have you kept in touch with the innkeeper's daughter—what was her name?—the one who had the accident? You were quite fond of her, I seem to recall.'

For a moment I sensed an intense pounding of blood in my temple. I had to call on all my facial muscles to compose a semblance of a smile.

'Once or twice,' I said, evasively. 'She was more frightened than hurt; she's been completely cured as of now. A nice girl, but rather provincial, if you get my drift. It's been a while since I saw her. She's still living in Blackfield, of course.' (Why "of course"? That was ridiculous.)

The super frowned, then absorbed the news in a meditative silence.

'And whatever happened to your novel?' he asked in a voice tinged with irony.

'Not much. All I have is my notes, for now.'

Had he asked me about Cora by chance, or did he suspect something?

I passed the rest of the day—and the week—agonising over that question.

The wind was glacial, although the sky was clear. Under the timid winter sunshine, I wandered the large thoroughfares of the West End, where cabs, omnibuses and cabriolets jostled for customers. It was how I spent most of my days off, tirelessly on the lookout for Cora's silhouette among the well-to-do crowds clustered in front of the sumptuous Regent Street shop windows.

I confined my field of research considerably. It was very unlikely that she passed her weekends in centres of commerce or industry such as the City and the banks of the Thames. And it was equally improbable she would wander the streets of St. Giles, Clerkenwell, Bethnal Green, Whitechapel and other squalid areas: the sad experience she had recounted to me would surely have turned her forever from such sinister places. On the other hand, the parks offered possibilities. But after several days spent in Green Park, St. James' Park, Battersea Park and Regent's Park, I decided to concentrate on the busy streets of the West End.

The reader could be forgiven for thinking I was on a fool's errand—and he would be right. I even thought so myself. But I am of an obstinate nature: as long as there was a chance, no matter how slender, that I would find Cora in this immense city, I would not give up my search.

By the end of March, I had still not seen Cora, and she had not shown herself, for none of the murders committed in that period seemed to be attributable to her. I went to Blackfield twice, out of desperation. Tony and his wife appeared as anxious as I was that their daughter had given no sign of life.

Where was she? What was she doing? These questions haunted me mercilessly, even though there seemed to be a flicker of light on the horizon. A tiny light, a brief glimpse of clarity, a logical deduction which my analytic faculties wanted to transmit, but which were blocked by a mental wall I had erected a long time ago. If I had thought more about this mysterious wall beforehand, and the reason for its existence, I would have known where Cora was and maybe have saved several lives. I say "maybe", because it's by no means certain. Fate had placed its pawns on the chessboard and things had gone too far to avoid the carnage. Already a smell of blood permeated the fog and darkness of London and had reached the tiger, who, after a long hibernation was about to unleash terror in the jungle.

On Easter Monday, the thirteenth of April, Emma Smith, a prostitute, was found dying in Osborn Street in Spitalfields. Transported to London Hospital, she only survived for a few hours, but was able to say she had been attacked and robbed by three men. It was a particularly brutal murder: perforation of the stomach by a blunt instrument wielded with considerable force.

Was Cora responsible? Were the three strangers the delirious imagination of a dying woman?

After questioning the inspector sent to see the victim, I was inclined to think Cora had nothing to do with it.

19

May 1888

A voyager travelling the troubled, yellow waters of the Thames could not help but be impressed by the forest of masts, the hustle and bustle of boats of all kinds, going up river and down or simply bobbing peacefully, the length of the drab banks full of hangars, warehouses and construction sites.

The closer he got to the city the more he would be struck by the increasing darkness caused by the clouds of smoke belching forth from sombre, gigantic factories working day and night. And if by chance a ray of sunshine should pierce those clouds, it would immediately vanish in the thick, viscous fog which was the scourge of London.

Traversing the labyrinth of streets bordering the Thames, he would see prodigious, feverish human activity. In winding, narrow alleys and passages devoid of sunshine, he would see nautical tackle, pulleys, jibs, rigging and boathooks swinging the heaviest loads imaginable above the heads of the continuous flow of the crowd below. This was the centre of all commercial and industrial activity. Against a background of deafening noise, a confused mixture of horses whinnying, clogs pounding on cobblestones, squeaking chains and axles and groaning pulleys, tireless workers killed themselves while shouting and raging. Vehicles, men on horseback and pedestrians transported merchandise towards the City, crossing on the way others coming to collect, all in an indescribable scramble which necessitated frequent intervention from police charged with keeping order in the never-ending double current.

A deep, voiceless murmur arose constantly from the rough-and-tumble of all the professions and all the nationalities moving ceaselessly. Inoffensive enough by day, but at night...Imprudent indeed are those who brave the neighbourhood of the docks with its incredible boozing places crammed with sailors seeking commercial love and drinking sessions which quickly degenerate into quarrels, fights and even murders.

It was on a misty night in May that Detective Sergeant MacNiel and I, suitably attired, wended our way to this perilous area. Joe Hawkins, a dangerous criminal, had evaded two arrests supervised by Walter.

He had been seen in a dockside tavern the previous evening. For MacNiel, it was a personal matter: nobody but he was going to clap the handcuffs on this miscreant.

Walter MacNiel, a redhead with a face more pleasant than handsome, was my right hand and best friend, who was at my side during most of my investigations. His modest detection skills were more than compensated by an almost mindless courage. But, for the moment, I sensed that my friend was congratulating himself for being in my company. As we made our way through the murky night, the masts of sailing boats emerged from the Thames-side mists like so many menacing lances: a last warning before entering the forbidden zone. A growing sound of muffled voices and guffaws reached our ears. We stopped before we reached the tavern, observing cautiously the shadows behind lighted windows, whose movements betrayed an advanced state of inebriation.

Walter turned to me, looked me up and down, and observed:

'You look really ugly tonight, John. You're so repugnant that the villains in there will take flight at the mere sight of you.'

I had taken particular care that night. Apart from my rough rags I had created a hideous scar which twisted the corner of my lips in a permanent rictus. If I shone in the domain of disguise, the same cannot be said for my friend, who had disguised himself as a sailor and had wiped ointment on his face so as to appear swarthy.

'What about you?' I retorted. 'You look like a redskin, which is bound to cause trouble. Well, let's go,' I said, patting the butt of my revolver.

Our stay in the tavern could not have been more brief: a lightning visit, to be precise. Less than one minute later, Walter and I were beating the world record for 100 yards, with pack of drunks on our heels. As expected, one of them had immediately been intrigued by my colleague's shining face. Unfortunately for us, he had just been released from Newgate Prison, where he had been put away for two years by none other than Detective MacNiel. Within a few seconds, we had been surrounded by vindictive-looking villains, none of whom appeared to nurture a love of coppers in his heart. Without further ado, and after I had fired a round into the air to make them hesitate, we slipped away quickly. It wasn't the first time it had happened to us, and Walter and I had become champions at the sport. Nevertheless, it was only after running a quarter of a mile that we succeeded in shaking off the last of our pursuers, whom gin and beer seemed to have provided with wings.

146

Out of breath, and hidden in a dark passage off Commercial Road, we listened to the noises of the night, alert to the slightest noise of footsteps.

'I think we've lost them,' I declared after a while, 'but let's wait a little longer, just to be sure.'

'My artificial tan nearly cost us dearly,' puffed Walter.

'Don't worry about it, tomorrow I'll start giving you make-up lessons—.'

Suddenly, we could hear steps resonating on the cobblestones.

Hearts beating faster, and ears pricked up, we remained motionless. But our anxiety dissipated rapidly, as the steps were regular and betrayed no sign of haste. Backs pressed to the wall, we watched two figures detach themselves from the darkness under the milky light of the gas street-lamp on the corner of the street. The first of the two, tall and thin, with an aquiline nose and determined chin, was wearing a long chequered cape and a deerstalker hat. The second man was of medium height; something about him made me think he was a doctor.

The taller of the two explained to the other in a weary voice:

'How often have I said to you that when you have eliminated the impossible, whatever remains, however improbable, must be the truth? Why do you obstinately refuse to apply my principles?'

The other gave an exaggerated shrug of the shoulders. Then they disappeared from sight.

'Did you recognise him?' I asked Walter.

'Of course. Who wouldn't have recognised the pretentious beanpole who claims to be the prince of detectives, accompanied by his friend and confidant? I remember meeting him during a particularly difficult affair, and I must admit that, for a while, his deductions seemed nothing short of miraculous. But I quickly realised they were theories thrown out at random and which, by an incredible stroke of luck, turned out to be correct. The fellow's a charlatan, who's not fit to clean your boots, John.'

'You're wrong, Walter, he's the best: without peer; people will be writing about him for a long time, believe me.'

On the way back, as we were hugging the walls of a sinister passage in Whitechapel, I almost stumbled over a box of rubbish.

'You can't see your hand in front of your face in this damned fog,' I grumbled.

A grunt came in reply.

We turned to look at the other side of the passage; the feeble light from a street lamp, which seemed to accentuate rather than dissipate the darkness, traced with a blue finger the silhouette of a down-and-out slumped on the steps of a dosshouse. He looked like a pile of rags or a coat thrown to the ground.

'Poor devil!' said Walter in a compassionate tone. 'Not only can't he afford a bed, but we wake him from his sleep.'

I shrugged and made a sign to my colleague to keep going. After a few steps, a thought suddenly struck me.

I stopped dead. Walter followed suit and gave me a questioning look:

'What's wrong, John?'

The words of the "prince of detectives" came back to me and I repeated them out loud:

'When you have eliminated the impossible, whatever remains, however improbable, must be the truth.'

I turned and peered back down the dark street. I was struck by a sudden flash of inspiration.

'Are you all right, John?' asked Walter, worried.

'It's nothing. I wanted to see if the tramp was still asleep.'

I think that Walter wouldn't have borne me a grudge for that small lie if he'd known the importance of my discovery. An incredible discovery. The response to a question which had been haunting me for months; I now knew the trick Cora had used to vanish into the night after killing Patricia Morrison. A diabolical trick, a minor masterpiece of ingenuity and simplicity!

Dreadful thoughts kept me awake the rest of the night. Since last summer, I had never had any contact with a woman. An act of fidelity, maybe? Yes, there was that, but equally a certainty that I would never find in another woman that unique combination of savagery and gentleness.

Cora, my darling, I know you are there, there in the big city, but where? You're afraid of me, my love...and I understand you. But, be assured, I shall never tell, never. What's happened is not your fault, it was a terrible combination of circumstances, a chance, an unfortunate chance. Don't worry, my darling, I am here to protect you whatever happens.

20

August 1888

'I've never had much luck with women,' said Walter, sadly, that evening of the sixth of August, 1888.

I'd given him plenty of advice on the matter, which, by and large, he had ignored. This was not the moment to re-open the discussion; I turned a deaf ear as I scrutinised the customers of the *Blue Anchor* through thick clouds of smoke.

On the eve of the Bank Holiday, the pub was packed. Soldiers, sailors, labourers, foreigners, love merchants, out-of-town bourgeois seeking thrills and adventure jostled each other, singing and laughing in a joyous atmosphere rendered practically unbreathable by tobacco fumes and the acrid vapours of the oil lamps; beer mugs raised high before their contents disappeared down avid gullets, barmen unable to keep up with the orders, soldiers kissing the girls without noticing the hands sneaking into their pockets.

Keeping an eye on the door, I thought about the incredible news I had received that morning and which had caused me to visit this Whitechapel tavern in the company of my friend.

As I did from time to time, I had gone to the bank where Luke Strange worked—he had become more human after the Morstan affair—to learn of any news from Blackfield and find out if anyone had seen Cora. Imagine my surprise when he replied:

'It's funny you should say that, John. Nobody had seen Cora since Christmas—until yesterday evening. I left work in the company of one of our customers who lives near Commercial Road. We stopped for a drink at the *Blue Anchor*. While we were there, a girl came in. I caught her eye and she immediately turned round and left. I only saw her for a couple of seconds, but it was enough to recognise her: it was Cora. Obviously, I thought it strange that she left as soon as she saw me, but I didn't think it necessary to follow her. She was very pale and her clothes were…Let's just say she made a curious impression.'

You can imagine the state of excitement in which I passed the rest of the day. Cora, whom I had sought in vain for months on end, had walked through the door I was now watching less than twenty-four hours ago.

And the place surprised me: a tavern in Whitechapel. Who would have thought I might run into her here?

As the minutes ticked by, my hopes rose and my excitement increased. I stared at the door, which might open at any time to reveal the woman I had vowed to protect, the love of my life.

'No, no luck at all,' lamented Walter, swallowing another glass of whisky. 'Not like you, John. You never had a problem like that. Quite the opposite. Look at the little brunette behind the counter, she hasn't stopped staring at you for the last quarter of an hour.'

I looked at the girl in question. She was a young girl of about eighteen years old, fresh from the country, and already with one foot on the slippery slope. Ignoring the sailor who was trying to flirt with her, she gave me a look whose meaning was unmistakable.

I looked away, disgusted:

'I must tell you that I haven't flirted for a whole year.'

'Yes, because that's what you want,' retorted Walter. 'And I ask myself why,' he added, frowning.

At that moment two prostitutes came through the door, each flanked by a military man. One was nearly forty and dressed in cast-off clothes. The other was masculine looking with a drooping lower lip and features ravaged by alcohol.

'Well, well, if it isn't Pearly Poll,' said Walter, speaking about the second woman.

'You seem to know all the tarts in the area—and Lord knows there are enough of them.'

Walter smiled knowingly:

'You know, John, we could get away somewhere, if you wanted.'

'With scrubbers like these? Are you mad?'

Detective MacNiel shrugged his shoulders and ordered another round.

The quartet disappeared to the other end of the room without my giving either of the soldiers a second look. Pearly Poll's friend was living her last few hours on earth, but I couldn't know that.

Constables Dickson and Schneider came into the tavern and sat down at our table. At midnight, having given up all hope of seeing Cora, and not wishing to spend the whole night brooding over my disappointment, I invited my colleagues to my flat for a round of cards to finish the evening. Dickson and Schneider took the route to 12, Shoe Lane, but without Walter who, over our insistent pleadings, preferred to go home, on the pretext his brain was too addled by alcohol to avoid getting fleeced.

I couldn't concentrate during the game. Cora paralysed all my faculties, and I am normally a canny player; Dickson and Schneider profited ruthlessly and lightened my wallet considerably. They left me in a similar state to Walter at around five in the morning, the time that John Reeves made a macabre discovery as he left his flat close to the *Blue Anchor*.

Screams had been heard that night, coming from 37, Commercial Road, a drab house bearing the name George Yard Building. But that was nothing unusual for the start of a holiday: boozy passers-by going home, shouts and laughter piercing the darkness. Mrs. Frances Hewitt, the landlady, paid no attention to the screams; the labourer John Reeves and his wife Louise were concerned, but not enough to do anything about it. Around half past three, the cabman Albert Crow, going up to his flat, noticed a human form on the first floor landing; thinking it was just a drunk, he passed by. At five o'clock John Reeves went down the same stairs on his way to work. When he first saw the body, he also thought it was a drunk, but a crimson puddle intrigued him: the "drunk" was a woman lying in her own blood.

A policeman brought me the news, and it was with a bad headache and an understandable anxiety that I arrived on the scene of the crime.

'About forty knife thrusts,' sighed Dr. Robert Keleene. 'The lungs, the liver, the spleen…only a madman could have done this.'

After a thorough examination, he concluded that the murder weapon could have been a bayonet. When my investigation showed that the victim was the woman who was with Pearly Poll the night we had seen them in the *Blue Anchor*, I experienced a glimmer of hope: maybe the killer wasn't Cora, but one of the soldiers.

I took Walter with me to interview Pearly Poll, who seemed eager to help us. Martha Tabram—the victim—and she had been approached in Whitechapel Road by two soldiers. One was a corporal. All four were among the last to leave the *Blue Anchor*, after Pearly Poll took the corporal to Angel Alley, and Martha headed in the direction of the George Yard with her soldier. That was at quarter to two in the morning. No one saw Martha Tabram alive again.

When I asked her if she was capable of recognising the friend of the unfortunate Martha, she replied in the affirmative, but accused us of being lousy coppers because we had seen her as well.

Nothing in Pearly Poll's testimony could confirm that the soldier who accompanied Martha was the killer. But I wasn't about to lose any trail which might prove something priceless: Cora's innocence. I pulled out all the stops and, having obtained permission from the military authorities, I took my precious witness to the Tower of London where all the non-commissioned officers and men who were on leave during the night of the murder were lined up. Wearing an extravagant plumed hat and dress with pearl buttons, Pearly Poll made a sensational entrance into the courtyard of the Tower and, just like a general, the little strumpet from Whitechapel reviewed the soldiers of Her Majesty, only to announce finally: "'E's not 'ere." This review without precedent in military annals was repeated in Wellington Barracks where she identified without hesitation two men, one of which was a corporal. Alas! to my great disappointment the two suspects had unshakeable alibis. The trail went cold and Cora's culpability now seemed certain. A Cora who knew how to make herself invisible, a Cora who—I had a sinister premonition—would not stop now she had started.

The bloody series was going to continue and London was going to walk in terror.

21

After having offered me a cigar, Superintendent Melvin chose one for himself and took his time lighting it.

'The soldier's testimony could have been crucial, supposing that he himself wasn't the killer.' He stared at me absent-mindedly, then added: 'No other avenues to explore?'

I shook my head. He cleared his throat and said:

'Fairy Fay on Christmas night, not far from Commercial Road, Emma Smith on Easter Sunday in Osborn Street, and now Martha Tabram, in George Yard, also off Commercial Road. Three prostitutes killed in the same area within a span of eight months. Don't you find that curious?'

There was a silence, during which I realised to what point I had been blind: three prostitutes killed in the Whitechapel-Spitalfields area, one of the few places I hadn't sought Cora. Where she had spent an entire year in company of a thug.

Cora at Whitechapel, it was unimaginable, and yet...there were the three murders. Three atrocious murders. Three murders of prostitutes. Why prostitutes? Difficult to attribute that to chance.

A name came to mind, that of a vile individual who had humiliated and debased an innocent young provincial girl: Larry Jordan.

'Three murders of prostitutes,' said the superintendent, stressing each word, 'which have never been solved.'

'Maybe an organised gang,' I improvised, 'who offer to "protect" the girls in exchange for part of their earnings, and liquidate those who don't pay.'

'It's possible. In any case, the killer or killers have to be found. One more murder and—.'

'And?'

A pained expression appeared on his face.

'It's none of my doing, John, it's orders from above. I saw the big chief this morning. He said that...actually, he demanded that I assign you to other matters. Public opinion is starting to get worried, and he wants results.'

No surprise that Sir Charles Warren wanted to move me to the sidelines. I'd had the misfortune to confide in a colleague my feelings about the "military methods" of the Police Commissioner, who had got wind of it. And since that day, he had been looking for an opportunity to punish me. If Cora were to strike again, I wouldn't be able to protect her. So be it. But I wasn't worried. I still remembered the way she had disappeared from the corner of the Morrison house: she was capable of defying any police force in the world.

'Let him do what he wants,' I replied disdainfully. 'Let someone else fall on his face for a change.'

Melvin looked surprised:

'You're scaring me, John. You talk as if you know there will be more victims.'

What a stupid thing to say! I could have kicked myself. Now it was more important than ever that I found Cora and stopped her.

As usual, the superintendent concluded the meeting by asking for news of my novel.

'I'm still where I was,' I said negligently, even though I was flattered on the inside by his interest.

'My goodness, John, all you have to do is to take the Morstan affair and change all the names. It would be a runaway success, I can assure you.'

'Probably, but I want to be sure. I want to do something out of the ordinary, a detective story that will put all others in the shade. Something that will haunt the reader long after he shuts the book. An immortal masterpiece! I want to—.'

Suddenly realising how outrageous it sounded, I stopped.

Melvin seemed amused:

'Something tells me you'll succeed. But you need to think of a pen name; John Reed is too banal.'

'What I need most of all is to find the end of the story. As you say, the Morstan affair is a sound base, but it alone doesn't seem enough. It needs an epilogue which stuns the reader and plunges him once more into fear and bewilderment.'

'You're making my mouth water. But at the rate you're going, it will never see the light of day.'

Without knowing why, I replied spontaneously:

'You'll be able to read it before the end of the year.'

A statement all the more ridiculous because I had never dreamt of placing Cora in my novel, which, without her and her diabolical trick, and her madness, wouldn't be possible. And yet, against all the odds, I kept my word.

I spent the afternoon digging up information about Larry Jordan. The results frightened me but, in a funny way, cheered me up: the very worst kind of lout, suspected of theft, blackmail and murder, as well as running a prostitution ring. This last point caused me to wonder: having discovered Cora's mental state, did he use her to punish any girl trying to hide her earnings?

This depraved individual lived in the most sinister street in Whitechapel, where many officers would not go at night: the infamous Dorset Street.

Late that night, passing myself off as a respectable gentleman in search of a little saucy adventure, I entered the villain's lair. I considerably exceeded my authority as a policeman...and left Larry Jordan in a state which removed all desire on his part to commit any further offences.

What he had said and what he had done had merited death. Never in my life have I hit a man with such ferocity, and only a last-minute reflex prevented me dispatching him to hell.

The despicable scum! Even as I pummelled him, he had continued to blaspheme, dared to shout obscenities about Cora...the dog! When I left his den I was foaming at the mouth, thinking I had never heard such a tissue of filthy lies, which collided with the mental barrier I had erected against all normal reasoning. But, inevitably, some of it got through and, subconsciously, doubts were sown.

Absorbed in my thoughts, with my head down, I wandered the dark alleyways of Whitechapel, deserted but for the shadow of the occasional tramp or prostitute.

'A little tipple with me, sweetie, what do you say?' said a voice in the night.

Without stopping, I glanced briefly at the questioner, wondering what such a pretty tart was doing in a place normally reserved for third rate trollops.

155

Suddenly, my legs refused to go forward and my heart beat as if it would burst.

'So, have we changed our mind then, ducky?' chuckled the voice behind me.

I was nothing but a block of ice, frozen in extreme anxiety. With a superhuman effort I turned round and almost fainted: it was Cora!

'Don't be so shy, dearie.'

'Cora....'

'Oh, we know each other already, do we?'

'Cora....'

'That's quite enough. And stop making that face, milord. You look as if you're about to kick the bucket.'

'Cora....'

'So, how do you know my name?...Blimey, it's the rozzer!'

She tried to run, but I caught hold of her clothes and heard the buttons of her coat burst. I was obliged to tackle her around her knees to bring her down; she fought with the ferocity of a wildcat and it was as much as I could do to control her. After I had ignored insults and wiped away spittle, she agreed to follow me to a pub.

That's when I grovelled, as I have never done before with a woman, explaining how and why I loved her and repeating ceaselessly that I was prepared to forget the past. In every way.

'Let's start all over again, my darling. We'll get married, we'll have children.'

But I was talking to myself. All sign of life had gone from her light blue eyes, lost somewhere over the horizon. When she looked at me, it was to say:

'I could do with another gin.'

There were several more.

'Right,' she said, finishing the last glass, 'let's go.'

'Go? Go where?'

She shrugged her shoulders and graced me with a smile, the first of the evening. (I prefer not to describe it.)

'Where? To my room. That's what you want, isn't it?'

My head was in a whirl and I no longer knew what I was doing. Cora was walking ahead of me, with her plumed hat, her black stockings and her ankle-boots. We climbed a rotten staircase which threatened to collapse with each step. Nauseous smells wafted up from the dustbins below. Her room was small, dirty, miserable and poorly furnished; in the open cupboard there were bottles of gin.

'Get undressed, I'll show you what I know how to do. I've made a lot of progress, you'll see.'

My God! Pray that it's not true.

She finished her work. Professionally.

I dressed without a word. I wanted to be sick.

'Wait a minute. You're not going without paying?'

I took five coins from my wallet and threw them on the bed. She smiled apologetically:

'You see, John, I haven't got a choice. If Larry learnt that I'd given you a pass, he'd drop me like a hot potato.'

For a brief moment, I caught a glimpse of the Cora I had known. She was beautiful in her nudity, graciously stretched out on the bed, her pearly-white skin gleaming in the flickering light of the candle, the exquisite line of her throat, her smooth stomach, her breast heaving after the effort.

She got up from the bed, tossed back a lock of hair on her forehead and came to embrace me. Licking her lips sensually, she stared and gave me a passionate look.

'You know, John, I like you well enough, even though you're not my type. But you can come back whenever you like,' she said with a wink.

She kissed me for a long time, pressing herself hard against me.

The look in her eye had always been a mystery to me. But now, I knew the significance of that strange, unfathomable light which shone there. I finally realised what I had subconsciously registered several times before: *she had the eyes of a harlot.*

'Larry's an extraordinary person, John, I'll have to introduce you one of these days. He threw me out once, because I hadn't charged one of my customers. You know, John, I used to be ashamed to take money from men who pleased me, it wasn't honest. Do you understand? I couldn't help myself, I just couldn't do it. He ditched me. It was hard, very hard. But he helped me get back on my feet when I returned to London last winter. I told him everything. He was thunderstruck. I think he may even have been afraid at the beginning. After a while he began to respect me. He's an extraordinary person, I

157

owe him everything. He taught me everything. Can you understand, John? I wouldn't let him down for anything in the world.'

She lowered her head, as if in thrall to a tricky matter of conscience. Then she went to the bed, picked up two of the coins and handed them to me.

'That's my share, John, that's all I can do. The rest is for Larry. Oh, I do wish you could meet him. I must introduce you.'

Too late, sweetheart, we've already been introduced. And I don't feel, somehow, that he'll be in a position to teach you anything new.

I stood there staring at her for a long moment, then left. Once outside, I was surprised by the orange tint of the wisps of fog drifting the length of the narrow street. Unhurriedly, I walked towards the river.

Cora had reached the bottom rung of the ladder into the abyss. It was all over. With a curious detachment, I was able to trace each step on the road of no return. The poor girl never stood a chance; luck—or, rather, bad luck—had seized her in its claws and never let her go. In her adolescence, a perverse monster had soiled her and undermined her mental state. Then another perverse monster, of unspeakable baseness and cowardice, had pushed her on to the streets and the poor girl had lost her head, abandoning herself to the vilest of pleasures. Luck—good luck, this time—had set her temporarily back on the straight and narrow path, until your humble servant intervened ill-advisedly. A disaster! In order to protect herself, the victim became a murderess once more and had killed and killed again before descending into madness. Although there was no tangible proof, I was sure it was she who killed the nurse. After a lull of several months, she returned to London…murder, reunion with Larry, prostitution again, murder and murder again, alcoholism. Fate had swallowed its prey.

Was it she who had killed those unfortunate streetwalkers? How was she going to react when she found her "protector" half dead? All these unanswered questions were of little importance to me at that moment. I sincerely believe I had tried everything in my power to save her. But she had gone too far already and I could not do anything more for her…whatever happened.

Shortly thereafter, leaning on the parapet of Blackfriars bridge, going over again and again the principle steps of my recent life and that of Cora, I looked at the melancholic but grandiose view in front of me: St. Paul's, the Mansion House and the Tower of London, like ghosts draped in shrouds of fog. Below me, dark and menacing, the river belched purple vapours.

Suddenly icy fingers grasped me by the shoulders and tried to thrust me forward into the black waters.

Resist, John, resist!

A strange, limpid, intoxicating music enveloped and cradled my senses, inviting me into the moving chasm.

I clung to the parapet with all my force.

I felt a burning fork in my back; a horned figure with eyes of molten lava, emerging from nowhere, pointed to the abyss with an imperious gesture.

It may seem ridiculous, but it's true: what saved me was my novel. *My* novel. *My* story. An *exceptional* story. My *work*, my *masterpiece*! I couldn't leave this earth without completing my masterpiece!

I gritted my teeth and tensed my muscles to the point of rupture. The terrible thrust intensified, giving me a glimpse of hell. I fought back with my whole body and all my force; my head seeming about to explode.

Suddenly, something gave way and there was a cracking sound in my brain. The terrible thrust had died away. An agreeable feeling of well-being overcame me. I looked up, as if to thank God, who seemed to be setting the sky alight, transforming the street lamps which dotted the bridge into flaming torches. Through the thick fog gleamed the Thames, its crimson waters swirling.

It was a daunting sight.

22

London is often described as a juxtaposition of towns, such is the startling contrast between its different quarters. The West End, a mixture of parks and palaces, opulent mansions and green gardens, immense squares, green carpets framed by trees and fenced by iron grills. Then, in the East End, the greatest and cruellest of miseries, an open wound typified by Spitalfields and Whitechapel. Overpopulated and squalid neighbourhoods, narrow, winding streets lined with large, leprous houses sweating with dampness, where all of life's human debris seem to have congregated; a teeming, haggard population suffering the scourge of poverty and vice in all its forms, including the most abject.

We have already spoken of the sinister Dorset Street but Buck's Row, with its knacker's yard, was just as bad. An evil-smelling street running with the blood of the unfortunate beasts whinnying in agony.

On Friday, August 31, at twenty past three in the morning, a carter by the name of George Cross was hurrying along the deserted street. Reaching the abattoir, he noticed, lying on the other side of the street, a vague shape which he took to be a tarpaulin. As he went over to look at it, he saw a fellow worker, John Paul, arriving from the opposite direction. To their horror, the "tarpaulin" turned out to be the corpse of a woman—and still warm. The two mates ran to the police station at Brady Street to report their discovery. At a quarter to four, the dark lantern of Police Constable John Neil illuminated the corpse, which had not been there when the previous rounds had been made a half an hour earlier. The victim's throat had been slit from ear to ear. In the subsequent medical examination, it was determined that the victim had been disembowelled: the wound was deep and partially revealed her intestines. There were also other wounds, several incisions to the abdomen and to the right side.

The results of the investigation were astonishing. Constable Neil's testimony fixed the time of the crime at between three fifteen and a quarter to four, narrowed down to between three fifteen and three twenty-five by the testimony of Cross and Paul. Three policemen pounding their beats nearby had heard nothing and seen no one. Three abattoir workers gave similar testimony. A woman living close to where the body was found, and who had not slept a wink that night, claimed she could not have failed to hear the slightest noise. Nobody had heard or seen the killer who, in less than ten minutes had chopped a woman to pieces before disappearing miraculously.

Polly Nichols—for that was the deceased's name—a forty year old prostitute, was one of those tramps whom debauchery and misery had rendered more repulsive than seductive. She had been married and was the mother of five children. But, preferring the company of the bottle to that of her children, Polly had ended up in the flea-ridden dosshouses of Spitalfields.

The investigation was not assigned to me. It was given to one of my colleagues who, as I had hoped, failed miserably.

The crime of Buck's Row awakened the interest of the press, the inhabitants of the East End, and above all the girls whose profession required them to be out late at night in dark alleyways. On the other hand, it didn't seem to excite the curiosity of the new head of the C.I.D.—who had just been appointed, following the resignation of his predecessor the day after the murder, as a result of a series of clashes with Sir Charles Warren—who left for a month's vacation in the Swiss Alps.

One week later, on Saturday, the eighth of September, another body of a prostitute was discovered in the same area. The news spread across London like wildfire, provoking widespread panic. In the streets, people grabbed the newspapers' first afternoon editions. By now, there was no doubt: the bloody series of murders was attributable to one single hand. Fear could be read on every face. And the victim's fellow streetwalkers asked themselves: who's next?

Their terror was justified, for this time the mysterious killer had demonstrated an even greater perversity: not only had the victim's throat been slashed and her stomach slit open, but her entrails had been removed and placed for all to see.

The victim, Annie Chapman, was the mother of two children whom, since the death of her husband, she had left in the provinces while she sought her fortune in the capital. She had been rapidly reduced to selling her charms in order to survive. At forty-seven, bloated and stinking of alcohol, she was even more degraded than the other Whitechapel ladies—which is saying a lot.

It was at five minutes to six in the morning when John Lavis, a warehouseman at the nearby market, discovered the body in the backyard of 29, Hanbury Street. The head had almost been severed from the body, the abdomen had been entirely split open and the intestines had been placed on the victim's shoulders; the uterus and one part of the vagina had disappeared. In addition, there were two miserable leather rings—ripped from Annie's fingers—and two coins placed at the victim's feet in a curious geometric pattern. The medical examiner, Dr. Phillips, noted the extraordinary dexterity of the criminal and the precision of the incisions, and opined that it must have taken the killer at least fifteen minutes to inflict all the mutilations: "It's obviously the work of an expert, probably using an autopsy instrument."

Sixteen residents lived at 29, Hanbury Street, and the interior courtyard was reached via a corridor from the street. Even though the partitions separating the rooms were made of very thin wood, none of the tenants had heard any sounds during the night. The son of the landlord affirmed that there was no body in the courtyard at a quarter to five. Annie Chapman was seen for the last time at half past five, in the company of someone wearing a coat and hunter's cap. The witness—one Mrs. Long—was unable to provide more information. The body was discovered at five minutes to six, and already Hanbury Street was swarming with porters headed for Spitalfields market. The puzzle posed to the police was similar to that of the week before: how could the killer—after having cut up the body in record time without anyone noticing or hearing anything, in a well-frequented area—have escaped, almost in broad daylight, without attracting attention, when he must inevitably have been covered in blood?

The police realised immediately that they were dealing with no ordinary criminal, who demonstrated exceptional virtuosity coupled with extreme audacity.

Needless to say, the acerbic criticisms of the police in the press served only to increase the panic: "The same criminal hand has killed four prostitutes and there is still not the slightest clue which could

163

lead to the murderer." People were being arrested left and right. Foreigners, beggars and thieves were apprehended before being released through lack of proof. An endless flow of suspects filed though the police stations. Meanwhile, throughout the city, there were tragic incidents; every gesture seemed suspect and the forces of order were obliged to intervene several times to prevent lynchings. There were denunciations and anonymous letters; it was a time for settling accounts; people saw the madman at the corner of every street.

There was a brief calm when the police arrested "Leather Apron," a Polish Jew who went by the name of John Pizer, a cobbler by profession. He had a cast-iron alibi for the murder of Annie Chapman, however, and the police were obliged to clear him publicly of all suspicion, to avoid him being lynched by a drunken mob hell-bent on vengeance.

From one day to the next, Whitechapel became the object of an unprecedented surveillance, and there was not a street in the quarter which was not subject to police vigilance. Scotland Yard had engaged a considerable number of detectives. In addition, the residents themselves organised Vigilance Committees.

The two hundred or so dosshouses for the poor were inspected with a fine-tooth comb because, for the Victorians, the monster could not possibly be an English aristocrat as some had suggested; that was out of the question.

After their successive failures, the police received no respite from the press. People talked of scandal, stupidity, total incompetence, and a desperate situation. But the anger was principally directed at Warren.

The fog was very dense when I left Scotland Yard one evening at the end of September. As I was stamping my feet impatiently waiting for a cab, I spotted the elegant silhouette of Superintendent Melvin, with its black cape and top hat, bearing down on me.

'John!' he said. 'Let's take a little walk together. We haven't had a chance to talk since that blood-thirsty madman started terrorising the town.'

'Willingly. Even though spending last night wandering the narrow streets of Whitechapel has left me with little desire to walk. The same goes for Walter, but he's worse off than I am because he's on duty again tonight.'

'What else can we do?' sighed Melvin. 'There's not a single lead. It's enough make you despair. We have the place flooded with men, but I still fear the worst. It's two weeks since the monster appeared. I can see him clearly in my mind's eye, lurking in the shadows, his hand on the knife, waiting for the slightest opportunity to kill again. A maniac! He must be a maniac, but an intelligent one, for he's diabolically adroit. You know, John, if it were up to me, the investigation would be in your hands.'

'Inspector Abberline seems to be handling himself well,' I observed, with a touch of irony in my voice.

Melvin shook his head.

'I think you're the only one who can put an end to it. The phantom killer is your speciality, if I remember correctly. Besides, this business, if you leave aside the prostitutes and the disembowelling, is strikingly like the Morstan affair: throats slit and a murderer who vanishes.'

Yes, Melvin, old boy. You're pretty close, but don't count on me to provide the answer. I replied:

'Nellie committed suicide. It can only have been her.'

'I know, John, but who could it be this time? A mad scientist? A religious fanatic? A butcher? An aristocrat who'd lost his mind? And why does he slaughter these poor women as if they're animals? You know, John, there are all kinds of rumours circulating. The frightful nature of the crimes brings out the most scandalous theories. The precision of his attacks puts the medical profession in the hot seat.'

'A doctor? I'd say that's a distinct possibility,' I replied, happy to have the general public thinking that way.

The superintendent observed a worried silence, then continued:

'Last week, we interviewed friends of Annie Chapman. You know where she was living, when she could afford it? In one of the most notorious houses of ill-repute in Dorset Street. Guess who else I saw there?'

A shiver ran up my entire body.

'The daughter of the Blackfield innkeeper. I was astounded to see her in such a place. I wanted to talk to her, but....'

I was starting to get very uncomfortable.

165

'She was bizarre. She seemed—how to put it?—mad. Mad with grief, perhaps. I couldn't work out what was consuming her. Anyway, she didn't answer me.'

I breathed a quiet sigh of relief.

Melvin cleared his throat before continuing:

'She…everything pointed to her being in the profession, so to speak. Curious, is it not? She'd made quite a good impression at the time.'

'I understand,' I replied rather tersely, 'but everybody leads the life they choose.'

I hadn't seen Cora since the night she had shown me her real self. The Cora whom I loved didn't exist any more; the other Cora was a human wreck whom I would avoid if at all possible if she crossed my path again. Mad with grief? Yes, that was certainly possible, because I'd learnt that her "protector," as the result of my attack, had become an idiot with the mental age of a baby and the appearance of a puppet without strings. And there was no chance of recovery. Just as well: that would have been too good for him.

We finished on that note and parted ways. I watched him disappear into the fog, and hailed a cab to take me home.

I saw Superintendent Melvin late in the afternoon of the following day, in his office.

'Read this letter, John,' he began, 'and tell me what you think. It was sent to the *Central News Agency*.'

Dear Boss

I keep on hearing the police have caught me but they wont fix me just yet. I have laughed when they look so clever and talk about being on the <u>right</u> track. That joke about Leather Apron gave me real fits. I am down on whores and I shant quit ripping them till I do get buckled. Grand work the last job was. I gave the lady no time to squeal. How can they catch me now. I love my work and want to start again. You will soon hear of me with my funny little games. I saved some of the proper <u>red</u> stuff in a ginger beer bottle over the last job to write with but it went thick like glue and I cant use it. Red ink is fit enough I hope <u>ha. ha.</u> The next job I do I shall clip the ladys ears off and send

166

*to the police officers just for jolly wouldn't you. Keep this letter back
till I do a bit more work, then give it out straight. My knife's so nice
and sharp I want to get to work right away if I get a chance. Good
Luck.*

Yours truly
Jack the Ripper

Dont mind me giving the trade name

*PS Wasnt good enough to post this before I got all the red ink off my
hands curse it No luck yet. They say I'm a doctor now. Ha! Ha!*

'So?' asked Melvin, in an aggressive voice, when I'd finished
reading.

'So now the murderer has a name: Jack the Ripper. We're making
giant strides,' I added, not without irony.

'Come off it, John. So, what do you think, a prank?'

'Even though it's just an impression, I'm inclined to think it's
genuine.'

He looked at me gravely

'So do I. And I'm afraid that he'll show his hand shortly, just as he
said. To some degree, the letter shows us something of his
psychology. A megalomaniac with an unshakeable confidence in
himself, not the slightest qualm, you get the impression he believes
himself invincible, as if he possessed....'

'...magical powers,' I concluded.

'Exactly. Look at the writing: it's elegant and precise.'

'Yes, but the style isn't, it's clumsy and vulgar.'

'A ruse, believe me, and a double bluff. He knows we're not going
to fall into such an obvious trap.'

He straightened up and his voice took on a professorial tone:

'John, I have the feeling we're dealing with one of the greatest
criminals ever. This fellow isn't as mad as we think. He is, in one
sense, but he's also endowed with a prodigious intelligence. He
knows it, and he knows we know. This letter is neither more nor less
than a challenge to the Yard.'

'Jack the Ripper,' I said, separating each syllable.

Melvin's eyes narrowed:

'Jack the Ripper…or Jill the Ripper!'

'The murderer, a woman?' I expostulated. 'But that's impossible. No woman could be capable of—.'

'And why not, may I ask?'

There was a deathly silence in the room.

'What exactly are you going to do with the letter, chief?'

'What the Ripper asks: keep quiet about it. Very few people know about it, and the ones who do won't talk.'

Three weeks had now gone by since the terrible murder of Annie Chapman. I had just finished greasing the hinges to the back door which had been squeaking as I entered in the small hours, when the front doorbell rang. I went to open it.

'Walter!' I exclaimed. 'Oh, that's right, you're on duty tonight, you poor devil.'

'I'd give a lot to change places with you tonight, comfortable under your warm bedcovers,' he grumbled as I took his bowler hat and rust-coloured coat.

He dropped into an armchair and looked longingly at the fire blazing in the hearth. I served him a whisky. He took a swig and sighed:

'You know, John, that I'm not a coward.'

'I know that better than anyone.'

'Have you seen the fog tonight?'

'Yes, but….'

'We received a message an hour ago.'

'A message? From whom?'

'I can quote it word for word: *"Beware I shall be at work on the 1st and 2nd inst. in the Minories at 12 midnight and I give the authorities a good chance but there is never a policeman near when I am at work. Yours Jack the Ripper."'*

After a moment, I observed:

'If this isn't a trick and if Jack the Ripper turns up…No, that would be madness, he would inevitably be caught. This fellow has the whole of London on his heels, the whores on the alert, even the tramps keeping an eye out and we're watching every passageway in Whitechapel.'

'Yes, but it's Saturday, there are lots of people in the streets and the whores have to make a living.'

'You told me the first and the second, which means Monday or Tuesday.'

'Up until now, he's always operated on weekends, and there's no reason why that should change. That's Melvin's opinion, anyway. Minories is a street north of the Tower which touches the southern part of Whitechapel.'

'Minories. He's leaving his sector. Don't you think that's a ruse to distract us?'

'I've no idea, John. Personally, I think he's going to strike tonight. And there's that damned fog,' he added, running a nervous hand through his red hair.

Walter emptied his glass to give himself courage, then stood up.

'Well, I'm off to see the monster. Goodnight.'

'Which sector are you in tonight?'

He gave a deep sigh before answering: 'Dorset Street.'

At the very moment Detective MacNiel left his friend, somewhere else in London a figure was sharpening a knife. "You'll soon be hearing about my knife and my joyful little entertainments," it said to itself, looking at its reflection in the mirror, which showed two half-closed eyes filtering the flames of Hell. "I'll carve up number one, and then number two in the Minories. Ha! Ha!"

Jack the Ripper was preparing a double killing of an unspeakable ferocity and incredible audacity, which would garner sensational headlines and plunge London into an abyss of terror.

It's very late, maybe midnight. Let us go slowly down the Thames and try to pierce the fog which is becoming more and more dense: the Palace of Westminster, Charing Cross Station, Somerset House, the Temple, Custom House, and let us stop at the Tower of London, because a shadow moving along the embankment has just turned north towards Whitechapel. The figure is wearing a long coat with the collar turned up and a deerstalker hat, with peaks front and back. It walks at an unhurried but determined pace. Nothing extraordinary so far. But an attentive observer could not help noticing the strange fixed stare in its pale blue, almost transparent eyes in which all spark of vital life seemed to have been extinguished.

169

As the figure advances further into Whitechapel, its pace slows so it can mingle with the night-owls who are beginning to leave the pubs. Nobody gives it a second glance, so harmless does it appear.

It glides smoothly into a dark, winding alley, treading stealthily on the cobblestones with its regular, sinister step. The swirling fog wraps itself around the figure to head height, like a fluffy, suffocating scarf.

Then it stops.

A few yards ahead, the dim light of a tavern projects yellowish patches on the slimy cobblestones. A tumult of voices—quarrels, bawdy songs, dirty jokes—breaks the silence.

The minutes pass, the figure is still there, stock still, in the shelter of the shadow.

Brusquely, the hubbub intensifies because the door has opened on a woman standing unsteadily who, between two shrieks of laughter, hums a popular air in her rasping voice. She is wearing a fur-trimmed jacket, a black satin dress and white stockings. Her laugh reveals the absence of several teeth.

The attentive observer will notice the frightening smile starting to appear on the figure's face, will deduce that the woman is a prostitute, but will certainly not know that her name is Elizabeth Stride, that she is forty-five years old, or that she is a widow and a mother.

But the figure does.

Elizabeth Stride shuts the door and prepares to leave when suddenly, seized by a premonition, she turns round to scrutinise the darkened passageway. A gap in the fog gives her a momentary glimpse of the stationary figure, but she attributes it to the gin and starts to walk, singing her tune.

The figure follows her.

At about ten minutes to one, Elizabeth Stride finds herself in a narrow courtyard off Berner Street, in total darkness save for a faint light from the windows of a club. She has just refused a client and is still wondering why she did it, when she notices a figure in a deerstalker coming stealthily towards her. She is frozen in terror until the figure speaks.

Suddenly, as if by metamorphosis, she is reassured and an amicable conversation begins.

'I've a little gift for you,' says the figure.

'Ah!' exclaims Elizabeth Stride. 'That's really strange, coming from—.'

Her voice suddenly stops, but she doesn't immediately understand why. Her hands go up to her throat, all sticky, and she understands just as she falls to the ground.

A few seconds later, Luis Diemschutz, a peddler, enters the courtyard. His horse shies, and he is almost thrown to the ground. Irritated, he gets down from his cart to see what has frightened his horse. He strikes a match and discovers Elizabeth Stride with her throat slit from ear to ear. He realises immediately that he is in the presence of another victim of the bloody madman and runs to the club to sound the alert. And the figure crouched in the darkness leaves furtively, cursing the person who interrupted its bloody work. Shortly thereafter Berner Street is swarming with police.

Ten minutes' walk from there, in the dark bowels of Church Passage, Catherine Eddowes, whose staggering walk reflects her drunken state, unleashes a stream of abuse about the coppers who arrested her. She had been held in the Bishopsgate police station before her release.

Hugging the walls, she is suddenly aware of the footsteps which have been dogging hers for some time. She looks over her shoulder and sees a figure wearing a deerstalker advancing slowly towards her. As soon as it begins to speak, the whore no longer feels the terror which had seized her.

Mitre Square is a quiet spot, bordered on two sides by the premises of Kearly & Tonge, tea importers. There are three points of entry into the square, which is situated close to Minories.

Constable Edward Watkins patrols the spot every quarter of an hour. He sees nothing out of the ordinary when he passes through at half past one.

It's at that moment that Catherine Eddowes and the figure enter the square. At one thirty-five, three men leave a pub in Duke Street and pass by. One of them pays attention to Catherine Eddowes' laugh; he looks briefly over at the whore and the figure and continues on.

Shaking with laughter, Catherine Eddowes looks into the figure's eyes. The softness of the blue eyes looking back has vanished; now they gleam with a strange intensity and seem to be getting larger. In a flash, she realises the horror of the situation.

Catherine Eddowes is lying stretched out on the cobblestones. The figure bending over her, seized by a frenetic pleasure, is busy in its mysterious work, of which the prostitute's stomach seems to be the centre of interest.

It's now a quarter to two and Constable Edward Watkins enters Mitre Square again. The beam of light from his dark lantern immediately picks up the corpse of Catherine Eddowes bathed in a pool of blood. The sight before his eyes is atrocious, unbearable.

Not only has the dead woman's throat been slit from the right ear to the left, but her face is horribly disfigured: the eyelids cut off, the nose and right eye removed; the lobe of the right ear has been sliced obliquely and that of the left is a vertical gash. The stomach has been ripped open its entire length and the entrails removed. The intestines are draped over the right shoulder and the digestive tube lies between the left arm and flank.

Watkins' reaction is swift. He hurries to the night watchman of Kearly & Tonge, an ex-policeman, who runs out of the square and gives a mighty blast on his whistle, while Watkins stays by the body.

And, from that point on, a relentless manhunt begins. Whitechapel becomes a concert of whistles, as the police try to work in the dense fog. Detectives come out of every corner, issuing orders to constables running around in all directions.

In Houndsditch, the figure in the deerstalker is running with long strides, a pack of policemen at his heels.

'We've got him!' shouts an inspector arriving from the opposite direction.

Jack the Ripper knows that the slightest error will be fatal. He is running so fast he is almost flying, yet his mind is calm and perfectly clear. Not the slightest sign of panic. He knows that his head depends on his extraordinary *sang-froid* and also on his trick—his diabolical trick which can, which *must*, save him.

At the very moment the police are about to overwhelm him, he ducks into a dark passage. They glimpse his silhouette for a few seconds before it vanishes, swallowed up by the fog.

Even though they have lost sight of him, the police aren't particularly worried; the madman must be covered in blood, the area is surrounded, it will be impossible for him to slip through the links in the chain. They follow his trail; a bloody scarf is discovered in

Goulston Street. He's going north, the whistles double in intensity, they hear hurried footsteps, they just miss him. Someone sees his furtive silhouette turning into the notorious Dorset Street. The officers run down the narrow street, only to encounter Detective MacNiel, who has been posted at the other end.

'He hasn't been past here,' shouts the detective. 'He must still be in there.'

Dark lanterns sweep every nook and cranny of the sinister street and finally illuminate, in a recess of fifteen to twenty feet, a fountain; the water is still red with blood! The murderer washed his hands before vanishing into thin air.

The following day, Sunday, a card was slipped into a letterbox in the East End: the handwriting was the same as that of the first letter signed Jack the Ripper. Furthermore, the card bore the imprint of a bloody thumb.

I was not codding dear old Boss when I gave you the tip, you'll hear about Saucy Jacky's work tomorrow double event this time number one squealed a bit couldn't finish straight off. ha not the time to get ears for police. thanks for keeping last letter back till I got to work again.

Jack the Ripper

At the time the card was posted, the press hadn't got wind of a double murder. Only the murderer could know that he hadn't had time to cut the ears of one of his victims. Which eliminated any thought of chicanery about the letter.

23

October 1888

When Londoners learnt about the double murder of such unparalleled ferocity and audacity, the panic knew no bounds and the city became one immense bedlam with inmates quaking in terror. People started to tremble as soon as the sun disappeared over the horizon, making the sky bloody; they holed up in their houses with their teeth chattering when the fog descended.

Jack the Ripper! A roving shadow who wandered the alleys and passages of the East End, foaming at the mouth, with his redoubtable blade ever ready to cause death.

Added to the unspeakable terror was the wave of indignation and anger towards the police, and most particularly towards Sir Charles Warren. Some demanded his resignation, some his head. Under a daily deluge of acerbic criticism, Sir Charles decided to recall the man who was hunting chamois and collecting edelweiss on the snow-covered slopes of the Alps, a man almost as difficult to find as the killer himself. Next, he ordered every available officer into the East End, to reinforce the considerable number already there.

It cannot be said that these measures bore fruit: a C.I.D. refusing to take any responsibility and a population increasingly angry. What a lamentable spectacle!

And all this time, Jack the Ripper, laughing up his sleeve, planned his next crime.

In the Whitechapel police station, where Scotland Yard had established its local headquarters, Inspector Abberline was pacing up and down under the attentive gaze of his officers.

With an irritated gesture, he waved away the smoke from his cigar, then growled:

'Let's look at it again. It's a quarter to one when Elizabeth Stride is seen alive for the last time. She's near the scene of the crime and accompanied by a man who, according to our witness, is wearing a long coat and appears quite corpulent. Was it the killer? There's nothing to prove it was. A quarter of an hour later, the peddler Diemschutz finds the body of Elizabeth Stride, still warm. It's clear he must have surprised the Ripper in the middle of his work, otherwise he would certainly not have stopped at slitting the poor woman's throat—.'

'Yes!' exclaimed a sergeant. 'Because, ordinarily he—.'

'We know what he would ordinarily have done!' barked Abberline, turning scarlet.

'The fact that the victim's ears remained intact is the best proof that Jack was surprised,' I intervened perfidiously. 'Don't forget, he promised them to us.'

A vein started to throb on Abberline's forehead. Although he seemed ready to explode, he continued in a calm voice:

'At a quarter to two, a second corpse was discovered in Mitre Square. Ten minutes before that, Catherine Eddowes was still alive. The witness who saw her gave us a relatively detailed description of the man in her company: he was dressed in navy blue serge, wore a deerstalker and sported a small blond moustache. In view of the state of the victim, found only ten minutes after that, we can reasonably affirm that it was the killer, indulging in his abominable occupation.'

'The ears had been cut,' I said, simulating compassion, 'but not removed. The poor fellow, what bad luck.'

There was widespread laughter, except from Abberline, who remained stone-faced. He evidently did not appreciate my jest, which he no doubt thought was in bad taste.

'Bad luck,' he continued acidly, 'is a point of view I don't happen to share. The constable who found the body did his rounds in the area and crossed Mitre Square every quarter of an hour. On top of that, the killer ran the huge risk of being seen by night-owls who could enter the square from three sides. And you say he had bad luck?'

Superintendent Melvin, who had been silent up to that point, declared:

'Evidently, the Ripper must have timed the constable's round. The crime was premeditated, even though he couldn't have known his victim in advance. And don't let's forget his message notifying us he'd be operating in Minories. Mitre Square is just next door.'

Abberline shook his head, infuriated:

'If only we'd known that the warning had come from the killer. We've received so many anonymous letters since the start of this business.'

Melvin suppressed a reproach, perfectly justified, but pointless at this stage.

'We know now; the card sent a few hours before the double murder speaks for itself.' He looked at a corner of the ceiling for a moment, then went on: 'I don't know whether you realise it, but that double murder was executed with a quite uncommon audacity and sang-froid. It was one o'clock when he finished with his first victim; it takes a good five minutes to get to Mitre Square from Berner Street; how many does it take to get rid of the traces of the first murder, make the acquaintance of another prostitute—who, like all her fellow streetwalkers, sees a possible suspect in every new client—reassure her, take her to a relatively well-frequented spot while avoiding Constable Watkins' round, and slice her up without being caught in the act by Watkins, who discovered the body of Catherine Eddowes at one forty-five?'

Melvin paused, as if to add weight to his words:

'Gentlemen, I repeat, we're not in the presence of a run-of-the-mill criminal who's slipped through our fingers because of a one-in-a-million chance. We're dealing with a sort of Napoleon of crime, as ferocious as he's intelligent, cunning and as agile as a tiger. And what about that infernal pursuit that followed the double murder? Our best men were on his heels. We just missed him, we crossed his path, we drove him into an alley and yet he vanished into the fog!'

At which, Inspector Abberline interjected:

'He even had the nerve to wash his hands under our very noses. Incredible!'

'In any case,' observed Walter MacNiel, 'he didn't get out of the other end of the alley because I was there, and he would've had to run into me.'

There was a profound silence. You could have heard a pin drop.

'One thing's certain,' continued Abberline. 'He hasn't taken refuge in any of the dosshouses in Dorset Street. The residents of those slums would have noticed his bloody clothes and lynched him before calling us.'

'That applies to all the other dosshouses in Whitechapel and Spitalfields,' observed Melvin. 'As far as I can see, the Ripper doesn't live in the neighbourhood. People here are packed like sardines and we've interviewed almost everyone, in vain. And yet, he does know the area like the back of his hand: the shortcuts linking the alleyways and passages, the buildings with escape routes and the ones without. He knows everything. Only the natives know about the fountain in the recess off Dorset Street. Better yet, he knows by heart the habits of the officers on duty and has timed their beats. He even seems to be able to recognise their footsteps.'

A murmur of agreement rippled though the audience.

'And, as if that wasn't enough,' sighed the superintendent. 'I'm forced to believe that he has, as a last resort, a stratagem for escaping when he's cornered. What it is, I haven't the faintest idea. But I'd give my right arm to find out.'

The stratagem in question would have flabbergasted Melvin with its simplicity, but I obviously couldn't tell him, even though I knew better than anyone how gnawing over a mystery like that could become an obsession.

'Now, let's address the motive,' he continued, in a firmer voice. 'It's customary to say that sexual crimes haven't got one. Nothing could be further from the truth, especially in this case, and it must be a terribly strong one to push such an intelligent man to commit such abominations. I propose to deal with the facts, just the facts.

'First of all, how many murders can be attributed to him?'

'At least five,' affirmed Abberline. 'The first being Martha Tabram, on August the seventh of this year.'

I murmured in Walter's ear:

'Do you remember? We saw her a few hours before her death, in the company of Pretty Poll and the two soldiers at the *Blue Anchor*, the night you were in your cups. Dickson and Schneider were there.'

Walter nodded silently and stroked his moustache.

'After that,' continued Abberline, 'Polly Nichols on August the thirty-first. Then Annie Chapman a week later. And now the double murder of—.'

'Fine,' interrupted Melvin. 'Let's move on to the second point: who were the victims whom Jack the Ripper attacked with an increasing perversity? They were prostitutes, we know that. But what seems to have escaped the journalists is their strange similarity of age, life history and appearance: they were third-rate whores, all over forty years old, married, divorced, or widowed, with children, not very appealing, with teeth missing...I don't think I need to press the point.

'Thirdly, the location of the crimes: Whitechapel and Spitalfields, the most sordid and squalid quarters of the capital. And, if we exclude Mitre Square, the area is even more restricted, an island of about four hundred yards square, in the very heart of the hellish misery.

'Fourthly: the mutilations inflicted on the victims. When he's not pressed for time, the Ripper slices up his victims with almost professional skill. The medical experts are agreed on that.

'Fifthly: the mutilated corpses are left abandoned in public places, at weekends. In other words, he deliberately seeks attention and displays his invincibility. Everything indicates a powerful case of megalomania: the letters, the challenges to the police, the name he goes by.

'Finally, I must draw your attention to the curious ease with which he gains the confidence of his victims, the prostitutes who—do I need to remind you?—need more than anyone to be on guard after nightfall.'

Scratching his chin, Melvin paused for a brief moment of reflection, then concluded:

'The situation is very grave. We're up against a master criminal and also a press doing their best to crank up the pressure, to ridicule us and turn the public against us. We must not spare *any* effort to capture this wild beast...before it strikes again!'

And Scotland Yard didn't spare any effort. Every officer gave his all in the pursuit of the phantom killer. There was one exception, however: your humble servant contented himself with being the attentive witness to the deployment of the forces of order in the East End, which had become a veritable human anthill. One night when I was on duty I spotted Cora. The other whores were trembling with fear; not she! Madness held her completely in its grip. I passed in front of her, but she didn't recognise me. I couldn't help her any more, she'd gone too far, *much* too far.

Each night there descended inexorably on London a blanket of terror, with a shroud of mist creating ghosts, distorting distances, and clouding your view when you wanted to put a face to him whose steps were resonating behind you. Those unfortunates whom hunger forced out on to the streets worked in an atmosphere of hysterical fright, expecting to see at any moment the outline of the madman who would pull out their entrails. The name of Jack the Ripper burned in everyone's brain.

The autopsy of Catherine Eddowes revealed that one of her kidneys had been removed. A slice of the missing organ reappeared on the sixteenth of October, in a package addressed to George Lusk, president of a Vigilance Committee, accompanied by the following letter:

From hell.
Mr. Lusk,
Sor
I send you half the Kidne I took from one woman and prasarved it for you tother piece I fried and ate it was very nise. I may send you the bloody knif that took it out if you only wate a whil longer

Signed
Catch me when you can Mishter Lusk

There were other messages, even poems, but nothing concrete. The six weeks which followed the double murder went by without anyone collecting any more macabre remains. Confidence returned little by little and a glimmer of hope seemed to dawn on the horizon as the nightmare dissipated. The atmosphere at the Yard, however, was far from relaxed, as the resignation of Sir Charles Warren was imminent; he was hardly ever seen and he no longer supervised Abberline, who, despite the apparent calm of Whitechapel, had maintained the strong police presence in that sinister quarter.

Was Jack the Ripper dead? If not, why had he put down his scalpel? While London was lost in speculation about him, it would not be long before the mysterious murderer would make his way to 13, Miller's Court—behind Dorset Street, there to commit a crime that London would never forget.

24

November 1888

For the ninth of November, Lord Mayor's Day, a day of great
solemnity, Sir Charles Warren, forever haunted by the ghosts of
anarchists, had reinforced the city police charged with protecting the
important procession. The parade needed to proceed without a hitch,
so Warren had studied the itinerary, trying to envisage all the possible
snags. All? Not quite. He hadn't counted on his old friend Jack the
Ripper who, by contrast, had not forgotten.

Mary Kelly, a young and pretty prostitute, lived at 13, Miller's
Court, situated in a passage off the ill-famed Dorset Street and
containing six lodgings. The owner of the building, a certain John
McCarthy, having noted that his tenant was six weeks delinquent in
the rent, enjoined his employee Thomas Bowyer to go to her flat and
recover whatever he could in the way of back rent.

At around eleven o'clock in the morning, Bowyer knocked at the
door of 13, Miller's Court. Not receiving any response, he shook the
handle and decided that the door was locked. The flat was on the
ground floor, with two windows overlooking a water tap and the
tenant's dustbins. One of the windows had two panes broken, and
Bowyer was able to put one hand inside to draw back the curtain.
What he saw took several seconds to register, and he stood there
petrified for several seconds before letting out a terrified shriek.

We entered Mary Kelly's miserable lodgings at almost precisely the
same time that Sir Charles Warren handed in his resignation.
Abberline and the medical examiner took a horrified step back, and
Walter and the other officers closed their eyes.

Mary Kelly lay there, scattered to the four corners of the room.
Blood had spurted over the floor and the walls, and had even splashed
on to the ceiling. Jack the Ripper had surpassed himself.

He had committed the most hideous crime it was possible to
imagine, a demented dissection which must have taken him at least
two hours, between seven and nine o'clock in the morning. What
incredible nerve when you consider that the other tenants of Miller's
Court were coming and going in front of the windows of number 13

during that time. Windows through which he had undoubtedly been obliged to escape, because he had pushed a heavy wardrobe in front of the door. The fact that he had struck on the morning of Lord Mayor's Day was not a coincidence. Jack the Ripper had pulled off a master stroke, unequalled in the annals of crime. His thirst for celebrity was evident: he had chosen the most propitious moment, the perfect place and the most brutal and revolting manner. The hideous crime paralysed London with horror and, if that was the Ripper's intention, it must be said he succeeded beyond all expectation. The prowling figure with the bloody scalpel had stamped itself in everyone's consciousness.

Two observations about this last murder. Mary Kelly was found dead, not in the street, but in her own lodgings. And, contrary to all the previous victims, she was young and attractive. She was also one of the few Whitechapel prostitutes who didn't need to walk the streets to pick up customers. Had Jack the Ripper decided to change his habits?

No. It was clear that, since the alleys were being subjected to an increased police presence, it would be difficult for him to execute the abominable dissections which he intended. As for his victim, young and pretty, one could well imagine that circumstances had dictated his choice.

It can be determined with precision who was the last person to see Mary Kelly alive. Around ten forty-five at night, a prostitute named Mary Ann Cox, also living in Miller's Court, saw her leaving the *Britannia* pub in the company of a man on the right side of forty, wearing a bowler hat and sporting a ginger moustache. She followed the couple, who went into 13, Miller's Court. Around two o'clock in the morning, George Hutchinson, an unemployed night watchman noticed an unknown man approaching Mary Kelly. He was of good bearing, and elegantly dressed in an astrakhan-lined overcoat, white shirt and black tie, and—quite a provocation in such an area—a gold watch on a chain. He had bushy eyebrows and a handlebar moustache; under his arm he carried a black package. Hutchinson followed the couple to Mary's flat and then took up a position at the entrance to Miller's Court until three on the morning, when he stopped his surveillance. The testimony, for who knows what reason, left Abberline sceptical; nevertheless, it did appear that the elegant man was the murderer. Between half past three and four, a couple in the building heard a cry of "Murderer!" which seemed to come from the courtyard. They didn't pay much attention. At a quarter past six, Mary Ann Cox heard somebody leave Miller's Court. A certain Mrs. Maxwell claimed to have seen Mary Kelly with a man in front of the *Britannia* at a quarter to nine—in other words two hours before Thomas Bowyer discovered the horribly mutilated body!

At the scene of the crime, the police found a great pile of ashes in the grate: the murderer must have burnt his bloody clothes. Even though there must have been a roaring fire, nobody appeared to have noticed anything, despite the thin interior walls. Finally, it was discovered that Mary Kelly was in the early stages of pregnancy.

It was now the end of November. Even though the Ripper hadn't claimed a new victim, the terror persisted and there were still no clues leading to the extraordinary criminal.

Who was he? How did he evade the increasingly tightly-drawn nets of Scotland Yard? What motive, supposing he had one, was driving him to commit such atrocities?

Those were the questions being asked everywhere. Comfortably installed on either side of the fireplace in my flat near the Temple, Walter and I were no exception on that Thursday night in November.

My friend stared pensively at the flames which highlighted his ginger hair.

Jack the Ripper had no idea he would be unmasked that same night, or his agile brain would have formulated an urgent strategy; but the die was cast, and had been for some time.

'They say,' said Walter, 'that Jack the Ripper is a member of the police force, which would explain why he hasn't been caught.'

I served him another whisky by way of encouragement.

'For my part,' he continued, after taking a swallow, 'I don't think they're completely right or completely wrong.'

'I don't understand. Either he is a member or he isn't. *To be or not to be.*'

'Leave poor Will in peace! Let me explain: he isn't a policeman, but he follows the same profession.'

'A private detective, you mean?'

Walter nodded and winked.

'So you know who he is?' I pressed him.

Walter was milking the situation, for normally the shoe was on the other foot: it was I who held the key and it was he who was trying to drag it out of me.

'On two occasions,' continued Walter, 'just before the murder, the victim was seen in the presence of a man wearing a deerstalker hat.'

'True, but I don't see what that has to do—.'

'As I was saying, a private detective who has the police's full confidence, a detective no one would suspect for a moment, a detective who knows the East End like the back of his hand, a detective respected and admired, even by tarts. A detective who always wears a deerstalker hat!'

'The celebrated Holmes! Whom we saw the other night with his friend and confidant, Dr. Watson. You're off your rocker, my poor Walter. Him? No, it's impossible. It's quite ridiculous.'

'And why?'

I shrugged my shoulders.

'Well, there's the motive, for a start.'

'Just so. Listen, up till now, nobody's ever seen him with a woman. He lives the life of a monk. Maybe he's impotent and—.'

'An impotence which, over time, has resulted in avoidance, bitterness, and eventually hatred for the female sex, and disgust for sexual relations?'

'Something like that. And I know for a fact he takes drugs. One could well imagine that under the influence of a strong dose, he—.'

'Jack the Ripper commits his murders with a clear head,' I cut in tersely. 'He proved it, I think, the night of the murder when he slipped through our fingers. Jack the Ripper making fools of the police under the influence of drugs? Hah! Ridiculous!'

'But he didn't slip through my fingers,' protested Walter, clearly offended. 'I tell you I never saw him.'

'Yet he certainly ran into Dorset Street with the police at his heels,' I retorted. 'You were at the other end of the alley....'

'And?'

After a deliberate silence, I said:

'There is another solution.'

Walter seemed disconcerted, then roared with laughter.

'I see,' he chuckled. 'When Jack the Ripper got to the end of the alley, he threw away his headgear, put on a bowler hat, and turned to face the oncoming police as Detective Sergeant Walter MacNiel.'

'Especially as I remember, on that night, you wore a rust coloured coat, which—.'

'There's one thing that doesn't square,' declared Walter, getting up and tapping me on the shoulder. 'The Ripper washed his hands in the fountain. If things had happened the way you say, he would never have had time to do that.'

I smiled at him:

'"Saucy Jacky" had more than one trick up his sleeve. He could very well have found a ruse to avoid suspicion. All right, that's enough, let's stop. You're not upset with me?'

He feigned outrage.

'That'll cost you a whisky for damages and interest, my good sir.'

While I obliged him, I observed:

'You can't go out in that condition. It's not even eight o'clock and you're on your third or fourth glass.'

Walter looked at his watch in horror:

'My God, quarter to eight already! I have to go.'

I looked at him in astonishment:

'You're not on duty, as far as I know.'

He got up, put on his coat and hat and confided in me, not without hesitation:

'I have an important rendezvous. Her name's Betty. She's very sweet...I think I've been bitten, John. It's serious, this time.'

My shoulders sagged and I sighed:

'I understand. I'll soon be losing a friend.'

'A friend whom you've just accused of being Jack the Ripper. That must be what the French call the English sense of humour. Goodnight, old sport.'

I accompanied him to the door and watched him go down the stairs. At the bottom, he turned, winked and waved his hand before disappearing. I heard his footsteps in the hall and the door opening and closing. I closed the door of the flat, locked it, and went back to my armchair to think.

When I heard the clock strike eight, I got up and went over to the glass-panelled door overlooking the interior courtyard. Behind a veil of fog, the windows of the flat opposite appeared as blurred splashes of yellow. Suddenly, I noticed a beam of light at the rear of the courtyard. Intrigued, I scoured the rest of the area, but the fleeting light did not reappear. I shrugged my shoulders and went back to my place near the fire.

In the dark courtyard, a figure looked up at the glass-panelled door behind which John Reed had been stationed a few moments earlier. Then its gaze alighted on the back stairs leading to that same door.

185

The figure approached carefully. At the foot of the stairs, it bent down and directed the beam from its dark lantern on the steps. It also illuminated the hand-rail, which it examined with interest. With infinite care, it climbed a few steps and continued its inspection.

I don't know what's wrong with me tonight, I said to myself as I served myself another glass. A strange impression. A sensation of approaching danger, just like the night Cora tried to stab me. I shivered at the terrible memory. Cora brandishing a kitchen knife with that terrifying look in her eye.

Cora....

Don't think about it any more, John. It's over and you know it.

Suddenly I heard a muffled creak.

I turned towards the glass-panelled door, because the sound appeared to have come from there. Was someone coming up the back staircase? Strange, because the other tenants didn't seem to use it. A kid? Not at this hour. A burglar, then? I looked at the logs crackling in the grate and shook my head, cursing myself for being such a fool. What are you afraid of, John Reed? But, as I tried to reassure myself, I became more and more conscious of the tension building up in the room. My pulse raced faster than usual and I was perspiring heavily. I knew somehow that this evening was not going to be like the rest.

There was a renewed creaking.

This time, there was no doubt: it came from the back stairs. I froze in my armchair.

There were three knocks on the glass-panelled door. I looked round: a figure muffled to the eyes stood on the landing of the back stairs. Its face was pressed against the damp glass of the door and a pair of pale blue eyes was visible.

'Melvin!' I exclaimed and went to open the door.

'Chief,' I stammered as I helped him out of his cloak, scarf and top hat. 'To what do I owe the honour? And why did you use the back stairs? You could have come to grief. You can't see anything in that courtyard. And why the dark lantern?'

Melvin did not appear to be his usual self. The muscles in his cheeks were taut, his lips were pinched, and his look, normally warm and sympathetic, was now hard and searching. Seeing my surprise, he smiled grimly and offered a lame excuse:

'There was a young couple in the front doorway and I didn't want to disturb them.'

When I didn't respond, he continued with a forced joviality:

'My dear John, what are you doing tonight?'

'Tonight? But—.'

'Have you eaten?'

'No.'

'Perfect. You'll be my guest.'

'But, chief, I—.'

'No further discussion,' he said, with an amiable authority. 'I'm your boss and you'll do what I say.'

'Fine,' I said with a smile. 'I'll be with you as soon as I've changed.'

Melvin took me to one of the poshest restaurants in the capital. We demolished plates of salmon, oysters, caviar, eels, lamb and grouse stuffed with truffles, all washed down with champagne. Throughout the meal he did his best to make the evening as pleasant as possible. As he had never invited me to dine with him before, let alone in an establishment of such quality, this intrigued me greatly.

We left the restaurant shortly after ten. Somewhat euphorically, I confided to the superintendent:

'Quite honestly, chief, that's the most pleasurable time I've had the whole year.'

'Glad to hear it, John Reed.'

John Reed? Normally he called me John.

'I…to what do I owe the honour of this invitation?'

His brow furrowed and he looked me straight in the eye:

'John, I'm about to entrust you with a very important mission. Undoubtedly the most important you've ever had. A very important mission, but a completely unofficial one, which only you can accomplish.'

'You know you can always count on me, sir.'

'I know, John, but this is rather special.'

'And what is it?'

'We'll talk about it at my place, if you don't mind,' he said, as he hailed a cab.

25

What Melvin was about to ask of me had to be of great importance, for he had never before invited me to his flat. The room in which we found ourselves was illuminated by two opaline lamps and the fire from the large hearth. A sumptuous glass-fronted bookcase, a Regency desk, two comfortable wing chairs, each with its own side table, comprised the furniture. A complete wall was reserved for fine paintings showing an eclectic taste and two French windows opened on to a lawn currently shrouded with fog. A superb Persian carpet lay on a perfectly waxed floor.

'I can see you eyeing my bookcase,' he said, filling two glasses with cognac.

'Quite remarkable,' I replied, impressed by the number of works on criminology.

Melvin smiled:

'As you can see, crime is my hobby.'

'I'm surprised that, man of letters as you obviously are, you've never written a crime novel.'

'I almost did better than that, once.'

Silence.

'Sorry?'

Melvin shrugged his shoulders and sighed:

'You're the first person I've ever told, John.'

'What are you talking about?'

'I came within a gnat's whisker of committing a crime. It was a long time ago.'

'A crime? A murder?'

'Absolutely. I was twenty years old and engaged to a sweet, adorable young woman. We were very taken with one another and I was waiting impatiently for the day of our impending marriage. One day, she failed to turn up for a rendezvous.'

'She'd changed her mind?'

Melvin shook his head, a distant look in his eyes.

'No. She was found dead two days later, in the woods.'

'Dead?'

'Murdered…and raped. By chance I learnt the identity of the culprit. Do you know what I did?'

'What anyone else would have done. You—.'

'No. I didn't act in anger, I prepared my revenge. I'll spare you the details, but it was a Machiavellian plan. The murderer was someone high-placed. I only joined the police for that reason.'

'I see. And I suppose you changed your mind at the last minute.'

'Not at all. The hand of God proved more rapid than mine. The man died accidentally just before the act I had planned. I had spent two years preparing for it, and I was furious with frustration. My anger subsided over time, and I ended up believing she wouldn't have wanted to be avenged in such a manner….She's always beside me now, young and pretty, gentle and innocent; an ideal image which the rare adventures I've had since then have done nothing to dissipate. I've tried to convince myself that my behaviour is ridiculous, that one can't live with a dream, that the dramatic circumstances were largely responsible for me idealising her, but to no avail. I was and I am her prisoner…her faithful prisoner.'

'Just as the wizard Merlin became Vivien's prisoner voluntarily, out of love.'

Melvin looked up and his face was very sad:

'My mind is wandering, John, excuse me.'

'Don't excuse yourself, please. I understand very well.'

He looked me in the eye:

'Yes, John Reed, you do understand.'

A shiver ran down my back I had the distinct impression that he knew about my adventure with Cora down to the last detail.

Another silence, then he began again, but his voice had changed:

'What you need to remember from all this is that a normal human being can, at a given moment in his existence and as a result of a specific event, become a criminal, a murderer even. Some act out of anger, others act differently. It's a question of temperament.

'I've often been criticised for my lenience. Now I think you understand the reason.'

I nodded.

Melvin indicated the bookcase:

'It also explains my great interest in the psychology of crime. But in your case, John, it's the mystery which attracts you, isn't it?'

'Yes, it started with Edgar Allan Poe and *The Murders in the Rue Morgue*. The idea of blood associated with mystery fascinated me, although I've never ignored the psychological side.'

Melvin smiled:

'For my part, I admit that mystery also exercises a fascination. I shan't readily forget the Morstan case which you solved with an almost magical skill.'

'I say,' I murmured with uncharacteristic modesty.

He handed me my glass of cognac.

'I propose a toast to mystery. Mystery with a capital M.'

'And to phantom murderers,' I added.

The cognac was consumed in an almost religious silence. Melvin stood up and went over to the fire, which he studied thoughtfully.

'Phantom murderers,' he repeated softly. 'Impossible crimes. Those are indisputably your specialties.'

I drank in his words (and his cognac) in agreement, and repeated:

'Indisputably.'

'Which leads me to the mission I spoke of. A mission which only a specialist like you can carry out.'

'And what is it, exactly?'

'The phantom murderer.'

I looked pensively at the superintendent's silhouette outlined by the flames. He turned slowly, fixing me with a steely regard:

'I ask you, my dear John Reed, to put out of commission the wild beast who has terrorised the city for the last few months, the phantom murderer who's demonstrated such prodigious skill: Jack the Ripper!'

'But we haven't any leads. How am I to—.'

His regard hardened:

'Only you can do it, John Reed.'

'But it's Abberline who's in charge of the investigation. He wouldn't appreciate it if I—.'

'I'm asking you unofficially.'

'I repeat, chief, there aren't any leads. How can you possibly expect me to arrest him? Even if, by some miracle, I were to identify him, his ruse and his ferocity would probably overwhelm me before I'd had a chance to put the handcuffs on.'

'I'm not asking you to arrest him, I'm asking you to *put him out of commission.*'

'But that's completely against—.'

191

'I'll take full responsibility, don't worry.'

In the space of an instant, my confidence was shaken. Had Melvin guessed the identity of the Ripper?

While I was rapidly analysing the strange comportment of my boss since the beginning of the evening, I heard his voice saying, with a gentle forcefulness:

'I'll put you on the right track, John Reed, and you'll realise that Jack the Ripper can only be one person.'

I experienced a rush of blood to the head.

After a moment's thought, he asked me:

'Do you remember the murder of Martha Tabram on the eighth of August? Walter and you saw her coming out of the *Blue Anchor* a few hours before her murder.'

'Perfectly. We ended up in my flat and played cards until dawn. During that time, the unfortunate woman met Jack the Ripper.'

'No,' said Melvin. 'It's a mistake to attribute her death to Jack the Ripper. Just like those of "Fairy Fay" on Christmas Night and Emma Smith in April. Those murders had nothing to do with the five that followed. The Ripper's victims had their throats slit and their wounds demonstrated a surgical precision and a sound knowledge of anatomy on the part of the murderer, which was not the case with the bodies of "Fairy Fay," Emma Smith and Martha Tabram. The Ripper has committed five crimes and no more: Polly Nichols on the thirty-first of August; Annie Chapman on the eighth of September; Elizabeth Stride and Catherine Eddowes on the twenty-ninth of September; and Mary Kelly on the ninth of November.'

I said nothing. Melvin continued:

'We know that he has a profound surgical knowledge, that's the first point. We also know that he knows the Whitechapel-Spitalfields quarter like the back of his hand and the position of each officer and their beats. Now I ask you, John, who could know that?'

After a few seconds' thought, I replied:

'A policeman.'

Melvin gave a deep sigh.

'Although we can't be sure, it's by far the most likely possibility.'

'So, it's an officer who knows the prostitutes in the area very well,' I observed. 'Only the constables patrol at night.'

'No, John, not necessarily. The ease with which the Ripper gains the confidence of his victims supports your hypothesis about a policeman, but you can't limit the field of suspects to constables pounding their beats. If the Ripper is a policeman, it's obvious he must kill on his days off duty, otherwise his uniform would be covered in blood and he would immediately betray himself. He may have known one or two of his victims, that's possible. But don't forget, at the time of the later crimes, the girls were suspicious of everyone, even the police.

'In my opinion, the Ripper is probably a good-looking fellow, used to charming women and who straight away inspires confidence. Which, of course, doesn't rule out his being a policeman.'

There was an icy silence.

'I've already stressed,' continued Melvin, 'that Jack the Ripper is no ordinary criminal. And, personally, I know very few men with the *sang-froid*, the audacity, the speed and the clear-headedness demonstrated by the killer during these crimes.

'I always thought he disguised himself in a different way for each of his attacks, so as to throw us off the scent, and the diversity of the testimonies seems to confirm that. As for his last murder, that of Mary Kelly, we're almost certain he dressed up as a woman.'

He gave me an unfathomable look:

'The murder of Mary Kelly, the most atrocious it's possible to imagine, which he doubtless considers his masterpiece. A genuine butchery, which shook even the medical examiner himself. Do you remember? The squalid room, miserably furnished…the bed, the little table, the cupboard offering a glimpse of crockery and empty ginger beer bottles, the engraving over the mantelpiece, the half-finished candle stuck in a broken bottle of wine, the bloody bedcovers strewn on the floor, and…Mary Kelly lying on the mattress, her head almost detached from her body, a pile of red flesh like some hideous stew. The face slashed beyond recognition, nose and ears removed. The stomach open from top to bottom, empty of entrails. Blood everywhere, even on the ceiling. On the table, laid out symmetrically, the heart, the kidneys and two bloody spheres, the victim's breasts. And, as the final flourish to this monstrous dissection, the intestines hanging on the wall, attached to the hooks of the engraving.'

Melvin stopped for a moment, cleared his throat, and continued:

'So, to sum up. A policeman, and no ordinary one, to judge by the qualities shown by the killer. A policeman with surgical training and a past master in the art of disguise. A policeman off duty on the nights of August thirty-first, eighth of September, twenty-ninth of September, and ninth of November.'

As I quietly withdrew into myself, Melvin went to his desk and lit a cigar.

With a nervous hand, I patted the contents of my pocket.

He turned to face me, blew out a cloud of smoke, and asked:

'What do you think, my dear John? The face of Jack the Ripper is starting to take shape, wouldn't you say?

'Everything points to the Ripper not living in the East End. Fine. But it's very likely he lives in a nearby quarter. One probably close to the Thames, so he could follow the riverbanks when he went back home covered in blood. His flat must have a second entrance, a concealed door, a back staircase, or something like that, to allow him to enter discreetly. He may have left traces of blood there. *We'll have to check in the daytime.*

'With what we know, we can also shed light on this person's psychology: a megalomaniac lusting for fame. He put everything in play and took enormous risks to prove what? His hatred of prostitutes, of course, but also his invincibility, his superior intelligence and his extraordinary agility…as if he wanted to create a masterpiece without precedent in the history of crime. A masterpiece which would put everything that had come before in the shade. Do you follow me, John?'

I squinted so as to see Melvin more clearly, hidden as he was behind a billowing crimson fog.

'Why does he attack prostitutes with such ferocity? Why, for that matter, did he suddenly emerge on the twenty-ninth of August to commit his first murder? Something must have happened shortly before then to set him off. But what? I draw your attention equally to the theatre of his crimes: an extremely restricted area—I exclude the Mitre Square murder for obvious tactical reasons—limited to five or six alleyways, centred around Dorset Street. Maybe it was here that our man experienced the most cruel disappointment of his life. A first experience with a prostitute which sickened him of all future sexual relations? Unlikely, our man is a seducer, and not without experience. A fiancée who turned to prostitution, which he discovered there?' I could feel his searching gaze on me. 'These things happen, John. Do you remember the innkeeper's daughter from Blackfield? Who would have thought such a charming and lovely creature would start down the slippery slope?'

I slid my hand slowly into my pocket.

'But all of that doesn't seem enough to justify such carnage. I suspect the killer was in some way predisposed to crime. The hatred of prostitutes must have been lurking deep in his mind. Notice the striking similarity of all the victims. Except for Mary Kelly, they were all ragged whores of a certain age who had reached the final stages of degradation. They were also all married and had abandoned their children. That last point is very important: that's where I see the root of the evil. The Ripper may not have been the son of one of the victims, but it's highly likely that his mother was a prostitute like them. That shameful knowledge is buried in the very depth of his being, until the day he discovers the woman of his life has taken the same road as his mother. How does he react? It's a question of temperament.

'Ah! One more thing: most of his victims had lost some of their teeth. That's nothing unusual, we know that those poor whores often fight amongst themselves when they've drunk too much and lost teeth are often a result.

'Last week I obtained the response to an apparently insignificant question I'd asked. I went to see dear Major Morstan. A good man who appreciates you greatly, John. He talks of you as if you were his son. *I do hope* you won't disappoint him. As I said, he spoke of you, your childhood, your father, your mother. Then the conversation turned to Miss Forsythe, your old neighbour, which naturally led to the mysterious body of a woman hidden in her garden. That's when I learnt a detail previously unknown to me. The skeleton was missing five teeth!

'That's when I understood everything, John.'

A shiny object sprang out of my pocket.

Melvin waited impassively.

I confronted him, my hand clenching the scalpel. His pale blue, almost translucent, eyes looked at me with the deepest sadness. It was no longer Superintendent Melvin in front of me, but Papa...my poor Papa.

Papa is opposite me, we're seated at the table, our meal is finished, when suddenly the door is flung open by a horrible woman: my mother! Papa shows her the door, she comes towards me. She wants money, they discuss, they quarrel. She threatens to take me away, Papa shows her the door again. "No one has the right to separate a child from its mother," she said, holding me in her arms and kissing me. An insupportable odour of alcohol mixed with a nauseating cheap perfume makes my heart beat faster. I hear her say: "John, my little John, you're coming away with me if your father continues to behave like this."

This woman with greyish hair, coarse features, a baleful smile; a mouth with flaccid lips and missing teeth; rotting stumps giving her the air of a witch... this woman is my mother? No I want none of it. It's not possible. This screeching voice which grates on my ears and echoes in my head with an insufferable stridence...The oil lamp diffuses a purple light, a crimson fog...The knife lies shining on the table.

This whore is my mother.

Put an end to this nightmare. My hand clenches the object shining on the table. The steel slices through the air several times, the face of the horrible woman is streaked with red, a hot liquid splashes me. Everything is crimson and I keep on stabbing...

There is a hand on my forehead
'Papa, is that you? Snuff out the candle, I want to sleep.'
'Here, son, drink. You'll be asleep soon, I promise.'

I'm hungry. What time is it? My head's spinning. Where's Papa?
The clock strikes four.
Oh! What a nightmare I had...Well, Papa had a big clean-up this morning.
'...You see, Celia, we're going to be able to seed the lawn tomorrow. This morning's heavy shower has cost us a day, but it's no trouble. And this autumn I'll plant another weeping willow in place of the other one. You'll see, it'll grow very fast. If you want, Baxter and Tony and I can move the old stone seat under the tree. I've also got some rhododendrons I can plant, if you like.
'You're too kind, Phillip, you've already done enough since yesterday. Is John still asleep? He must have been very tired last night.'
'I'll have a look.'
'Wait, I'll get the cake I baked for him this morning.'
...Papa came back and kissed me, squeezing me tightly against him, maintaining a silence I dared not break.

I knew now that my nightmare was real. I guessed what Papa had done during the night while I was sleeping, and why the kitchen had been washed down so thoroughly.

And the corner of Miss Forsythe's lawn! Oh! I thought I would go mad. Papa was distraught. We didn't speak any more, and yet I had a great need to speak. I tried to confide in Celia Forsythe, but her stern, enquiring look reduced me to silence.

Then Papa started talking to me, softly and gently, as if he were talking to someone sick. Time passed. I forgot my mother and that terrible night. Alas! that terrible memory returned when I enrolled in the faculty of medicine. Worse still, I noticed that I derived a certain pleasure from cutting people up. During each operation, I sensed the madness building inside me. I fought against it with all my force, but in vain. So as not to end up in a lunatic asylum, I left the faculty the year I was supposed to graduate.

I know full well, Papa, that you worked your fingers to the bone to pay for my studies, but I couldn't go on: each time I picked up a scalpel, I felt a mad urge coming on...I fought it, Papa, I fought it really hard...

'Papa, my poor Papa, how happy I am to hold you in my arms. You must think it strange to see me crying my heart out like this, but I can't help it. And why did you go away for such a long time? What did you say? Ah! Yes, in the armchair. That's better. Thank you, Papa, thank you. Your cognac is excellent. Yes, another, please.'

'I'm not your father, John, but I acted as if I were, I think you'll agree. I hope I shan't come to regret it. My conduct wasn't just aimed at protecting the honour of the Yard: if the Ripper had been any other member of the force than...the one we're thinking about, I can assure you I would have personally taken care of the matter, and by my own hand.

'We can't do anything more for him, John. His is a hopeless case: even if he were cured, he would never be able to forget his monstrous acts; his life would be hell, wouldn't it?'

The die had been cast a long time ago. The situation and Melvin's presence made that crystal clear.

'My opinion doesn't count,' I sighed. 'Three weeks for me to—for him to be put out of commission. Why the respite?'

'Why, John, you have to finish your novel. I'm assuming you've got all the material you need?'

'Of course. I'll have finished it by then. I'll hand it to you just before I ...terminate the Ripper.' Melvin looked away. 'I'd like to know at what point you started to suspect him.'

'I can't pinpoint the time exactly. It dawned on me gradually, one might say instinctively. He had an unshakeable alibi for the murder of Martha Tabram; at the time, I couldn't know that murder had nothing to do with the ones that followed. After the infernal pursuit on the night of the double murder, I became aware of just how agile and cunning the killer was. Furthermore, he'd managed to disappear under the noses of the police; just as in the Morstan case. Then I thought of all your theories and studies on impossible crimes, a subject on which you seem to be an undisputed expert. Jack the Ripper was, too, and he didn't hide it. Quite the opposite: at each turn his reputation as the phantom murderer grew by leaps and bounds. Obviously our man had a trick, a stratagem, which allowed him to appear invisible. But I still didn't want to believe the evidence.

'Last week, while I was juggling with your initials in the hope of finding an alias for your novel, it struck me: this time J.R., Jack the Ripper, had been too clever by half.'

Despite the circumstances, I had to smile.

'After which,' concluded Melvin, 'I returned to Blackfield.'

I stood up and served myself another brandy, which I drained in a single gulp, after which I bid my boss goodbye:

'Thank you for the evening. I won't see you tomorrow, for I assume I've been suspended.'

'Don't forget the novel, John.'

'Don't worry, in three weeks the Ripper will cease to exist. I've never refused an order, and this one will be brought to a satisfactory conclusion. You have my word, sir.'

26

The delay granted by Melvin is almost over. My manuscript is almost finished and I'm going to catch a few hours' sleep. Tomorrow—or, rather, today, for the hour hand has already made four turns since midnight—I'll complete it and hand it in.

Writing this has already required a considerable effort and I have rarely gone to bed before three in the morning.

I'm glad to have finished, because of late the fog has been acquiring a crimson tint.

My scalpel sits on the desk in front of me. It asks nothing more than to slice the air. It's a marvellous object, a perfect accomplice, docile and silent, responding to every order. I owe it much; it guided my hand when my thoughts were unclear. I'm sure Edgar Allan Poe must have had one in front of him when he wrote.

I've just re-read the text and I must say I'm rather pleased with it. (The astute reader might have had his suspicions aroused when he read of the two coins at the feet of Annie Chapman's body.) I've dreamt for a long time about writing a novel, a great novel. And now I've done it. It seemed to me a good idea to withhold the identity of the Ripper until the end, for the reader's pleasure. Which wasn't easy, because I made it a point of honour from the very beginning to underline the psychological clues which pointed to me: the bloody vision of the night I killed my own mother; my obsession with mystery; my surgical studies; my gift for disguise; the parts of Whitechapel I knew like the back of my hand; my agility, etc. In addition, I was scrupulously honest in my accounts of the facts and my impressions at each stage of the story. Remember the moment after I had just left Cora, after discovering she was a whore like my mother, the moment when everything changed in my head—the moment Jack the Ripper was born.

In order not to be tedious, I've kept to the essentials regarding the events sparked off by the crimes of Jack the Ripper. Two thick volumes wouldn't have been enough to contain all the material. For one thing, there was the story of Sir Charles Warren's dogs. Someone had the bright idea of setting dogs on the Ripper's trail. Can you believe it? I almost died laughing, along with a lot of other people. The brave animals were taken to Whitechapel to begin the hunt, and as soon as they were unleashed they were off like bullets from a gun. The next day, the press announced a reward to anyone who could provide information, not about the Ripper, but about Sir Charles' dogs. All London burst out laughing.

The Police Commissioner's methods were the opposite of my own. The man, certainly jealous of my past successes, lost no opportunity to discredit me. I was his *bête-noire* and he was mine. When I mentioned him in the text, it was solely for the purpose of showing how I had led him up the garden path and contributed to his downfall.

In August, the Lyceum Theatre had offered a new production: *Dr. Jekyll and Mr. Hyde*. The story concerned a split personality: a perfectly normal man who became a monster at nightfall. The theme, captivating though it may be, in no way applies to Jack the Ripper, even though it spawned a thousand imitators.

I was perfectly lucid when I killed Polly Nichols, Annie Chapman, Elizabeth Stride, Catherine Eddowes and Mary Kelly, and perfectly aware of what I was doing. My acts helped shed light on the frightful misery which reigned in Whitechapel, an open wound in the heart of the city. As a result, Victorian society can no longer avert its eyes. But let's not delude ourselves: the Ripper's scalpel was never wielded for that purpose.

I still love Cora. For a brief moment I thought about "purifying" her as well, but it would have been impossible to modify that anatomy. Fate will soon put an end to her cruel existence. I know that she will soon be delivered to me *up there*, and I'll be able to introduce her to Papa.

The more I think about it, the more I'm sure that our time here has only been a test, to prove to us that nothing can destroy our love, our perfect union. We had both been sorely tested in our adolescence— she had killed a monster of perversion; I had killed the woman whose vice had stigmatised her face and robbed me of the tender souvenir each child should have of its mother. Subconsciously, I had registered the word "murder" in Cora's mysterious regard, mirror of my own latent folly. I had understood from the first, and so had she, the secret bond which tied us and will tie us for ever: *we were both murderers*.

Was it really by chance that she gave me the name Bluebeard, I who had killed my mother and who would slit so many more female throats?

There remains one more point to clear up: Cora's trick for disappearing in the night, the ruse the Ripper employed to avoid capture. In a word, the means to render oneself invisible....

But, in fact, does such a method exist? Did I ever specifically say there was *one* method? That the Ripper did what Cora had done? That her stratagem could be used by anybody at any time? No, I never expressed myself in such a way. I let it be understood, it's true. An ingenious and extremely simple means to make oneself invisible; I thought the idea very seductive and I couldn't resist the temptation to suggest such a miraculous recipe existed.

In fact the mysterious disappearances of the Ripper have nothing to do with those of Cora. With regard to the murder of the schoolmistress, where Cora managed to disappear from a dead end, according to Baxter, I don't think one needs to search too far for the explanation: the fugitive must have hidden herself behind the buttress of the first house, just at the corner of the alley. Baxter, who was not drunk, but certainly tipsy, carried away by his own momentum, must have rushed past her, leaving her free to retrace her steps.

The way she slipped through my fingers when Patricia Morrison was killed was rather amusing, in the sense that I fell for a really childish trick which would never have worked in broad daylight. As I already said, the solution came to me from something I glimpsed in a Whitechapel street, coupled with a phrase from the famous detective: when you have eliminated the impossible, whatever remains, however improbable, must be the truth. Remember the circumstances of Cora's disappearance. After having heard a noise in the garden, I turned to see a shadow vanish around the corner of the house. I took off in pursuit and ran round the house, where I met Nellie, who told me she'd seen no one. Following the foregoing dictum, a normally constituted person could not have disappeared in front of our eyes. That being the case, a different thought came to mind: then what was the shape I saw? The sight of the tramp laid out on the steps of a doss-house in a sordid Whitechapel street caused me to think he looked like a pile of rags or a coat thrown to the ground.

A coat thrown to the ground!

What could the shape I saw vanish round the corner of the house have been?

It was hard to avoid the glaringly obvious truth, the solution to the problem which had become a blinding obsession: after having attracted my attention by throwing something into the garden, Cora had thrown a coat from the window, extending her arm far enough out to get near to the corner of the house…and I had mistaken it for a shadow disappearing. A vulgar coat thrown from a window, which I had mistaken for a fleeing figure! And to think such a childish trick had defied my analytic faculties for months!

Needless to say, it was a very risky business, for it depended—for the illusion to work perfectly—on the precise moment I turned back to resume my surveillance of the house. But look at the situation from Cora's point of view: she had just committed a murder and knew she was under observation. There was no possibility of escape as long as Nellie and I stayed at our posts. She had to do something to draw one of us out of position. If I had turned round any earlier, I would have seen *someone* throwing a coat out of a window, without knowing who—it was much too dark for that—or why they were doing it. It would have intrigued me—I had no idea at that point that Patricia Morrison had just been killed—and it was highly likely that I would have gone to see Nellie to discuss it. Hence, whether Cora's ruse was successful in fooling me or not, I would have left the field clear for her to escape. Which she would have done while Nellie and I were talking elsewhere, picking up the coat on the way.

The method that Jack the Ripper used after the double murders is not without a certain humour. In fact, it was Major Morstan who had given me the idea when he asked me to play the role of a policeman…when I was already a Scotland Yard inspector! Looking back, I'd found that particular situation greatly amusing, and it occurred to me that it would be a clever idea to disguise myself as a copper on the beat after committing my crimes. This ruse offered two obvious advantages: first of all, the official uniform—carefully hidden beforehand—inspired confidence and respect; secondly, it would hide the bloodstains on my other clothing. The greatest risk, obviously, was from the other constables patrolling the area. But, there again, I'd taken all the precautions necessary to avoid them. I'd studied their beats, I knew where they would be and when. And even if one of them—intrigued by a colleague he didn't recognise—started asking questions, I felt sure I could bluff my way out of it, given my evident familiarity with police procedure. And, as a last resort, I could always run away; I was much too fleet of foot for any of them. It goes without saying that I disguised my face. A simple copper on his beat, that's how Jack the Ripper found his way home.

But, to avoid capture, it wasn't enough just to disguise oneself as a policeman. Even though I say so myself, very few men could have done what I did. Several times, I owed my survival to my *sang-froid*. I sliced up my sluts rapidly and skilfully, with a perfectly clear head, my eyes and ears on full alert. At the slightest sound of a footstep, I stopped.

I owe much to my *sang-froid,* my exceptional *sang-froid,* at Buck's Row especially, where the carter who had just discovered he body of Polly Nichols passed within inches of me. In the courtyard at Berner Street, also, where I was literally caught in the act. I took risks, considerable risks, but they were calculated risks. What was important was to demonstrate a growing audacity; the more intense the hunt, the more savage and reckless the murders, and the more elusive the figure of Jack the Ripper became.

As for the chase on the twenty-ninth of September which ended in front of the little fountain in Dorset Street, leaving my pursuers dumbfounded by the sight of the water tinged with blood, that was already set up beforehand. I had washed my bloody hands *before* enticing the police into the alley, where I hid in a doorway before mingling with them dressed as a fellow officer.

I changed my approach for the murder of Mary Kelly, in several ways. It had become too risky, even for me, to do my handiwork in the street. I also thought it more prudent to disguise myself as "Mary Kelly" for my escape. The impersonation seems to have been perfect, for a witness reported seeing me alive in front of the *Britannia* at a quarter to nine in the morning.

Dear Melvin, you have to acknowledge that, in the realm of crime and mystery, mine was an exceptional accomplishment, never to be surpassed. I plunged London into unspeakable terror for several months and I know that the dreaded name of Jack the Ripper will forever haunt the memory of men. For, whenever anyone finds himself in a dark alley and hears footsteps behind him, he will inevitably shiver at the memory of the prowling killer with the bloody knife.

Much has been written about mystery throughout this story, and I shall conclude on the same theme. Dear Superintendent Melvin, if my explanations about the mysterious disappearances of Cora and the Ripper didn't live up to your expectations, because you seemed to believe there existed one single method of diabolical ingenuity to render someone invisible, consider this: *if such a method did indeed exist, do you really believe that Jack the Ripper would reveal the secret? For someone else to use?*

By the time you read this, I will have kept my promise. Mission accomplished, sir.

Yours sincerely

J. R.

EPILOGUE

"There's husbandry in heaven,
Their candles are all out."

-Macbeth, Act 2, Scene 1

The fog is so thick that even the nearest street lamps scarcely illuminate themselves. There is no sound in this sleeping city, plunged into darkness, behind doors double-locked out of fear. But wait...listen...were those footsteps?...calm, regular footsteps...no, nothing now....but over there? Just for a brief moment, that silhouette in the dying light of the gas-lamp? Illusion, phantasmagoria due to the fog? The only living thing is the Thames, whose powerful, reassuring pulse can still be discerned, muffled, through the fog. The voice of Big Ben breaks the silence. One...two...three strokes, as if a curtain were about to be raised. But it will not be raised tonight, for it has already fallen.

Sleep, good folk, sleep in peace.

Made in the USA
San Bernardino, CA
20 November 2013